# KILLING IT

# KILLING IT

## MIKE BOCKOVEN

Copyright © 2023 by Mike Bockovan
Cover and jacket design by 2Faced Design

ISBN 978-1-957957-19-7
eISBN: 978-1-957957-23-4
Library of Congress Control Number:
available upon request
First published August 2023 by Polis Books

62 Ottowa Road S
Marlboro, NJ 07746
www.PolisBooks.com

POLIS BOOKS

# INTRODUCTION

It was a great space.

Maybe "great" was a little strong. It was dirty and still carried that specific "bodega smell" that he would have to scrub out of the walls, but Jaff Maul was more than ready to apply as much elbow grease as the job needed. After all, this place wasn't just going to be his work. It was his goddamn calling, even if it did currently stink of decay.

He had first pictured this spot in his mind more than a dozen years ago, shortly after hearing George Carlin's voice fly out of the speakers of his father's car and directly into his brain. Jaff's father, who was an old-school military man with a perfectly square haircut and a mean sense of humor, had decided his young son was old enough to hear the truth from Saint George one day as they drove across the I-80 on some long-forgotten road trip. He had put *Class Clown* into the tape player and by the end of the album, Jaff's face hurt from smiling, his old man had a grin like a Cheshire Cat, and Jaff's brain was in a different shape than it was before.

He had asked his father a million questions. Who was this guy? What was he doing? Did people do this a lot? Did people pay to go see people like this? Are there more? Can we listen? His

1

father, who more often than not told Jaff to shut up when he asked questions of any kind, showed remarkable patience and answered his questions. Before long, Jaff had graduated from *Class Clown* to the much more caustic *Jammin' in New York*. When the "fucks" started dropping, his old man smiled in a way that said, "It's okay, just don't tell mom." He hadn't.

What he did get was a clear picture of his life stretched out before him. He would graduate high school and move to the big city. He would find performers and artists who could make people laugh and whoop and holler and cry, they were laughing so hard. He would know these people and they would be his friends and he would chase the high of that car trip every day until he died. By the time they reached the end of that trip, he even had the name of the club picked out.

He never shared a moment like that with his father again, as the old man was all about discipline. George Carlin had sent Jaff out on a different path. He started by finding comics his father had never heard of and wouldn't approve of in a million years and soon was shaped by the likes of Cheech and Chong, and Sam Kinison, and Eddie Murphy, and Bobcat Goldthwait, and Steven Wright, and Andrew Dice Clay, and Bill Hicks. He stole money from his mom's purse to buy cassette tapes at the local music store and lied about it when confronted. He started smoking at age sixteen and couldn't believe how dumb, intentionally or otherwise, his parents were about all the "long walks" he would take. He used other comics' lines to impress girls and would loudly have sex with them in his room, almost daring his parents to say something. They never did, but they came down hard in other ways.

Jaff's father beat him after a particularly bad report card, his fists connecting with Jaff's stomach like some sort of metal. He got caught sneaking out of the house a few weeks later and the ensuing argument got so vicious that the old man slashed the tires on Jaff's car so he couldn't leave. His mother would shake her head at his appearance, which now included longer hair and tight jeans, and would wonder, out loud, where she failed as a mother. It was during this time, when Jaff was seventeen or so, that he learned to get by, he had to both control his temper and learn how to take a punch. Turns out, in the world of comedy, both are a valuable thing to know.

College came and went with more of the same. Jaff majored in business, went to every stand-up show he could find, realized he wasn't good at the craft himself but never lost his desire to be around it. He talked to open mic organizers, comics, bar owners, talent bookers and made a field trip to New York over spring break each of his four years to go to the clubs and talk to the owners. There, he met comics doing amazing things on stage, conceptual comics, prop comics, comics who only did crowd work, comics who moved the audience outside into lanes of traffic, comics with giant hair and bigger egos, comics who told the most depraved stories on stage who were the kindest and most gentle people when they got off. Through it all he never lost his buzz for his dream and he learned how to make friends inside the community.

His father, on the other hand, had spoken to him less and less as time moved on. The night before his graduation, the old man had come by Jaff's apartment to mend fences and reveal that he was battling cancer. Four years and countless medical horrors later, he had suffocated on a sterile hospital bed, but his estate had afforded Jaff the money he needed to open his own club. Which smelled like a shitty bodega and needed a lot of work.

Located on the island of Manhattan in the upper north area known as Inwood, the space had been a bodega for years according to the realtor, and it showed. The floor was a lime-green linoleum, there were still two upright coolers along two of the walls, the upstairs was spacious, and downstairs was more storage than any club would ever need. Getting the right amount of tables inside would be a bit of a tight fit, but Jaff had seen clubs located in Italian restaurants where they just moved the tables at a certain point in the evening. It would be fine. He could make some magic out of it.

As he stood, trying to figure out where to begin, Jaff heard the jingle of the bell attached to the front door and saw a young man, likely not yet eighteen, come through the door. The kid was lanky but hunched in that way teenage boys sometimes are, and the boy's bangs hung in his eyes. He wore a white t-shirt that could use a wash that promoted some clothing brand Jaff had never heard of.

"You buying the place?" the boy said, already knowing the answer.

"Yeah," Jaff said. "I'm turning it into a club."

"My dad owned this place."

"Yeah?" Jaff said, trying to size the boy up. He didn't seem like a threat, but you never knew. Plus, Jaff could defend himself, if need be.

"You didn't do your research."

There was a long pause as Jaff tried to figure out what to say as the kid's gaze held firm. After a few seconds, Jaff just started talking to fill the void.

"I…I guess. I know the neighborhood, I know, like, the other clubs…"

"Move the freezer," the kid said.

"What?"

"That freezer, there," the kid said, pointing. "Move it."

"It's heavy. You gonna help me?"

"I am helping you. Move the freezer."

Jaff stared for another few seconds but did what was asked, his footsteps clacking loudly on the hard floor. There were two freezers against the dirty walls and Jaff had a brief flash of something terrible jumping out from behind them. It was silly, but he couldn't shake the feeling like he was walking down into a creepy basement, despite the bright sunlight.

"This one?"

"Either one," the kid said. "The same thing is behind both of 'em."

With a grunt he scooted one of the freezers from the wall, which didn't move on the first try. Jaff had to really push, and when the scraping of the freezer against the worn floor finally started, it didn't take long to see what the kid was talking about.

There were dark stains the color of dull rust running down the wall. Even now, a long time after the stain was first made, he could tell a lot of…something had been thrown against the wall and had run down toward the floor. The freezer had been tight against the wall, and moving it released another smell, not strong, but definitely worse than what was plaguing the space as a whole. Jaff couldn't put his finger on it, but it made his stomach churn and lurch.

The kid had taken a few steps toward Jaff and was pointing at the freezer.

"That was Mr. C. He was the second of third, I don't remember. The other cooler was Rosa, she came in every day for cigarettes and tuna."

Jaff wasn't a stupid man, but it took longer than he would have liked for the kid's meaning to dawn. When it did, his stomach lurched even further and it seemed, for a second, he was going to vomit. He didn't have a weak stomach normally, but he did now.

"People were murdered here?" he finally asked.

"Yeah," the kid said, dropping his voice and mocking Jaff's

tone. "People were murdered here."

"What happened?"

"My dad," the kid said. "He...listen, I just want to tell you, don't listen to her. She's going to come to you when you're sad or when you're stressed. She's going to try to tell you things—"

"Kid," Jaff said. "What are you talking about? Who died here?"

"Fucking listen to me!"

The shouting was enough to kill all motion in the room, and suddenly everything felt very still except for the buzzing of a few loud flies off on one side of the room. The kid's eyes were wide and pleading

"Okay," Jaff said softly. "I'm listening."

The kid dipped his head again, composing himself a bit, and when he raised it, he looked younger, more like a child. A scared one.

"I can't explain it, but you'll know it when it happens," the kid said. "If you stay here, at some point, she'll come to you and it'll sound like a good idea. It'll sound obvious. That's what my dad said. He said it was obvious. Don't listen to her. That's all I've got to say."

A tear dropped, and then another fell straight from his eyes onto the floor as he spoke. Jaff had the urge to hug the kid, but that seemed creepy, given the circumstances. His voice wasn't shaking and he was sturdy on his feet, but the tears were spilling quickly.

"Okay," Jaff said. "I won't listen to her but...you're right. I'm still not sure what you're talking about."

"You'll know when it happens," the kid said, turning to leave. "Just...don't listen."

A few lanky steps later, the bell on the door chimed and the kid was gone. For a second, Jaff considered running after him, but to what end? Chances were excellent he had just had a run-in with a mentally ill street kid. If he was the son of the former owner like he had claimed, he could call and ask the realtor. The deal was done, but maybe he could get some sort of break on the commission or something if she had not revealed he was moving into the local murder bodega. Even if he stretched and tried to grasp what the kid had meant, the best Jaff could come up with was a kid full of shame and grief had just come to talk to him about his father's mental illness.

Bottom line was this had nothing to do with Jaff, or the kick-ass comedy club he was about to open.

As it had for the past few days, the excitement of what he was about to do washed over him. His face broke into a small smile as he thought about what the place was going to be, the comics he was going to bring in, the laughs that were going to explode from this place onto the street. He'd live upstairs, the bar would be in the back, the green room and storage would be downstairs, he even had his office picked out. It was going to take a lot of work, but his bohemian dream was about to become a reality, dire warnings from spooky street kids or no dire warnings from spooky street kids.

He was going to live the life of an artist, round and full and lively, which was why he had decided to call his club The Square, after the man who had funded it by gasping and dying on a hospital bed a few months before.

The excitement wiped away the kid's warning, and by that evening, he had forgotten the kid completely. The Square opened a few months later and it was everything young Jaff had dreamed it would be.

And more.

# Emcee Set

Live From The Square in Manhattan
*Friday, October 12*
*Braden Bond Set*

*Yes! Hello. Thank you for coming out to The Square tonight. Who's ready for some live, raw stand-up comedy?*

*[crowd claps]*

*Yeah, it's gonna be raw. My name is Braden Bond and, uh, I'm having a weird night, man. I mean, that's nothing new, I have a lot of weird nights. You can kinda tell by looking at me. I've got a "throw cottage cheese at him out of nowhere" kind of face. A "got shit on by a pigeon during a first date" kind of vibe. If you see a bum following a guy for six blocks for no reason, then you see that he's following me, you're like, "Oh, that makes sense." It's a very specific look that I have.*

*All those examples are dead serious, by the way. See me after the show, buy me a drink, I might let you throw cottage cheese at me. I take it really well. Right on the chin. I've had some practice.*

*The one that people gloss over but that give me the best stories is the fact that I attract transients. I'm a bum magnet, man, which is an unfortunate thing to be in New York. The unhoused will seek me out in a crowd. It's not like I'm overly generous with my cash or anything, but something about this face says "this guy needs to hear my theory about 9/11."*

*The one time I was in Times Square, of all places, and the costumed characters are jumping around trying to get tourists' money, you know, and right between Dollar Tree Batman and*

*Pikachu with terrible unnamed stains all over him, I see this guy. You know how you can tell some people don't smell the best from a distance? If not, don't worry, it's a basic survival skill in New York. Hang out here a week or two and you'll develop it. In Mexico, it's learning to ask where the bathroom is. In New York, you develop smell-o-vision whether you want to or not.*

*Anyway, this guy sees me from, like, two crosswalks away. Like, he has to wait for a light, then wait for another light, and then he gets to me, but I can tell, from the second my bum-sense starting tingling, that he's coming, man. He is coming, and unless I abandon my plans and run in the other direction, the two of us are going to have a conversation. And this fucker, he cuts diagonally across the street to get to me like I was mother's milk, like him talking to me is the thing that is going to get him a house and a shower and a job and a girlfriend and a blowjob and the keys to the city, and he's pushing, you know, dick-shaped minions and Spider-Man who had a big lunch out of the way and tourists are flying off the sidewalk, and when he gets to me, he looks me in the eye and, out of breath, he says, "Man...man...I like your hat."*

*So I gave him my hat. And later that day I went on a date and a pigeon shit on my head. True story.*

*Ah, enough of me. Let me tell you how this is going to work. Again, I'm Braden Bond, bum magnet. I'm one of two white guys you'll see tonight, so don't confuse me with the other one. We all look alike. Here's how this works, my job is to "warm you up," so I hope you're feeling sufficiently warm and cozy, maybe ready for another drink, and I'm going to bring up our actual, professional stand-ups tonight, many of whom you will recognize from the TVs and the YouTubes. We're going to start off with the extremely funny Jerrod Seybourne, who you might recognize from all over the damn place. Jerrod is, what's called in the business, the "opener." Then we'll move*

*on to Jackie Carmichael, who you might have seen on the Showtime
series The Dapper.*

*[crowd cheers]*

*Right, you know Jackie. Very, very funny lady. She is what's
called the "middle," which is more a verb, such as, "I'm middling on
a shitty show in north Manhattan tonight." Finally, we'll say What's
Happening to our closer and the host of What's Happening on the
FX network, Sammy Platter. He's the other white guy. Plus, there
are always special guests showing up, so please don't be surprised if
someone else is on the bill, so please, drink a ton, tip your waitresses
because they're working their asses off, and, if you end up in possession
of some cottage cheese, please keep it to yourself.*

*Okay, our first comic tonight...*

# Chapter 1

The second Jaff lost control and bashed Calista's head in with the printer from his office, the headache vanished.

The unearthly pain had started on Wednesday as he sat in his apartment upstairs from the club watching some bullshit on Netflix with Calista. As they had settled into late middle age after years and years together, energy seemed to drain out of them at a certain time of night and television was the unconscious routine in which they had settled. He didn't even like most of the shit they watched, but his butt always ended up on the couch, the "love of his life" on the other side, scrolling on her phone. Being in your early fifties will sap your energy, as will being together for a couple of decades. They never married because saying things like, "It's just a piece of paper, man," and, "I don't need to conform to society's standards" is a lot easier than talking about deep-seated abandonment issues. If you didn't mind missing out on a fairly significant tax break, it wasn't that hard to get around. They were comfortable, they worked well together, and nothing needed to change, so it didn't.

The show had ended and she had gone to bed, but he was antsy, which was not like him. Since he was a boy, Ronald Jaffee Maul had been rebellious first and lazy second. It wasn't a very potent combination, which was why he had peaked at twenty-five, opening a comedy club just as the alt-comedy scene had exploded in the early '90s. He was there to be one of the first clubs to book comedians like Dana Gould, Patton Oswalt, and David Cross to sold out shows in New York. There were pictures on the wall of his upstairs apartment of Jaff with a young John Stewart, a young Chris Rock, a bunch of the old *Saturday Night Live* cast, all sitting at the bar, smiling widely, their arms around each other. The money he inherited when his father died had bought him the life he had dreamed about way back when.. That and naming his boy after *Mad Magazine* cartoonist Al Jaffee were the only two gifts his father had ever given him, but it had been enough. He'd been tied to The Square since the day it opened, never wanting or needing to do anything else. The question "what's next" had been ignored and had rotted away on the vine.

Those early days had pulsed with energy, and Jaff had fed off it, staying up late, meeting people, making connections, and making mistakes. He was a terrible bar owner at first, but he put in the time and energy to get better and had worked hard enough to keep everything afloat. The club had endured, even though the popularity of live comedy came in peaks and valleys. Nowadays, over twenty years since starting the business, he relied on just a handful to bring in most of his revenue (two weekly podcast recordings, of all things, were the most popular ways to put butts in seats and sell drinks) and was glad to let comics play around or put together their own regular shows during the remaining nights of the week. Seeing a comic develop something, struggle, fail, regroup, then really knock it home during one of the smaller shows still gave him a little bit of that early juice. It was one of the only things that did anymore.

Part of the issue was the comedy community could be

egotistical, needy, and infuriating most of the time. The comics themselves were often moody and in need of some heavy-duty therapy (he was one to talk), but they were some of the funniest people Jaff had ever met. On a good night he laughed until his sides hurt and he started to sweat around the top of his receding hairline. Even on a bad night he was guaranteed a few chuckles from a well-executed joke or a well-timed riff. He had even gotten some media attention in those early days, with *GQ* doing an article about The Square, calling it a "bastion of alternative comedy." It quoted Jaff as saying he wanted to "make some magic" in the club, and the phrase had stuck. He'd been using it ever since, more sparingly as of late as things had become more routine in one sense and more terrifying in others.

The comics had always been crazy in one way or another, but in the early days he had the patience to deal with it and there was less drama, or so it seemed. There were always those ones who were guaranteed to bring drama with them, be it alcoholism (a common one) or other addictions, mental illness, relationship problems, severe, debilitating need for approval, or a hundred other issues Jaff had fought with for the past two decades. But back then he loved it, and he stuck with it because he loved it. And where else was he going to go? He was very short in the marketable skills department.

As age caught up with him, Jaff had settled into an easy groove. Calista, who had been a waitress, then a lover, then a partner, had settled into that groove with him. They worked, they watched TV, they went out on occasion when time and money allowed. Every so often they were taken out and shown the high life by a comic whose career Jaff had seen blossom over time. Once every two or three years they took a big trip. Things were what they were. No health problems to speak of if you don't count the five to ten drinks

Jaff was likely to down on a daily basis, and that hadn't caught up with him quite yet, though his doctor said he could see trouble from where he was standing. As it was now, he was a five-foot-eleven, two-hundred-ten-pound comedy club owner with a bit of a gut, a reputation for being solid, and debt that had been slowly mounting since around about 2008. Some days, it put him in a foul mood, but mostly, things were good.

But on that Wednesday, after they had watched whatever show they had watched, the headache started and wouldn't leave Jaff alone. It wasn't the unpleasant background kind or the "I drank too much" kind. It was a full fire from stem to stern one that burned in spite of two, then four, then six Advil and kept him from getting any sort of meaningful sleep that night. To make matters worse, the headache seemed to be fueling his legs. His fitness tracker said he usually took between 15,000 and 20,000 steps a day in the general business of keeping The Square up and running, but with his newfound, unwanted energy he was easily doing that at night as well, back and forth from the stage to the bar, back and forth from the bar to the green room in the basement, back and forth from the door to the end of the street and back. His feet and legs ached and shadows started dancing in strange ways along the walls of the apartment and the bar downstairs. He didn't find it creepy. Quite the opposite. In the dead of night, as he paced and paced, he felt like he was almost at the precipice of something important, but every time his mind got close to whatever revelation lay in the dark, it flittered away, leaving him to pace and pace and pace some more.

Calista never asked what was wrong. She didn't care. Had she ever?

She seemed to be a good stop for his anger brought on by the headache and pacing. The next morning, he snapped at her and she snapped back. The show on Thursday night was fine, it was one of the podcast recordings and people had shown up in droves and bought plenty of drinks. It was a good night, but it didn't feel like it, and it was one of his regulars who finally noticed.

"You look like shit," Bass Sherman said. Bass was a former radio personality who did a show once a week where he made fun of entertainment news. It wasn't Jaff's thing, but, again, it brought in the crowds.

"What?"

"Gaunt, man. You look skinny. Stretched. Like you haven't been eating."

"Same as always," Jaff said, it only then occurring to him that he hadn't eaten much of anything all day. "I don't like that word."

"What? Stretched? Not as bad as moist. Or lugubrious."

"What the fuck is lugubrious?"

"It's like gloomy," Bass said. "Like you right now."

"How about 'go over there for a while before I beat your ass.' People like saying that?"

Bass ignored him. The comic part of his brain was working.

"Oh, how about squirt? Curd? Chunky?"

Jaff ignored him, but could have sworn some voice had whispered something terrible in his ear. He felt a brief urge to punch the comic, which was strange as Jaff had only punched four people in his entire life and each one of those had been in the service of running The Square. He remembered every punch vividly, from the anxiety of the wind up to the surprising joy of aggression to the pain in the hand afterward.

The fire continued raging in his head and Jaff left to go refill the ice containers from the machine next to one edge of the bar, grunting against the pain as he went. When he came back, Bass had moved on, but his constant headache companion hadn't. And it persisted.

Later that night, Jaff had hoped sex might alleviate some of the pain, but Calista wasn't in the mood. Though this was a frequent source of tension in their relationship, he found himself raging and screaming at her to the point where he had to sleep on the couch. He briefly considered a comedy bit where he would wonder, on stage, why men always had to sleep on the couch and what women were doing when they had the bed all to themselves, but then he remembered he hadn't been on his own stage in front of a crowd in over a decade. He didn't have the patience for it and had been around comedy long enough to know that he didn't have the chops to ever make a serious run at comedy. Or so he told himself. He didn't sleep much again that night and what sleep he had was plagued with images of fires, knives, and terrible things happening to people he didn't recognize. In one flash that he remembered upon waking, he had punched someone at the bar and their head had split apart, thick, black and red goo splattering on Jaff's arms and face. Instead of waking up and shaking it off, the images from his subconscious stuck with him long after breakfast.

The next day, Friday, Jaff couldn't remember ever feeling so foul. His head was still on fire, sure, but his guts were starting to roil from the second he stood up. Everything from the light streaming in his living room window to the constant sounds of cars and foot traffic outside pierced through whatever barriers he had put up over the years and penetrated like a spike into his brain. How had he ever lived in this city, much less for so long? The sounds were constant, the filth was everywhere, the rot too deep. How could this be his life?

Calista had run off to yoga or some such and even the pleasant thought of her in stretchy pants was soured by memories of last night and how she had, politely but firmly, turned him away and how he had, not politely and forcefully, called her terrible names because of it. He remembered briefly wanting to throw something at her. He would have done it had something been handy. Maybe he could still do that later on.

"Come on, Jaff," he said to no one. "You're not that guy."

The words were swallowed by the empty apartment with its strange shadows, seemingly cast by nothing at all. He took another handful of Advil, emptying the bottle, and went to work.

Keeping the books, dealing with talent, and running a bar was more than enough work for one person, and Jaff had always prided himself in getting a lot done in a short period of time. Friday morning, he fell into a familiar groove—returning calls, prepping the bar, sending emails to the night's talent, and paying bills. Everything had gone fine, the headache even receding a bit, until he opened two letters in a row, one from the electric company saying rates were going up and another from his wholesale alcohol distributor saying the same thing. He scanned the letters, reading words like "kilowatts per hour," "tariffs," "political climate," and "glad to serve you," and all of a sudden, without forethought, he spun around in his chair and punched the nearest wall.

He got all of the wall (which didn't budge) and expected to feel pain radiate through his body. Nothing came.

"How the FUCK," he yelled, again to no one, "am I supposed to stay in business when I'm getting nickeled and fucking dimed to death every second I fucking turn around?"

No one answered, but it didn't seem like he was yelling into the void. Far from it, as a matter of fact.

Truth was, business had been bad for a while. He had done his best to hide it from Calista, which wasn't hard because she had no legal financial stake in the business and they both kept separate checking accounts, but the place was in bad financial shape. Part of it was the consistent, oppressive rise in all aspects of the business—taxes, booze, taxes, electricity, taxes, competition for help. Paying comics like shit for the right to get on a stage that had some mystique and still drew crowds was the only part of his business model that still worked. He had done that math and there was no way he could survive another year without serious changes. The Square was moderately famous for its one-drink minimum, which had been a calling card in the early days and was now an anchor dragging the place down.

As things stood, he'd be out of the business and on the street by the summer, which was a slow time anyway. He was in the endgame. His time at The Square was going to be over soon.

The numbers had been there for a while, but that afternoon, feeling foul and angry, was the first time it had ever really sunk in. Closing time was a long time coming and was barreling at him like a freight train on fire. In months, not years, he would be out on his ass, unqualified for any other work on the planet.

A kick to the bottom of his desk sent items rattling and falling around him, the loud bang echoing in his ears to the point he didn't pick up immediately when the phone in front of him rang. When he did pick it up, his hand was shaking.

"Hello."

"Jaff Maul."

"Yes."

"Please hold for Terry Stafford."

There was a rustle and a sharp noise on the other end then the surprisingly deep voice of comic legend Terry Stafford crept across the line. He sounded slow and tired.

"Hello, Jaff?"

"Yeah, this is him. I'm here."

"Hey, I'm in town doing a few sets and I'd like to come do some

18

time."

"Absolutely," Jaff said, stumbling for his smart phone where he kept the evening's schedule. "When do you think you'll be here?"

"Between nine and ten," Stafford said. "I don't need to tell you this is not a promoted performance, right?"

"No, I…I got that," Jaff said, the previous moment's troubles melting away like butter on a hot skillet. "I know the drill."

"Good man," Stafford said. "See you tonight. You still with that skinny girl…what's her name?"

"Calista. Yeah, still living above the club."

"Keeping the light burning for us comics. Good on you. See you around nine."

"Thanks for thinking of us."

"Yeah. It's been a while."

And with that, one of the most influential stand-ups of the last forty years hung up. Of course Jaff had met Terry Stafford before. He had met damn near everyone, but Stafford was legendarily gregarious and had a politician's gift for remembering names, faces, and venues. It had been at least a decade since he had last performed regularly and more than twenty years since his seminal comedy album *Fartknocker*, which was labeled as both revolutionary and the end of western civilization. The man could work blue, and when he got cooking, he could absolutely destroy a crowd, or at least he could twenty years ago. His career had given way to subpar movies and cancelled TV series. Either way, it was going to be an interesting night.

This was what he had gotten into the business for—crazy nights where crowds would leave with a story they'd never forget. For a second, he forgot how lousy he felt and enjoyed the light buzz that came with having a secret.

He heard Calista come in and yelled for her. She did yoga

wearing jewelry, big, jangly bracelets and necklaces that had some sort of mystical properties that Jaff neither understood nor wanted to understand. All that mysticism and "soul repose" bullshit was obnoxious to him in the extreme, but he tolerated it because…why had he tolerated it again?

"What?" she said, still sweaty from yoga.

"I just got off the phone with Terry Stafford. He's stopping by tonight."

Her mood lightened, as she had seemed ready for a fight.

"It's been a while since he's been on stage"

"Yeah," Jaff said. "Hope he's still got it.

"It'll be nice to have some energy in here."

Both the headache and the rotten gut made themselves known.

"What did you say?"

"I just said it'll be nice to have big energy in here. It's nice."

"That's not what you said. You said, 'It'll be nice to have some energy in here.' Like there's not any energy in here."

"Jesus Christ."

She walked away and he stood up to follow her.

"I've sunk every bit of energy I ever had into this place!" he yelled, but she was already well past the bar and opening the front door of the club, disappearing onto the street, presumably toward the entrance to their apartment.

"You're tired," she yelled back. "Get some sleep tonight."

It was a popular refrain, the solution to whatever ailed him. He got cranky when he was tired, she would say. Get some sleep. Like he was a fucking toddler and she was the mommy.

"Bitch," he muttered. In the back of his head, a small voice spoke up, objecting to the word and the sentiment lobbed at the woman with whom he shared his life. The pain quickly made too much noise for that voice to have any sort of impact and Jaff descended the steep concrete stairs to the basement where the green room was to lie down on one of the filthy couches. He was suddenly tired, and if he could grab a few minutes of sleep, it would be a blessing.

The green room was an oddity among clubs, or performance spaces, really, as far as Jaff could tell. When comics first walked into The Square, they walked past the bar into the seating area. The stage was at the front, the tiny office was off to one side, but the green room, where comics often hung out before, during, and after the show, was down a flight of stairs and down a very short concrete hallway, actually underneath where the audience was sitting. The staircase that went down there was a dank affair to the right of the stage. Realizing it was always going to be a dank room in a basement, Jaff had leaned into it, leaving a single, uncovered bulb leading down the stairs that made it seem downright scary if you were in the right headspace. If they wanted, comics could wait in the stairway to go on stage, but most waited in the back of the room which had closed-circuit cameras hooked up to a big television so everyone knew when to go on.

Over the years the green room had earned the name The F Pit. It had happened when a road comic by the name of John Rabbit, who often played up his legends of debauchery on the road, refused to go to the green room at any point, telling anyone who would listen, "I ain't going down in that fucking pit." Fucking Pit became Fuck Pit, which didn't sound good and was unfriendly to female comics, so it was eventually shortened to F Pit. Jaff didn't mind. It gave the place character, and it was cool in the summer and held heat surprisingly well in the winter. Besides, comics don't need much to hang out. The Hang was one of the few perks of the gig.

Years ago, a comic named Matt Campbell, who had gotten on a hot streak and made a bunch of money, bought Jaff a big neon sign that said "F Pit" on it. It had naked, small light bulbs surrounded by thick wires and a plastic background, but it was heavy, and when it was the only light source, cast a rather lovely soft glow over the subterranean room. He stumbled down the stairs, swung the big wooden door (from what he could figure the room used to be a secure office of some sort), clicked the light on, and collapsed on the couch. Mercifully, sleep came quickly, sinking him deep, low, and empty.

His nap was dreamless, mercifully, and he felt pretty good when he awoke. He checked the phone, saw that it was 6 p.m. He had woken up at eleven, meaning he had worked for three hours and slept for another four. This was not typical, nor acceptable if he was to be ready for tonight.

"Holy fuckballs," he said, rolling his frame off the couch. Colorful and creative profanity had always been part of the gig at The Square, and most other comedy clubs. Jaff was always able to hang with the comics, at least a bit, in the green room after the show, to shoot the shit with the guys and girls after they got off stage. Most of the time he was no match for the rapid-fire jokes that comics tossed around like it was nothing, but on a good night, he enjoyed watching them go. At least, he had at one point. This was not going to be one of those nights, as he felt worse than he had before he took a nap.

On weary legs he made it up the stairs before his phone exploded. Either because of the underground locale or some other reason that Jaff honestly couldn't care less about, cell phone signals were never able to penetrate into The F Pit. For some it was a feature, others a bug.

By the time he hit the top of the stairs he had twenty-two missed calls, thirty-two texts, and one pissed off common law wife working feverishly to prep the bar.

"You were down there?" she said, dumping ice into a bin. "What were you doing?"

"I...took a nap," Jaff said, still shaking out the cobwebs. "Didn't mean to sleep that long. Sorry. I'll be there in a second."

Calista didn't say anything, but kept working. She was clearly pissed and had decided the cold shoulder would solve all her problems. The word "bitch" floated across Jaff's mind again, a word he had railed against and tried never to use, and he swatted it away.

Calls and texts were from comics looking for time, distributors he assumed Calista had handled, his mother (again), and a few other calls he could ignore. He worked through them just in time to open the doors at seven for the show to start at eight. Even in his hyper annoyed state, he took a stab at making nice with Calista.

"I'm sorry about the, uh, the nap," he said. "Not like me. Haven't felt myself recently."

"Yeah, what's up with that?" Calista said, breaking her self-imposed silence.

"I don't know. My head's been pounding, my brain's been all over the place..."

"Go see a doctor, maybe?" she said. Her body language was still distant and it was starting to piss him off.

"Not yet."

"Okay," she said "Don't say I didn't warn you."

Rage crashed over him, quicker and harder than before. It happened so fast and with such force he wasn't able to stop it.

"It's not a fucking contest," he said. "You either care about me or you don't, you passive aggressive cunt."

Jaff had never used the C word in his life, nor had he ever been tempted, but it tumbled out like it had come from another person all together. Comics in his club had debated the word's use, most landing on the idea that it wasn't worth the baggage, no matter how good the joke, but he had tossed it out like it was nothing. If he had been thinking clearly, he would have realized he had basically just ended the relationship. Calista was a good partner, but could be 135 pounds of fire and fury when called upon, usually with drunk bar patrons, and Jaff could see her gearing up to unleash.

"What. The fuck. Is wrong with you?"

Instead of answering this very salient question, Jaff bolted for the office, part of his head screaming to go back and finish the fight with her, to end it good and proper, and the other half screaming at him to get it together. He wasn't this guy. He was the guy who spent his life providing a spot for people to laugh and drink, the guy who had high moral ideals at one point and had vowed to never wear a tie in his life, the guy who had taken care of Calista when she had back surgery, who had nursed her and cared for her and given insane thought to her presents and drank gallons of her spit and other fluids over the years. He was not the guy who called is girlfriend the "c" word. That was some other guy comics made fun of. It wasn't him. It couldn't be him.

As he moved quickly toward the door, knocking over chairs in the empty room, his headache started screaming and he felt like an ice pick had been jabbed through his eye and into his brain. The pain kept pushing and pulsing, starting at the base of his skull and piercing all the way to his nose. He had never endured so much pain, and he stumbled into his office, grabbing the desk for support.

"Get back here, you piece of shit," Calista yelled, following, tears already in her eyes.

*Don't come in here,* Jaff thought. *Please, baby, don't come in here.*

He tried to speak the words but they didn't get near his throat, choked in his brain before they could go anywhere. Something else was talking to him. He couldn't make it out, but he heard it, like a song in the distance, about to get stuck in his head. It was whispering, whispering, and though the words were a jumble, he understood.

Then she was there, in the office, pushing on his back, yelling at him.

"You do not get to call me that," she said. "I do not fucking care what's wrong with you, I will never be treated like that."

She shoved him again, pushing his head forward toward the desk. Jaff shut his eyes and tried to will the rage away and silence the voice. He didn't even come close.

*Kill her.*

Finally breaking through, the voice was clear and strong and he greeted it like a friend who had finally showed up to party that was already in progress. It cut through the pain and the anger and, in its sweet, lilting way, gave him a clear course of action.

"I will burn this place to the fucking ground before you say that to me again!" Calista screamed, so near his face that he could see the burst capillaries in her eyes.

The thought of the place in flames suddenly appeared in his brain, bright and vivid as anything that had ever happened to him, and suddenly, it was all clear. There was nothing holding him back, nothing stopping him. He was alone with Calista and he could do anything he wanted. The flames licking in his mind were replaced with terrible images. He could cut her. He could pull out her tongue and make her stop talking. If he wanted, he could bash her head in.

And he really wanted to.

*Kill her.*

There was no obvious candidate on the desk with which to do the deed. Some items were too big, some were too small. The first strike had to do some damage, he had somehow decided, and if that was the criteria, he guessed bigger would have to do. The printer beside his computer monitor was big but not unwieldy. When he picked it up, he was slightly disappointed at the weight of the thing. Too much plastic, not enough metal, but you worked with what you had. Calista was about ready to storm out.

"We are done, do you hear me!" she yelled. "Do you? Answer me…you cunt!"

The voice had already taken over, but her language made him put some extra stank on the swing. She didn't see it coming and put up no defense at all. The printer smashed into her cheek, shattering bone inside the flesh and knocking at least one tooth out from deep near the back of her mouth. Her body tumbled hard to one side of the office.

He couldn't finish the job with a printer. That was just stupid.

Calista had not lost consciousness, but immediately realized things were wrong in a profound way. Blood poured from her face and she had lost vision in her right eye where the printer had found its mark. She felt another tooth wiggle in her face, loose enough to pull out and gushing blood into her mouth.

After a bit of deliberation and finding no perfect options, Jaff's vision settled on a plaque hanging in his office, a cheap award from the Comedy Club Owners of America given to him for twenty years in the business. It was heavy enough for the job. It came to a point on the top, which didn't hurt. Calista was trying to crawl toward the door, the streets of Manhattan within view through the windows of the club.

"All right, baby," Jaff said, taking it off the wall. "Let's make some magic."

Jaff felt energy course through him, energy he couldn't explain but didn't want to stop. The headache he had been fighting against suddenly turned into energy moving in his direction, fueling his senses, his emotions, his muscles. It was more than a cloud disappearing from around his head, it was as if something had emerged from his mind, something that had been there for a very long time. It was glorious and he couldn't wipe the smile from his face as he watched the blood pour from Calista's.

He beat her until she stopped moving, spilling blood on the already filthy carpet, splitting her head, stabbing her in the back, literally, and eventually shutting her head in the door over and over and over until the rage inside him was satisfied. She hadn't screamed, hadn't begged and hadn't thrashed, just taken all the punishment he dealt, and after he was done, he wordlessly threw her body over his shoulder and carried it downstairs where there was a broom closet just off The F Pit. He would deal with this at the end of the night.

Right now, he had a club to open.

# CHAPTER 2

Seeing folks in Manhattan with ear buds in was a frequent occurrence. As Braden Bond walked down the street, he wondered how many of those people were listening to their own voices filter into their ears.

He had absolutely killed a few nights ago at Caroline's, writing a few jokes on stage and fleshing out a few more ideas, which was a skill great comics had but that he was just starting to discover. As he replayed the set, over and over, he concentrated hard on what was working, the words and rhythms the crowd responded to, and just how his mind was working. Digging into the specifics of the set allowed him to avoid the cringe factor of hearing his own voice in his ears, something he hated but was necessary to hear the crowd reaction, which was putting him in a good mood. Killing it felt good.

Twenty-three and lean in that way being poor in the city makes you lean and tall in that way a corn-fed Midwest upbringing can make you tall, Braden temped and worked in bars while working up the nerve to try stand-up. Once he finally did, it infected his blood and all his misgivings about moving to the city melted away.

He was still scared and homesick on occasion, but he was doing exactly what he wanted to be doing and, at six foot six and not bad to look at, he was getting some attention. There was much to love about stand-up—the way you had to "think like a comic" and constantly take in the world and notice the things others didn't, the thrill of speeding across town to make a set, the waves of applause that fed the soul like sugar fed a fat kid. It was almost too much and he had decided it was what he wanted to spend his whole life pursuing.

That being said, The Square was not his favorite New York club.

There wasn't a good reason for it other than the vibe. The place was, by all accounts, very nice but seemed danker than it was. Some of the jokes that played there would get you kicked out of other clubs. There was also the smell, stale, with a hint of something sharp and metallic. It wasn't the normal unclean smell you'd get at other places in New York suffering from neglect or bad trash placement. It seemed to run a little deeper. That being said, it was a shining beacon of the alt comedy scene in the early '90s and had a good history. Most importantly, it had a stage and it put him in front of an audience, and that was all Braden wanted at this point, no matter what it smelled like.

The show was at eight and he tried the doors at 7:10 to find the owner, a past his prime drinker named Jaff, coming up from the basement where the green room was, wiping his hands, coming to unlock the door. It was very quiet for a club that was going to be booming in fifty minutes' time and a few people were mulling around, presumably waiting for the club to open. No one had come in yet, employees included.

"Welcome," he said. "Ten-dollar cover, one-drink minimum."

"Oh yeah," Braden said. "I'm your emcee. I'm Braden."

The man did not make any indication that he understood, but gave him a once over and opened the door. The place looked like it always did, kind of a dive, kind of atmospheric, with deep shadows and dark wooden tables. The stage was lit up like noon, clearly where the attention should be. Definitely a comedy club. Jaff was busy trying to get the place open and was clearly behind schedule.

"If you want, grab a beer and head to the green room. You been here before?"

"Yeah," Braden said. "I did a set for you two weeks ago. You asked me to emcee tonight."

"Sorry, man," Jaff said, shaking his head. "You get to be my age and things start slipping, you know?

"Not a problem," Braden said. "I'll hang out up here, if it's cool. Can I hang at the bar?"

The last time he had done a set and had ventured to the green room to talk to a few comics, the green room had not impressed him. In fact, it activated his mild claustrophobia. The room was cramped, but comfortable, but it was the sort of place where fluorescent lighting really made you look bad. Plus, there was no signal down that deep for his phone, which didn't make him keen on going back.

"Whatever," Jaff said as the other folks outside got the message and started coming in. It was weird, Braden thought, that there was no security, no bartenders, no nothing. Just one guy, and a guy acting weird at that. Braden noticed that Jaff's hands were shaking but he didn't seem rattled or like something was wrong, just overwhelmed, which was probably a regular state of affairs when it came to running a comedy club.

Over the course of a few minutes, staff did start to appear, and Braden clocked them. There was a bartender, a tall, sandy-haired dude named Bryce he had hung out with a few weeks before, three servers, two of whom he recognized, and a dishwasher/runner, a really friendly Hispanic dude named Raoul who gave Braden a high-five as he passed him.

Raoul was short, with skinny arms and big, muscular legs. His eyes were bright and his energy was contagious, flushing away whatever uneasy feelings Braden had.

"I remember you," Raoul said. "You told that joke about a plumber being a guy who plumbs, right? Dude, you killed last time I saw you."

Not that he got it a lot, but it always amazed Braden what people took away from his work.

"Yeah, that's me."

"You telling that joke tonight, man?"

"You know what, for you, my man, definitely."

"All right! Thanks. Hey, if you're still around at the end of the night, would you mind helping me out? I've been working on an act to show to Jaff over there, like, to be on stage, and I'd love to hear what you think."

Raoul was shuffling his feet, shy, but desperate to ask the favor. Unlike getting recognized for his jokes, this happened to Braden all the time. The second someone learned he was an aspiring stand-up comic, the jokes and observations started flying. It could be terribly annoying, but Raoul made it feel like fun. Plus, he seemed like the kind of kid who could take some honest criticism if his jokes weren't landing. Some new comics said they wanted feedback, when what they really wanted was validation.

"Absolutely," Braden said. "But I don't do well with people crying in front of me. It reminds me of every girl I've ever dated."

Raoul stared back blankly.

"If something doesn't hit me as funny, I'll say so. That okay?"

"Brother, that's what I want!" Raoul said, reaching out his

hand and pulling him into a forearm shake. "I'll track you down. Thanks!"

And Raoul was off, enthusiastically attending to his job. It was time for Braden to do his. He got up from his seat and started rooting around for the other comics in the room, trying to figure out who the hell he was introducing and what he should say about them. While Braden had been lucky and had emceed once or twice before (which meant his career was off to a pretty decent start), he didn't want to leave anything to chance if it could be helped. For a room that looked big when he was in it by himself, it filled up fast, and now no more than thirty people made the whole place look almost jammed. The floodgates had opened and the audience was getting ready.

There was a time when Braden would have preferred to chew on a wooden beam than find a stranger in a crowd and chat them up. He was a shy kid who had turned into a shy teenager who realized, early on, that a lot of the successful people he saw in the world were outgoing. Upon this realization, he watched YouTube videos and read books on how to overcome his naturally shy personality and was doing okay at it. Stand-up had been a big, sweaty risk when he first tried it a few years ago, but it had paid off. He had directed a crowd to laugh and they had. That simple act of laughter had done more for his confidence than anything else in his life, he figured. He was even talking to women and doing okay for himself, as far as that went.

But as quickly as that first rush of success had come, he found himself quickly realizing how little he knew and, if he was going to make a run at this seriously, how hard he'd have to go. Which meant pushing people to give him a shot, which meant not eating some days, which meant listening to his voice on the street when there was other stuff he'd rather be listening to.

He found the first comic, Jackie Carmichael, right off the bat. Her hair had been big since she broke in the late 1980s and she was tall, clocking in at a solid six feet. She also had one of the most legendary set of lungs in the business. There was a rumor flying around that Braden wanted to ask her about. In the early '90s, rumor had it, some comics paid her to come to their shows and laugh because her volume and resonance was a joke in and of itself. "If Jackie is in the audience," one comic had told him, "your show is instantly twenty percent better."

"Ms. Carmichael," Braden said, lightly tapping her shoulder. "Hi. I'm your emcee tonight. I wanted to check in with you before the show."

"I don't know you," she said, the straw from her gin and tonic never once leaving her lips. "Let's change that. I'm Jackie."

"I'm Braden," he said.

"What's your last name, Braden?"

"Bond," he said. "But Braden is—"

"You gotta be careful with that last name of yours," Jackie said, grinning widely, her voice lilting upward in a distinctly New York way. "You say the last name first and all of a sudden you're a movie spy that Jeff Bezos bought for his mantle."

Braden liked her instantly, especially the way her accent hung out but didn't over assert itself. She was old enough to be his mother, which probably helped. He had always liked strong women, and strong women tended to be older women.

"Yeah, you've got that right. I've never done…that thing. But if you've got any of that Bezos money, I'd take it off your hands."

"Ha! You and me both," she said, her guffaw loud and lovely. "Hey, use that Showtime show *The Dapper* when you introduce me, please. It's what people seem to know me from. Also, tell Jaff to play The Kinks when I come up there. 'Come Dancing.' I usually go up to that song."

"Why that song?"

"It's upbeat but kind of spooky, you know? Like me. That's my song. The Kinks are fucking magical and if you haven't figured that out yet, you should get on that fast and hard."

"Kinda spooky? You seem like a good time to me."

He produced a small notebook and began to write down her request. She let the line slide, the toothy grin never leaving her face.

"Hey, hey, you ain't taking that notebook up on stage with you, right?"

"No, no," he said. Some old-school comics had very strong feelings, but most comics didn't care unless the notebook was a crutch. Personally, he saw no problem with it, but didn't want to make an enemy. "I just go over it a few times before getting on stage."

"Good, 'cause this isn't a show where people show up in sweatpants and don't give a shit if you read them a poem," Jackie said. "If I was stuck with a notebook and couldn't see what was going on with the audience, that'd be the end of me. Pay attention to the audience if you can, young man. There's my advice. That's for free."

"Can't wait for the stuff I gotta pay for," Braden said, smiling.

"Aww, you're one of those flirts, aren't ya? I'm gonna watch out for you. You've got mischief in you. I can see it."

Braden smiled and motioned that he was moving on.

"Go do your thing."

"Yeah, I will. Talk to you later."

"Hey..."

She grabbed his arm as he walked past.

"You heard anything about Terry Stafford dropping in?"

He shook his head, a sinking feeling in his gut. Of course, Terry Stafford was one of the guys who Braden had listened to as a kid, one of the comics who made him think this life was possible. He was also the subject of some nasty news of as late. If he was coming, this night had just gotten very interesting.

"If that son of a bitch does show up, I'm liable to take an ice cream scoop and hollow out his eyeballs," Jackie said. "He better keep away from me or there's gonna be blood. That's for free, too."

"You're giving away the store today in terms of advice."

The joke didn't land, as something darker had found its way into Jackie's face. Braden made a joke of making a note in his book and moving on.

He found comic number two, Jerrod Seybourne, not far from Jackie, talking to a group of white men in their late thirties who had clearly just come from work with their ties askew and drinks going down fast. When Braden approached, he thought he saw a flash of appreciation cross Jerrod's face, as if he was happy to get out of the conversation.

A little thick but solid, with big glasses and no hair, Seybourne had one foot in comedy and one foot in the cable news game. No one was really sure which one he preferred. He had racked up dozens of appearances on talk shows like *Anderson Cooper Live*, *The View*, and even *Fox and Friends* as a goofy guy with razor-sharp wit who could be counted on for bringing the pain when it came to politics and deliver it with a joke and a glimmer in his eye. But as a comic, he was as good as they came, which made the fact that he was opening the show somewhat of a mystery. He could very well be on TV right now, but Jerrod Seybourne was at The Square, about to do a set in front of a weekend crowd.

Braden walked right up and introduced himself, which was easy because Jerrod saw him coming and pulled out of the conversation with the businessmen.

"Hey, Mr. Seybourne, I'm Braden, I'm the emcee."

"Nice to meet you, man," Jerrod said, shaking his hand warmly. "Thanks for coming over. I was hoping you were the emcee and not someone else wanting to tell me about how their little slice of the country was falling apart."

"Yeah, I'm about comedy tonight," Braden said. "Glad I could help. Glad you're on the lineup. Whenever you're on CNN it seems to go viral."

"Yeah, that's me. Fighting the good fight, earning all those clicks."

Curiosity got the better of Braden and he had to raise his voice to be heard over the noise of the crowd, which now topped forty. The room suddenly seemed small and cramped, which was, of course, by design.

"I have you opening. I'm making sure that's right. I mean, you agreed to be first up tonight? At least I assumed you agreed. Jaff emailed me the list, so…"

Jerrod put his arm around Braden and pulled him in, not tight, but close. He smelled slightly of pot and mostly of the cologne he hoped was covering up the smell of pot.

"You ain't twenty-five yet, are you?"

"No, just getting started."

"This is great," Jerrod said. "You know Jackie over there?"

"Just met her a minute ago."

"Well, I met her fifteen years ago when I was still bouncing off the walls and she's been nothing but sweet to me, which is weird because laid back black guys and big loud Jewish ladies can sometimes end up hitting each other. But I've never had a bad time with her. She's funny as fuck. So, I see she's on the list, I say, 'Put her above me.' Helps maintain the relationship."

"Okay," Braden said, suddenly distracted by the whiff of burrito on Jerrod's breath. There was a killer burrito joint a few blocks down but it was pricey enough that Braden could never quite afford it at this stage of the game. He'd heard it was worth the trip to The Square just for the burrito by more than one comic.

"Second thing," Jerrod continued. "You said you seen me on CNN and MSNBC and all that shit?"

"Right."

"I'm trying to turn that juice into a show of my own, which is where Sammy comes in. Sammy's got his own little empire, right? He's got his big-ass talk show and on FX and he's always got something popping on YouTube and he's got that podcast? Turns out, he's tight with one of the execs at Comedy Central, who's considering my show right now as we speak. He's also kind of a bigger pull right now than I am, so I actually called Jaff and had him kick off some other comic to put me on the bill. I usually hate pulling that shit, but this is a very important time for me and it took me twenty fucking years to get here."

He released Braden from his grip but kept his hand on his shoulder.

"I've done so many shitty one-nighters at so many shitty clubs and now it's my time. That's why I'm opening, and you're my MC. So bring your A-game."

"Definitely," Braden said, feeling his blood pressure rise a bit. "Any way you want me to introduce you? People know you from all over the damn place."

"Say that," Jerrod said. "Makes me sound accomplished."

"You are, man."

"That's nice of you to say."

"Yeah," Braden said. "Thanks."

Braden walked away shaking his head. It was strange that

someone shared so much of their hopes and dreams within seconds of meeting someone else, but that was pretty mild compared to some of the things Braden had already seen in his brief career. He'd had run-ins with hardcore drug addicts, exhibitionists who'd show you their asshole if it came up in conversation (and often if it didn't), proud drunks, guilt-stricken Catholics, gamblers down to their last few bucks, active psychotics, compulsive liars, painfully sad sacks, hicks in over their heads, thieves who stripped the wires from buildings when they weren't telling jokes, and much worse. But they all had the same sort of gift and curse—they were able to make people laugh. Compared to some nights, this was shaping up to be a pretty great group, which brought Braden to Sammy Platter.

The next uncomfortable half hour was spent trying to track down Sammy Platter, and when that didn't work, tracking down Jaff to see where the hell he was, only to learn that Sammy never showed up on time. If he was closing, was likely to show up thirty minutes before his set, if they were lucky. A lot of comics did that sort of thing, Braden had noticed.

It was about twenty minutes before he was going to take the stage for one of the biggest sets of his young career when Taylor Tracks caught his eye.

"Shit," he muttered, riffling through his notebook to look busy. "Don't come over, don't come over…"

She came over.

"Hey there, you little asshole."

It was better than he thought he'd get.

Taylor, all five feet two inches of her, was looking sharp in a shiny, faux-leather jacket over a tank top, jeans, and her hair back in a "don't fuck with me" ponytail. They had been on a couple of dates a month or so ago and had slept together a couple of times.

After that, Braden had pulled back, almost to the point of ghosting her. The last message the two had sent each other was Taylor unleashing her considerable comedic chops on all his soft spots via text message, some of which kind of hurt, if he was being honest. There was also a long Instagram rant that was probably about him, but it was vague enough to where she could deny it.

It wasn't that he hadn't liked her. It's that she was, what was known in the profession as, "a lot." High energy, very pretty, and came with a pedigree. Braden remembered her grandfather had been a big wig at an amusement park at one point in time, but he couldn't remember which one.

"Taylor, hi," Braden said, trying to sound busy.

"The fuck!" she said, hitting him in the shoulder harder than he would have liked. "Did you honestly think we'd never run into each other. Idiot…we're both comics! We run in the same fucking circles."

"I know," he began.

"And you had the nerve to ignore me? Jesus, Braden, I don't sleep with people that dumb. At least, I didn't think I slept with people that dumb."

Clear that this confrontation was going to happen, he tucked his notepad in the back of his pants and turned to face her, trying to look deferential, but not too deferential.

"What do you want me to say?"

"Sorry would be nice."

"Okay. I am sorry," Braden said, putting the emphasis on "am."

"And tell me why you basically ghosted me, you pile of giraffe shit."

She punched him again in the same shoulder.

"Ow! Okay, you want a line or the truth?" he said, holding his shoulder for dramatic effect.

"Is the line funny?" she asked.

"I could make it funny."

"Betcha can't."

"Okay..."

Braden turned around and acted like he was facing an audience. He couldn't tell if it was cute or weird and feared it was some terrible combination of both. But he was already committed.

"I'm no good when it comes to dating, because it's so easy to screw up. You've heard of dealbreakers, right? Things that disqualify you from dating a person?"

He snuck a look at her and she seemed moderately amused, or at least not gearing up to hit him again.

"Well, I was out with this girl who was funny and sexy and kind of a bad ass, so already I'm a little intimidated, and it also turns out she was really good at sex. Like, shockingly good. Like, I'm struggling to make the JV squad and she's dunking all over me...it was like she was the Harlem Globetrotters, doing all those trick shots, and I'm standing at half court wondering how my pants ended up around my ankles."

She snorted, which made Braden feel good in that way that only comics truly know. The line had landed. It was a miracle considering he was making it up on the spot.

"So I knew how it was going to go," he said, still addressing the nonexistent crowd. "Once the new relationship energy wore off, I'd be left with the girl who was obviously more experienced and worldly than me and...shoot, I don't know how to end the bit yet. Give me a couple more swings at it, I'll figure it out."

"Yeah, that button sucks."

"I'm working on it."

"You made it...twenty percent funny," she said.

"I'll take twenty percent and I'll tell you what, I'll even prove to you how sorry I am by telling you a secret about tonight."

"Oooh, a secret," Taylor said. "Is it about how you're a giant pussy with anxiety issues?"

"What's secret about that? No, I'm talking about a big-time name that recently got into some big-time trouble that's coming around tonight"

"So, Terry Stafford?"

"Maybe."

"Introduce me to him and buy me a shot of Jameson before you go on and I'll consider you more than twenty percent forgiven."

"Sold," he said. "But the shot will have to be after the show. There's no way I'm getting through that crowd now."

The Square was now at capacity, a minor miracle considering the doors had opened roughly thirty-five minutes ago. There was a line at the bar, servers were hustling their asses, and Braden didn't see so much as an empty seat in the place. As he had come to expect, his shyness started to bubble up, and he pushed it back down and smacked it around a bit.

Just as Braden felt good about the upcoming set, excited about hosting this gig and generally happy with his decisions up until his point, he felt a sharp *whack* on the back of his head as Jaff, passing by, smacked him hard with an open hand. It was harder than Braden had been smacked in some time and he saw stars.

"The hell...?" he said.

"Get up there," he said. "We need a mic check. You're on soon."

Dumbstruck, Braden gave a small thumbs-up to Jaff, who flipped him the bird and disappeared back into the crowd.

"That was...shitty," Taylor said, the playfulness in her voice dying a quick death. "Deeply."

"Yeah," Braden agreed. and the implications of the slap began to settle in his brain. Jaff had a reputation as a bit of a grump, but a grump with scruples. He didn't pay the talent much (nobody did, really), but understood his place in the New York comedy scene as a stepping stone and treated comics well. He also had supporters who spoke highly of him and it wasn't unheard of for industry people to make their way to The Square now and again. In short, if he wasn't a good dude, he was at least an okay one in the eyes of everyone Braden had spoken to on the subject, and if he was in the business of hitting his emcees, that rep would have caught up with him by now.

*It'll certainly catch up with him now*, Braden thought. *I'll make sure of it.*

In the meantime, what else was there to do but get up and do the show?

"You gonna be okay after that?" Taylor asked.

"Oh yeah," Braden said, smiling. "I only act shitty toward people who let me see them naked."

"Fuck you."

"Yup," he said, smiling, getting ready to climb on the stage.

"Oh, real quick," Taylor said. "Who's first up?"

"Jerrod Seybourne," Braden said

"Okay, if you get the chance, tell him to eat a bag of dicks for me. He bumped me off this show and I didn't have time to reschedule. I could have found another set somewhere tonight if he hadn't been such an asshole about it."

Braden gave a small nod and jumped on stage, trying to put the slap, the drama, and the fact that a comedy legend who was in some hot water, whose appearance would definitely make waves, would be on this stage in a very short period of time. And he was in charge of keeping it all together, running smoothly, and making sure no one punched anyone.

Even with a few cobwebs still shaking out of his brain from Jaff hitting him, Braden had a good feeling. The crowd looked healthy and were giving off a good vibe. He recognized Raoul pulling double duty, running the sound board in between doing his job in the kitchen. It was so typical of a comedy club, Braden could hardly stand it. Raoul gave him a little wave and a big grin broke out over Braden's face. He had partially made up with a really hot girl. He was going to have a great story by the end of tonight no matter what happened. If his set went well, this could be one of the best nights of his life.

"You got this," he said to himself. "They're gonna love you. Everyone's gonna love you."

# CHAPTER 3

When the naked man opened the door to his hotel suite, Jackie Carmichael was momentarily unsure what she was looking at.

She had seen naked men before, to be sure. Some were pleasant enough to look at and do things with, others were complete horror shows of cascading flesh and discolored floppy bits. The one she was looking at was particularly problematic. Between the gut and the thick thatch of pubic hair playing backup to an off-colored five-incher she had not asked to see, the whole scene took a second to register, and when it did, panic set it. Then anger.

How dare he do this to her? How fucking dare he?

The man, who was older, richer, better connected, and in every way more powerful than her, paused a beat, letting his nakedness sink in. Then hit her with his best, most poetic pickup line.

"So, you gonna suck it or what?"

So charming. So romantic.

Under the normal run of things, Jackie would have thrown one-liners until the guy felt so bad about himself that he covered up. She would have hit him with a, "Got the AC cranked in there?" Or a, "That dick sucks enough already without my help," or a, "Die in a fire in front of your mother, you wrinkly piece of shit." She would yell at that dick until it retreated into the soft flesh, never to return. She had a way with words.

But this naked man and the fact that he had made himself naked with no encouragement or permission from her made all the difference. For one of the first times in her young, comedic career, Jackie had said nothing. Instead, she had run to the elevator on the fifteenth floor of the hotel, banged on the button for the longest twenty-five seconds of her life, and then spent hours walking the streets, trying hard to figure out what to do next. She had never felt so panicked or so alone because her dreams may have died when she refused the naked man's request in the doorway of that hotel room.

*What city was it?* Jackie thought. *It was hot and sticky. Houston, maybe?*

Cities, towns, clubs, and sets all faded and bled together at Jackie's advanced age of forty-nine. She had spent decades toiling in clubs and the naked man represented not the first or the fifth or the tenth time she'd been inappropriately propositioned in them. It had gotten better as she had gotten older and more established.

"And fatter," she said to herself in the bathroom of The Square, which was just as dingy and small as one might expect. She always made sure to pee before sets after a really rough one-nighter in Toronto where she pissed herself on stage and was able to hide it from the audience who was laughing so hard they hadn't noticed. She also wanted to be alone for a second and collect herself. On the outside, Jackie was a kick-ass broad in the best sense of the term and, truthfully, very few things rattled her. But the image of the naked man with his wild pubes and his wrinkly member and his sneering, superior sense of entitlement to her body and her sex, it rattled her something fierce.

"If Terry Stafford sets foot in this club," she said to the mirror in the bathroom, "I'm going to cut his fucking balls off on stage and throw them to the crowd."

***

Jackie arrived at The Square in the best professional position of her life. The crowd seemed to sense it.

The first time she grabbed hold of a mic was in New York City, where she grew up. She was sixteen, used a fake ID to get into the bar, and didn't know a soul in the joint. What she found, quickly, was she had a decent sense of what was funny, had a decent on-stage presence, and was scared of absolutely nothing. The audience laughed at her material but they also laughed at *how* she said it, which was part of that special sauce that made comics distinct and successful.

Most comics will tell you the first time they get a laugh on stage it's like heroin hitting the bloodstream, a pure, clarifying high that is never matched, and that was very much Jackie's experience. She started sneaking out at night to go to comedy clubs. She got good. Then she got very good, and by the time she was old enough to get into the bar legally, she was a legit rising talent.

Over the years, she had developed all the skills you needed to make it as a stand-up—she could craft a story and kill, she could do crowd work, she could bob and weave and write on the fly, she could callback with the best of them, and she had figured out who she was and brought a heightened version of it to the stage: big, loud, brash, and funny as fuck. She wasn't rich by any stretch but she made a living off stand-up and various writing gigs, which was her definition of success. She loved her life as a comic for years and years until age started to slow her down. She was prepared to do Vegas or maybe, God forbid, find somebody and settle down. But nothing had prepared her for peak TV.

Four years ago, a fellow stand-up who had done well for himself as a TV exec gave her a call and personally asked her to audition for *The Dapper*, a "prestige comedy," meaning it was a drama with more than two comedians in the writer's room. The part was the mother of the main character, an unlucky in love sad sack who was trying to learn to be a better man. There was really no plot to speak of, and, to be honest, Jackie didn't a hundred percent understand why everyone was so gaga over the show, but she understood her part in it and nailed it to the fucking wall.

By the time they had been renewed for season two there was honest-to-God award buzz around her work. Turned out, she wasn't a bad actress. Not that it was her first time, but stand-up was always her bread and butter, and TV changed her standup in big, bad ways. First off, it wasn't just comedy nerds and repeat customers who sought her out—it was couples on dates, parents away from the kids, aspiring actors, super fans of the show who all kind of resembled the lovable sloths they saw reflected on their screens, industry types who wanted "meetings," and more. She couldn't do a show anymore without people coming up and asking for her autograph, which, after more than twenty years on the road, was surreal.

It also meant every now and then there was a walkout when someone hadn't taken the time to google "Jackie Carmichael, comedy" before coming to the show. She sure as shit wasn't going to tone down her act now that she was on TV. Not after clawing to make a name for herself on her own terms. The act she had developed was raunchy and rough and involved a lot of yelling at the crowd. It wasn't everyone's cup of tea.

So, things were getting complicated in the best of ways, and if there was any group of people in the world who understood that, it was other comics.

"You really smacked the shit out of Frank Luntz on CNN the other night," Jackie said after composing herself in the bathroom and leaving to find Jerrod Seybourne waiting for her. She gave him a big hug—she was a hugger—and talked shop.

"Frank Luntz doesn't feel pain," Jerrod said. "He's had all his nerves removed and replaced them with money. He drives a fucking Lamborghini. Like, unironically."

"Douchebag," Jackie said. "I wanted to talk to you. Thank you for taking the first spot tonight. I figured you could have put up a fight if you wanted."

"Ain't no thing," Jerrod said. "You're a big star, Jackie."

She blushed. As much as she loved the cast and directors and zeros on her paycheck that came with TV work, it still made her a bit embarrassed to talk about it. For all her brashness, she had never learned the fine art of taking a compliment.

"Figured you'd have your own show by now," she said. "You could be the black Jon Stewart."

"Larry Wilmore was the black Jon Stewart and Comedy Central cancelled his ass. And Trevor Noah is South African black and he sucks. Get with the times, Jackie. What I figure I'll do is just be me and see where that gets me."

"As long as you keep beating the shit out of Frank Luntz."

"That ain't hard," Jerrod said. "Now beating the shit out of Frank Luntz and making 'em laugh while you do it, that's a challenge."

Jackie chuckled. She always liked this kid and he gave off a really relaxed vibe.

"Can I ask you a favor?" she said.

"What you need?"

"Backup."

The fact that Terry Stafford was rumored to be coming out to a club was a big deal. At this point, Terry Stafford leaving his house would be a big deal. Earlier in the week, four women had gone on the record in the *New York Times*, claiming Stafford had forced them into situations where he could proposition them, and when they turned him down, assaulted them. He had denied the allegations and given one of those "I'm sorry to whoever I offended" sort of half-assed apologies. Within thirty-six hours of the paper hitting the street the once legendary comic's career was starting to circle the drain.

He lost his job as the voiceover pitchman for a rental car company right away. Shortly after, his short-running but much replayed sitcom had been taken off a streaming service, a development costing a lot of people a lot of money. Then, worst of all, two of the women brought criminal complaints, meaning Terry might be in an orange jump suit by the middle of next year.

Why he was coming out to a show was anyone's guess, as was why Jaff would let him anywhere near his club. Jackie figured he'd want another crack at stand-up to remind audiences why they loved him. It was hard to understand if you hadn't been doing stand-up for most of your life and didn't have an ego the size of a blimp.

"So you heard Terry Stafford might be showing up?"

Jerrod nodded.

"I have no idea why Jaff is letting him within a hundred yards of his stage, but let's just say I know him to be a creep firsthand, if you follow me."

"I follow you," he said, suddenly grave. "Was your…experience as bad as the women in the *Times*?"

"Not as bad, but I can tell you what his dick looks like."

"I definitely do not want that in my brain. You're going to confront him, I figure? That's what you need backup for, right?"

"I knew you were smart, Mr. Seybourne."

"Yeah, I've got your back," he said. "I'm no fucking good in a fight, but I'll definitely stand behind you and look black."

"I appreciate it."

She went in for another hug and went and got another drink from the bar. To her surprise, she was shaking a little bit and it pissed her off. Part of her wanted to go back into the bathroom and slap herself upside the head and pull it together. In the meantime, gin and tonic would have to do the trick.

Before the show kicked off, Jackie pulled up a seat at the bar, said hi to the bartender, and gave some basic advice to a very enthusiastic busboy who said he wanted to be a comic. From there, everyone was taking their seats, so she let her mind drift a bit.

The green room at The Square was underground, far away from everyone. It had a closed-circuit TV hooked up so you could watch the show, but she never liked it down there. Something about it smelled too old for her. You could air freshen the shit out of that room and the dank would bleed through, ghosts of a thousand sweaty comics and just as many beers spilled, coke lines snorted and God knew what else the filthy comics in this club did. A lot of places smelled like that, but The Square smelled worse. It was weird.

Her mind drifted to another green room on the set of *The Tonight Show*. She had gotten to do the show with Carson before he retired, an honor that she had found underwhelming. When she first started taking the stage, comics built up *The Tonight Show* like it was the gates of Oz itself, with a wizard who could make or break your career right there. You put together the Clean Carson 5, got a sitcom, and were a success. For years that was the way you did it, and any other route led to a dead-end taco with a sadness shell.

Jackie had gone on, killed like she knew she would, and never heard a thing. Not a sniff. Not a fucking phone call. Nothing. And in her gut, she knew Terry Stafford had a hand in that.

She had gone back to the clubs, made some decent money, had an HBO special, rode the wave of the new media like a champ and landed on her feet. So fuck Terry Stafford. She was going to hand him his ass tonight. She didn't usually kick people when they were down, but in his case, she'd made an exception and kick him right in the balls.

The show started and the emcee seemed a bit shaky at first, but ultimately landed a solid few minutes and got Jerrod up on stage no problem. Just as he started, the bartender shooed away a customer and Sammy Platter had a seat next to her at the bar.

Platter, who started life as a morning radio DJ and worked his way up to talk show host on basic cable, wasn't a great stand-up in Jackie's opinion. He could make a crowd laugh, which, technically, is the one and only requirement for the job, but Jackie had a technical term for his brand of stand-up, and it was "pandering bullshit." Some comics had one act for the clubs and another for those precious few corporate gigs that came along where you needed to be PG-13 but got paid a lot more. Sammy had never separated the two.

"Sammy!" she said, and gave him a hug. "Nice to see you."

Her big frame wrapped neatly around his trim one and she noticed he had worn a suit to the occasion. Jackie was old enough to remember Sammy in jeans and t-shirts, drunk every night in the back of the room. It was weird seeing a guy who used to be a raging alcoholic get his shit together and go the other route— corporate boards, business speak, suits when you were on stage. Not that it helped his stand-up any.

"Nice to see you too," he said. "But closing after you is a pain in the ass."

"The audience will recognize you from TV," she said. "You'll be fine."

"*You're* on TV," Sammy said back. "And you're still the best stand-up I've ever seen."

"Damn right."

Jerrod was up and into his set, and she sat and watched with Sammy. After a few seconds of paying attention, he took out his comically oversized cell phone and started taking notes. Jackie figured interrupting him might be good for a laugh.

"That's a big fucking phone there, Sammy," she whispered.

"Yeah, It's a Note 12. Not on the market yet."

"Seriously, you ought to be able to call in air support on that thing."

He snorted but kept typing.

"If I didn't know better, I'd say you were compensating for something."

He tapped faster, and when he finished, she had a big grin on her face. Both of them knew Sammy was doing very well for himself and a good part of his income was tech companies who liked anyone who was reasonably plugged into their culture. Given that Sammy was an entitled douche more often than not, he fit the bill.

"You're a brat," he said to her.

"Yeah, kinda. You hear Terry Stafford might come by tonight?"

"I did, yeah. Why do you think I'm in this shithole?"

A loud bang from behind the bar startled Jackie, and when she looked back at Sammy, he had a weird look on his face. Across the bar, shards of glass were still vibrating and moving across the bar. A few patrons turned their heads but quickly went back to Jerrod and his jokes about pot.

"Don't talk shit about my club or I'll bust your head open for you."

Jaff Maul stood behind the bar, blood trickling from the hand he had used to smash the glass. From the looks of it, the glass hadn't been delicate either, with thick chunks still visible as he went to clean it up.

"Whoa, Jaff, sorry," Sammy said. "I didn't mean anything by it."

"The fuck you didn't" Jaff said, wrapping a cloth around his injured hand. Jackie immediately saw blood soak through the already brownish rag and bloom into odd, red blotches. As quickly as he had appeared, he stormed off, leaving the bartender, who was already extremely busy, to pull double duty and clean up glass from around the bar.

"Sorry about that," the bartender said. "He's been extra grumpy tonight."

"There's grumpy and then there's psychotic," Sammy said. "Jesus Christ, what the hell just happened?"

"I don't know, but there are a lot of bad feelings floating around tonight," Jackie said, stirring her drink. Jackie's mother, God rest her soul, had been a bit of a psychic, and while Jackie wasn't big into mysticism and such, if you nailed her down, she believed in energies, positive and negative. And there was negative energy coming off The Square in waves tonight.

As a veteran stand-up, bad energy was not enough to keep her from doing her job. Far from it. She had performed after a drunk had punched her in the face, performed on a stage after it collapsed, worked while microphones were on the fritz and still killed, screaming her jokes to a crowd who ate it all up. Good comics could stand on a street corner and get a crowd on their side by the time their set was over. Hell, after Terry Stafford had exposed his wrinkly cigar dick to her, she performed the next night as if nothing had happened because that was her job.

But something about tonight was telling her to run. Bad energy, Terry Stafford, Jaff being a psychopath—it was all adding up to something bad that was pulling her toward the door.

She waved it off and got ready to do her job.

# Chapter 4

For an extra two hours added on to his day, Sammy Platter would straight murder another human being with his bare hands and do it with a big smile on his face and gratitude in his heart.

In the beginning of his career, Sammy had nothing but time. He chose, at that stage of life, to fill that time with booze, women, and stand-up comedy, most of the time in that order. For a while, that was more than enough to make him insanely happy. He and his stand-up or writer friends would spend late nights, three sheets to the wind in diners, recounting their stories of sets they'd done, projects they finished, ladies they had banged. After a while, he had landed a job on the radio doing the morning beat and things only got better once there was steady money coming in.

He was living the mothafuckin' dream, as he used to say, but, like others before him, he burnt out right quick on booze, pot, and bad feelings. After the burn out, the resulting husk couldn't make his job or his gigs. He was fired from the radio and was very quickly not good for very much. After a while, the only thing he was really good at was the Final Fantasy series on the PlayStation and getting girls to go home with him from bars, both of which weren't highly valued on the job market.

Bloated, alone, and drunk most of the time, he had a revelation on stage at one of the only comedy clubs he'd managed to maintain a professional relationship with—if he didn't get his shit together, he was going to die like this. It was something his mother and his friends and, hell, his one-night stands had told him, but for some reason the message finally penetrated his skull and sunk into the soft gray matter when he opened up about it on stage for the first time.

"You all wanna hear a secret?" Sammy told the crowd. "I think I'm an alcoholic. And you all laugh, but I'm serious. In about a minute or so you guys are going to be looking around the room saying, 'Is he really serious?' and the answer is yes, I'm really serious."

The crowd kept laughing, waiting for the punch line that never came as Sammy spilled his guts about the flaming wreckage that was his life. He talked about waking up and having hard liquor with breakfast, about pregaming with a twelve-pack of beer before going out at night, about throwing up on a stripper (which got a pretty good laugh). Little did he know that someone was filming and the clip was uploaded to YouTube and watched hundreds of thousands of times. Before Sammy knew it, people were reaching out, his phone was ringing nonstop, and for the first time in his life when he wasn't on stage, he felt like somebody gave a shit about him.

A year to the day after that video was uploaded, Sammy went on Oprah to talk about his recovery, and, with the magic touch of Oprah in his corner, things blossomed. He wrote a comedic self-help book which shot to number three on the *New York Times* best seller list, he started getting very lucrative speaking gigs at corporate events, and, because of his years on the radio and in stand-up, he eventually landed a talk show on basic cable. It all happened because of getting clean, working hard, and, let's face it, talent.

*What's Up with Sammy Platter* wasn't a traditional talk show format with five-minute conversations with celebrities promoting their latest projects. He wouldn't have done it if that was the pitch. Through his journey of self-discovery and recovery he had learned that a person's most valuable commodity was their experience and their story. Before he started his own show he made the rounds, talking to anyone and everyone who would talk to him about what they'd do if they had a show. Finally, when he went in to pitch, he made it as simple as possible—"what makes you so great...with jokes."

The resulting show wasn't exactly a sensation, but it was a solid performer, and as it grew, Sammy kept getting bigger and bigger guests. While it started with some of his comic and actor friends, it eventually drew titans of industry, politicians, and, in the end of the second season, Oprah herself. It was his highest rated episode, obviously, and announced to the world that Sammy Platter was in the upper echelon, a man who came from the humble beginnings of the comedy club and accomplished something big.

Through it all he never stopped doing stand-up, even when everyone told him to. He had lost tens of thousands of dollars in speaking gigs to keep his chops sharp in clubs and he bragged to anyone who would listen about how stand-up was the only constant in his forty-one years of life and how he'd be lost without it. Sure, he was in the best shape of his life, he drove a Jaguar, his bank account had seven figures, and he was bringing home eights and nines instead of fours and fives like in his bar days, but he never wanted to forget where he came from. In his book he'd written, remembering your roots was one of his seven keys to success.

But that's not why he was at The Square.

Over the years, it was one of his least favorite rooms and he didn't much care for Jaff Maul, who didn't much care for him. And that was cool. Not everyone had to be into you and you could be okay with that (key to success number four). He wasn't here to ply his trade, because, as much as he talked, it was getting easier and easier for Sammy to sacrifice stand-up to his many, many more lucrative ventures. He was enduring time at The Square because Terry Stafford was going to be there and he was going to land the first interview since allegations came to light that he had sexually assaulted at least four women, with more coming out of the woodwork every day. Stafford was a comic's comic, and only a comic could land the interview. At least that's what Sammy was banking on.

But first, he wanted to have a word with the owner.

Jerrod had finished his set (which Sammy hadn't heard due to the glass incident) and Jackie was just getting started with some crowd members ("You're a dentist? Got a thing for sticky wet tongues, do ya?"), when Sammy saw Jaff duck into his small office of main floor. He moved quickly and shut the door behind him, a strange move for someone in the middle of their prime business hours where he surely had more than enough responsibilities to keep him busy.

Given that Sammy was on a mission and didn't give half a fuck about Jaff Maul and his emotional state, he didn't bother knocking and felt a little thrill when he realized the door was unlocked. He swung the door hard, itching for a fight, and it banged into the back of a chair.

"The fuck?"

Terry Stafford, looking fatter than Sammy had ever seen him, had thrown his bulk into a rolling chair and the momentum had brought him within the door's proximity. Jaff must have snuck him in, which was easy to do in a comedy club where the attention was literally focused on one spot.

Stafford, known for years for his amazing stand-up chops and leading man good looks, looked like shit. Aside from his considerable bulk, his hair seemed a little shaggy and much whiter than Sammy had ever seen it. His clothes looked too tight and the bags under his eyes could send him on a European vacation. Even still, his presence still invoked a bit of awe. He was, after all, one of the inventors of modern comedy and a guy who little Sammy Platter had listened to for years in his youth.

Jaff was immediately pissed off by the interruption.

"Get out, Sammy."

"Hey, Terry. How are ya? Jaff, what the hell?"

"Get the fuck out. I'm not asking."

"What you gonna do, break another glass?"

The expression on Jaff's face went from white-hot rage to almost calm in a fraction of a second and it genuinely unnerved Sammy. He had seen that sort of change before, right before bar fights, and it never amounted to anything good.

"Tell you what. Stay here another few seconds and I'll come over there and show you."

"I'm done with this club," Sammy said, shutting the door.

"You will be missed," Jaff yelled, and continued whatever important conversation he was having with Terry. Most comics can tell you horror stories about dealing with club owners who don't pay you or short you or generally treat you like shit, and some had reputations for being openly hostile to the talent, but this seemed beyond the pale and Sammy was pissed.

Chances were pretty good that Jackie was going to go a half hour, maybe longer if she was really cooking, so Sammy hung out in front of the office, waiting for both of them to emerge. He watched the crowd, not quite sure what he was going to do. Maybe he'd confront Jaff, maybe he wouldn't, but either way, he wasn't going back to the bar. There was nothing there for him anyway. He'd been sober for more than eight years and had stabbed that particular demon in the eye until it stopped moving. Key to success number three.

As he sat at the bar, sipping a Pellegrino and waiting, his annoyance gave way to genuine anger. Who the hell was Jaff to treat Sammy like that? On the street on his way here, he had been recognized three times. He had taken five selfies with people at the club. He reached an audience of millions every week. He was one of *People Magazine*'s Sexiest Men Alive - Comedy Edition. They were lucky to have him here. The only thing that pulled him out of his head was watching Jackie, who had not only won over the crowd, but was taking them for a ride.

Jackie really was a good comic. She was five minutes into her set and hadn't touched her material yet, just poking at people in the audience and getting killer laughs because of it. He was never a crowd work guy, but one of his favorite moments, ever, on stage involved a drunk lady who tried to insert herself into his show. He came down on her with everything he had, and when he was done, she was in tears and the crowd was still on his side. He's still not sure how he managed that and would pay handsomely for a tape of that night. Ever since then he not only knew he could handle himself, he knew he could handle himself well.

As he hung out, he clocked a small girl in a faux leather jacket working her way toward him. The crowd was good, but not standing room only, so anyone standing up immediately stood out, and she was moving toward him at an appropriate speed, keeping her eye on the stage. He prepped for the inevitable approach which he recognized. He was famous, after all.

"Hey," the girl whispered. "You're Sammy, right?"

"Yeah."

"I'm Taylor. Big fan."

"Thanks."

"I'm a comic, too. Can I talk to you after the show?"

"Sure. I'm watching the Jackie show right now."

"Yeah. She's really good. Right, I'll track you down, then."

He's not sure why he said it, or why it even occurred to him, but it probably had more to do with the girl being petite and pretty than he would have liked to admit.

"You know where the green room is?"

"Yeah, downstairs."

"That's where I'll be."

The girl gave a big, radiant smile that made her eyes sparkle and she was off, back to the bar. Jackie was on her prepared material, which was polished and structured and damned funny. Sammy started thinking about his set, which was probably for the best, because in less than ten minutes, he'd be up in front of an audience with high expectations who had just seen a great comic do a great set. He could do his bit on how celebrities were different from normal people, that always worked as a way to get him on the audience's side. A story about a sexual mishap as a young man worked well for a closer. He wasn't sure what would happen in the middle, but something would occur to him. It always did.

Wrapping up with a great bit about her audition for *The Dapper*, Jackie left the stage to applause and a few coveted whoops from the crowd, always a good sign. Sammy ran his fingers through his short hair and got ready to go on.

"Jackie Carmichael, everybody," the emcee said. "So, before we bring up Sammy Platter, I have a bit of an announcement. Here's the club owner, Jaff Maul. Come on up here, Jaff."

"What the hell?" Sammy said to himself.

Sammy hadn't noticed it before, but Jaff was looking like he'd been hit by a car. His ever-present stubble was a bit scruffier, his shirt was untucked, he was pale, and he seemed like he wasn't entirely with it. Then he opened his mouth and removed all doubt.

"Yeah, uh, hi," Jaff said.

"Strong start," Sammy muttered.

"Look, I run this place, and something truly brave is about to happen," Jaff said, immediately bringing the room down. "So you've all probably heard about a bunch of guys losing their jobs recently because women said they grabbed their titties or whatever."

Though the crowd didn't make a sound, any experienced comic could see he had just lost the room something fierce. As someone who had lost a crowd or two in his day, Sammy knew Jaff was only hurting matters by doing this introduction. It felt wrong on several levels.

"Well, that happened to a friend of mine just the other day and he called and asked me if he could come do the one thing he loves doing, stand-up comedy. He's a brave guy for doing it and I want you to show him some love. So, everyone..."

"You son of a bitch," Sammy said.

"Please welcome to the stage legendary performer and a great guy, Terry Stafford!"

"He bumped me," Sammy said. "Motherfucker bumped me."

Getting bumped was a unique form of rejection that never failed to sting, but Sammy, who was not usually an angry guy (key to success number nine), was suddenly red hot and wanted another word with the owner. For a terrible moment he wasn't sure whether to head to the back of the room and confront Jaff or listen to what could, in all actuality, but one of the great stand-up train wrecks of all time. Terry Stafford was good, but no one was good enough to win a crowd after you'd been publicly accused of sexually assaulting several women. Thanks to Jaff's awkward introduction, Terry had an even bigger hole to dig out of.

In the end, he figured he'd watch for a few minutes then track down Jaff and maybe take a swing at him. As he made that decision, Stafford lumbered on stage, unsteady and unsure as a newbie taking an open mic for the first time.

"Thanks," Stafford said after a slow round of applause, his husky voice sounding even heavier. "So, uh, I had a bunch of material written about my wife, but I'm not thinking that's going to go over very well."

It got a small laugh and was smart, Sammy thought. Gotta point out that elephant. He looked at the crowd and noticed two young women, both with phones out, capturing the moment. They were dressed differently than a normal comedy club patron and were most likely media that had been tipped off or called to the club.

After the first joke, the room had gone completely still.

"My...uh, my job here is to make you laugh, right?" Stafford said, his voice slow and lumbering. "But I've being accused of some pretty heinous shit recently so...why the hell am I even up here? Well, I got a reason. See, when I was fifteen, my dad beat the hell out of me, just laid into me each and every day when he got home from work, so...I found the best way to deal with that was to not be there when he pulled into the driveway."

Another small ripple of laughter ran through the crowd.

"I would wander around this city and I'd make friends. One of my friends, this dude named Anthony Plinn, he and I snuck into this bar in hopes of finding half-full bottles of beer, right, and turns out it's an open mic night. As a goof, I got up there and started making fun of people and telling them how ugly they are, and next thing I know, they're laughing.

"It was the best moment of my life," he continued. "I was a broke, punk kid and comedy gave me everything I ever had, my houses, my, cars my—and, look, I know some of you are sitting there thinking, 'He's a piece of shit who deserves everything that's coming to him,' and maybe you're right, but I'm wondering if, as an act of mercy, all you would be willing to let me, maybe for the last time in this life, I could tell you about the time I called my dad a fartknocker."

"Holy shit, that's brilliant," Sammy whispered to himself..

Sammy knew, as did the rest of the crowd, that one of the first things that made Terry Stafford a star was this story, which was also the title of his breakthrough comedy album. The empire that was now crumbling around him was built on this story. It was his signature and Sammy found himself saying the words along with Terry, beat for beat, joke for joke. Many in the crowd were doing the same thing.

"...and when Jimmy Collins had called me a fartknocker, it was a term of endearment. When I called my dad a fartknocker, it was something else..."

On one level, this was genius, Sammy thought, and on another level, it was one of the most sociopathic things he'd ever seen. The world was telling him to go away. Lawyers must be screaming at him to lie low. The law was, rightfully, telling him he was done as a free man. Yet, here he was, feeding his ego one last time, reminding everyone of how great he used to be, that he had once been something great instead of the old, fat rapist currently occupying the stage. He couldn't help himself. How sad.

After fifteen minutes, Stafford smiled real big, used his giant hand to wipe away a few tears, and told the audience good night.

The woman in the back stopped filming and that was that. No yelling, no protesting, no fuss, just the end. That was the show. Sammy checked his watch real quick and it wasn't anywhere near a normal time to end a comedy show on the weekend. In fact, it was prime time for any club, but people were getting up and leaving like that was the end. He clocked Stafford heading toward the stairs to The F Pit, where he assumed the other comics were.

Sammy ran his fingers through his sandy blond hair again.

"Go get him," he said to himself by way of a pep talk. "He's not getting away."

# Chapter 5

She couldn't hold on to anything, so the fall never stopped.

Moments and memories, all tainted by something terrible happening beyond the edge of the frame, kept floating by like clouds. They were made of nothing, and as hard as she tried, she couldn't anchor to them, couldn't pull herself back, couldn't stop the fall. Every time she tried, the red creeped in around the edges of her eyes and she fell.

*FLASH.*

Pain and panic would consume everything, and then, a moment later, she was adrift, trying desperately to grab onto anything, even the electric current of pain. Nothing worked. Instead, the pain vanished and was replaced by her past, presented in second-long chunks by her dying brain.

Her ninth birthday party where she punched Susie Wren in the face for taking too much cake.

Snorting cocaine with a few of her friends while in their cap and gowns for high school graduation.

Being on the streets of New York, hustling, stealing, doing any drug she could get her hands on. Eventually she got clean and found her niche working in a comedy club, co-running it with her friend and lover, a laid-back guy who had a mean streak, apparently.

Lying in bed as the sun streamed through her window, realizing she had found something close to a purpose.

*FLASH.*

The voice was there, telling her terrible things. It demanded she let go, succumb, give way to whatever was at the end of this. The voice wanted her to die and to bleed, and its laugh was sweet and terrible. She could almost feel tendrils of the voice in her brain, spiking its way through the grey matter, unyielding and hungry.

*FLASH.*

The pain was back and it brought with it a pathway. She didn't really understand how or why, but she knew that if she followed the pain, she could find a way out, away from the hole, away from the voice worming its way through her mind. If she hung on to the searing, intense feeling, she could escape.

*FLASH.*

She followed, psychically gripping with everything she had, everything she was, and the pain stayed with her, not a compatriot but a companion. The voice fought back, but she felt the grip loosen, felt her control return. Before she knew it, smells flooded her nostrils and pain bloomed across her battered body—her back, her neck, her face, her legs. Thought returned as well and flooded into her brain.

*I can't move one of my arms.*

*Jaff called me a cunt.*

*I'm bleeding and I'm going to vomit.*

*Why do I smell ammonia?*

The smell, that acrid chemical scent with a top note that whispered "danger," was the clue she needed, the thing she could hang on to. She was in the cleaning closet at the bottom of the stairs in The Square on the island of Manhattan in the city of New York. Her boyfriend had attacked her, beat her, stabbed her, and had seemed to take glee in doing it. He had beaten her and she had taken it and she had held on. She was in a desperate situation. If she didn't move, she was going to die.

She was not going to die.

As she struggled to pull herself out of the fetal position in which she'd curled, willing her limbs to start moving, Calista Jones-Maul started the long process of getting out of the closet at the bottom of the stairs.

***

Jerrod was not going to miss this.

He was not a fighter. Or, more accurately, he wasn't currently a fighter. He had grown out of a fierce temper when he was younger, throwing down early and often, with a few fat lips and school suspensions to show for it. But he wasn't a fighter now, and the sheer amount of fun he'd have watching Jackie Carmichael throw down with Terry Stafford in The F Pit at The Square, that was worth maybe getting punched in the mouth over. He could take it, but it wouldn't come to that, he thought. Just a lot of talk and one hell of a great story afterward. If that meant hanging out in a dingy-ass green room, that was a price of admission he was willing to pay.

*Someone's going to bleed.*

Being a man who was familiar with the inside of his own head, Jerrod didn't recognize the voice throwing the dark thought out there. For a second, he had to check himself to make sure he was alone in the room, but he was. He shooed away the dark thought, not sure what else to do with it. Normally, his darker thoughts were of women and power, not blood.

He grabbed a bottle of water from a small mini fridge, took a long drink, and arched his eyebrow as a diminutive woman, her hair pulled back in a harsh pony tail, came in.

"Shit," he muttered. Jerrod had been in this situation enough to know, in broad strokes, what was coming.

"Hey, man," the woman said. "I'm waiting for Sammy."

"Cool," Jerrod said. "Sit, if you like."

"Well, I would, but I'm afraid as I was sitting, you'd jump in quick and snatch my seat from me."

Jerrod waved his finger, a smile blooming on his face.

"That's a good joke."

"I thought so," she said

"You're funny. I'm gonna remember that. I'm Jerrod."

"Taylor," she said, shaking his hand and smiling. "You bumped me."

"I wish I was sorry about bumping you, but I had a very good reason."

"I'm sure," Taylor said. "And hey, shit happens. I'm sure it was nothing personal."

"That's right," Jerrod said, pointing the bottle of water at her. "Nothing personal. I'm glad you didn't come down here to bust my balls."

"Nope," Taylor said. "I'm waiting for Sammy. He and I have some business."

"You make that sound like a mob hit or something."

"Oh yeah. I'm not gonna just break his knee caps, either. There's gonna be blood."

That sounded familiar, Jerrod thought.

The two chuckled and joked around a bit more and Jerrod flopped down on the couch. The room itself was actually nice as far as green rooms went. What The Square sacrificed in convenience to the stage it made up for in decor, with two full-sized couches, three chairs, a mini fridge, two coffee tables, an old-school exposed brick exterior, a closed-circuit TV showing what was going on upstairs, and, of course, the big F Pit sign made of metal and light bulbs on the far side. It was a cool space, Jerrod decided, if a little cramped. He'd definitely been in worse. Recently. It was dirty, but all green rooms were dirty.

He pulled out his phone to check messages. There was no data connection at all.

"Really?"

"Really what?" Taylor asked.

"I can't get email or nothin' down here. Dude needs to put a second router down here. It's just good manners anymore."

"I kind of like it."

"You kind of like not being able to get online?"

Taylor motioned to the screen.

"It forces me to watch the show."

Jackie was finishing her set and people were rolling.

"I get to see why she's so good. She's been doing it for decades, so if I can't learn something from someone like Jackie Carmichael, it's my own fault."

"Yeah, I got all the advice I need," Jerrod said, going back to his phone. A few minutes later, they heard a shuffling sound as Jackie came down the concrete steps and burst into The F Pit with the force with which she had just left the stage.

"He's here."

"Who?" Jerrod said, still working on his phone to no effect. "Oh, yeah, Terry Stafford. Right."

"You stoners," Jackie said, smiling. "If I asked you to find your ass with a flashlight, you'd lose the flashlight."

"Yeah, but we wouldn't give a shit, and you can buy another flashlight, so..."

Taylor, who had never met Jackie before, jumped in.

"Great set," she said. "So, Terry Stafford is up there?"

"Yeah. If I'm not wrong, Jaff bumped Sammy to get him on stage."

Over the closed-circuit, they saw Stafford take the stage and make his plea to the audience. By the time the crowd gave him a small round of applause and he launched into his old routine, Jackie had had more than enough.

"Jesus Christ, are they serious? He's a pig. He's always been a pig and everyone knows he's always been a pig and he comes in, plays the sad sack, and all of a sudden he wins the room? Are you fucking serious?"

"I don't know," Taylor said. "His *Live From Reno* was my favorite comedy album for years."

Jackie shot Taylor a glance that almost had a physical effect.

"Who are you?"

"Oh, sorry, Taylor Tracks. Big fan."

"Taylor Tracks? You sound like a Ben and Jerry's ice cream flavor. How about it, girl? You got a chocolate swirl in ya?"

Jerrod snorted, despite himself.

"Hey, little miss Taylor, why are you even down here? I didn't see you on stage tonight."

"Yeah, ask Jerrod about that."

Jackie turned and smiled. She knew the score.

"You bumped the adorable up-and-coming stand-up comic so you could get on the bill?"

Finally breaking contact with his phone, Jerrod made a large "what are you going to do" style gesture, he palms up, shoulders back. He had his reasons, and if Jackie found out he had bumped a comic to get a word with Sammy about a possible show, she would chew him a new one and spit it out hard enough to make another new one. She was old-school like that, plus she was currently in the mood to help out a young female comic who was just starting out.

"See, that's why this Terry Stafford thing has me so goddamn hot," Jackie said. "It's the entitlement. You men just think you can walk all over us forever, don't you?"

"I think I said the same thing on Kumal's CNN show a couple weeks ago," Jerrod said, smiling a little bit.

Jackie took a breath with the intent of laying into Jerrod, but Sammy opened the door and walked in. Jerrod immediately sat up a little straighter.

"Hey, Sammy," Jackie said, immediately changing her energy. "I didn't see your set."

"Yeah, because fuckin' Jaff kicked me off completely so Terry Stafford could do his 30-year-old material," Sammy said. "I get that it's newsworthy, but why not have me on, then bring Terry up? I'm not nothing. I've got a fucking following, man."

Rant over, he looked around the room and realized he didn't know two thirds of the people in it.

"Hey," he said, a bit sheepishly. "I'm Sammy."

"Jerrod Seybourne," he said. "I was the opener."

"Oh yeah," Sammy said. "I've seen you before. You're a political comic, right?"

"I did most of my set tonight on smoking weed, but yeah, I do a lot of political shit."

Taylor saw the opportunity to jump into the conversation and pounced, albeit ackwardly.

"I'm Taylor Tracks," she said. "We met upstairs. I was supposed to be on tonight, so I guess we have something in common."

"Taylor Tracks?" Sammy said. "That sounds like something a cartoon character would feed to his dog."

"I went with an ice cream flavor," Jackie said.

"I didn't make a joke at all," Jerrod said.

Taylor blushed and the three comics chuckled to themselves, riffing a bit more on what the name sounded like. It was a nice reprieve from the anger that had been thick in the room and was more indicative of what the post-show hang was like— an AP English class full of kids in therapy hanging out in detention after the teacher had left the room. Taylor jumped in, suggesting her name sounded like a toddler's toy they stopped manufacturing in the '80s.

On the television, Terry Stafford had transitioned to a bit of crowd work, and once the bit sort of died (and Taylor's cheeks stopped flushing), attention slowly turned back to the old comic.

"I know he's a piece of shit, but he was really great once," Taylor said.

Everyone sort of nodded.

"I remember the first time I met him," Sammy said. "It was the early nineties and he had just peaked. He had done that HBO special, remember when that was a thing?"

"I remember when they tried to make him a romantic lead, do you remember that?" Jerrod said. "They put him with, like, three of four interchangeable white ladies and he did the same movie a bunch of times and they all bombed."

"That was so stupid," Taylor said.

For a split second, Jackie tried to decide whether to let the group in on her little interaction with Terry years ago at the door of his hotel room, which was strange because Jackie's mouth usually worked faster than her brain. In this case, the brain and the mouth were in total agreement. Fuck that guy.

"I remember when I was twenty-four, he called me to his hotel room and told me to suck his dick."

The mood in the room rocketed downward, everyone going

silent.

"I remember the look on his face. I remember how he just expected me to fall down and worship him, like my sexuality and what I wanted were something he was entitled to. Yeah. You guys remember his albums and his movies. I remember that."

"I…I didn't know," Taylor stammered. "I'm so sorry."

"Don't be sorry, sweetie. He's a charming guy, but deep down, he's the guy who takes advantage of you when he thinks he can get away with it."

"Think he's coming down here?" Sammy asked.

As if an answer to his question had fallen from the sky, Braden came around the corner. His black hair was disheveled and he looked like he'd been running around. He'd also had a solid few short sets in between the featured performers, which typically put emcees in a decent mood most of the time. He was clearly somewhere else.

"Good, some of you are down here. I have a situation and I don't know how to deal with it."

"You look like you just found a dead body," Taylor said, half teasing.

"No," he said. "But Jaff just told me nobody's getting paid tonight."

***

As Stafford was doing his thing, Braden had found Jaff at the back of the bar, a tumbler full of fine-looking scotch in his hand, a glass of water on the bar. His intention had been to ask if he wanted Braden to say good night to the crowd or if there were more performers coming up. Things had gone a bit wacky in terms of the lineup and he had missed one of his spots and wasn't sure if Sammy was still going up or not.

Jaff had been less than helpful.

"Everyone's going home after Terry's done," he said. "Everyone."

"Okay," Braden said. "I can get that done. I'll go up and tell everyone good night and we can get paid and out of your hair."

"Fuck off," Jaff said. "You goddamn comics have been bleeding me dry for years. I ain't writing any checks tonight."

Not sure how to proceed, having never been flat out told he wasn't getting paid for a job he had done, Braden went the diplomatic route.

"One fifty is really reasonable for emceeing an entire night, man. I came here to do a job and I did it. I expect to get paid."

"Okay," Jaff said. "Here's something for you."

There was a quick motion of Jaff's arm, and for a split second, Braden thought he had been slapped. It certainly sounded that way, but then he felt wetness on his shirt and looked down to see water running down from his chest to his stomach. He ran his hand through his hair and it came away wet. Jaff put the glass, now not full of water, down on the bar with a *thunk*.

"What the hell, Jaff?"

"I don't want to talk to you anymore."

Slowly, Jaff walked away toward the other end of the bar, leaving Braden to figure out what the hell had just happened and if he bore any blame. A few of the patrons around the bar chuckled, one even quipping, "Looks like that guy has a drinking problem." Aping forty-year-old movies. Nice.

Braden smiled, hiding quite well the fact that he'd never felt quite so terrible and angry in his entire life.

\*\*\*

The comics in The F Pit were shocked.

"I've known Jaff for years and he's never done anything like that," Jackie said.

"Yeah, when I was just starting out, that guy was a prince,"

Sammy echoed. "That really doesn't sound like him. Are you sure you didn't call him an asshole or something?"

"I didn't then, but I will now," Braden said. "But something's up with him. He hit me in the back of the head earlier, so I don't know if he just hates me or what, but I'd bet none of us are getting paid tonight."

On screen, Terry Stafford was just finishing up his set to a pretty enthusiastic round of applause, given the circumstances. As he lumbered off, Jaff came on stage from the other side, grabbing the mic and immediately speaking over the still-applauding crowd.

"That was something wasn't it? All right, that's our show for the evening. Good night, everyone."

The announcement surprised everyone because, normally, sitting and having a drink in a bar after a comedy show meant money for comedy clubs, and any comedy club owner who didn't squeeze every penny out of potential drinkers were out of their minds. The kid was right, Jackie thought. Something was way off.

"That's it?" Jackie said. "What the hell is happening tonight?"

"Suppose they'll come down here?" Sammy asked. "I'd like a word."

"You all seem really interested in whether they're coming down here or not," Jerrod said. "Got plans for the man, do you?"

"You know it," Sammy said. "When you have your own show, you'll be the same way, too."

"Yeah, about that…" Jerrod said.

The group heard shuffling outside in the hallway, a narrow affair with exposed pipe and brick, not wide enough for two people to walk down at once but comfortable enough for one person walking. Or stumbling. The sound was weird from inside The F Pit and it sent an unease over the room that stopped conversation cold and heads slowly turned to the door as the sound got closer.

Calista's hand snapped into view and clung to the doorframe, fingers white from blood loss. With a grunt, she pulled head around the corner. She was missing several teeth, some of her hair was gone, and the rest was matted with blood and sticking out in wild directions. Bruises were already forming on the parts of her face that weren't covered with blood, and if it wasn't for her black dress that served as her waitress uniform, the extent of her injuries would have been all the more apparent.

As it stood, she looked like a woman who had been badly beaten and was trying, with every fiber of her being, not to die.

"Please...help me," she croaked, the words pulling all the energy she had left out of her body. She fell forward, into The F Pit, blood from her wounds immediately staining the carpeted floor.

# OPENER

**Jerrod Seybourne**
**Live From The Square in Manhattan**
**Friday, October 12**

*[crowd claps]*

*Thanks, you sexy-looking motherfuckers.*

*So, yeah, I smoke weed. I like to open with that so y'all know what you're dealing with. You might have seen me on CNN or something, but it's good for y'all to know what's up right off the bat. You don't open with that when you're doing panel discussions on cable news.*

*[FORMAL VOICE] On our panel today is former Trump Treasury Secretary Steven Mnuchin, Biden Secretary of Agriculture Tom Vilsack, and guy who hit a skunk on the way to the studio, Jerrod Seybourne.*

*I remember the exact moment when I decided to try weed. I was at a Redman and Method Man concert when I was a kid because my mom was fucking dope, and Method comes out at the end of the show and he has the biggest blunt…well, the biggest blunt you've ever seen. I've seen some pretty fuckin' big blunts, I don't mind telling you. You could get on this blunt and ride it around like a benevolent witch and get everyone in the neighborhood high. That's how big it was. It was cartoony big. If Bugs Bunny or some shit suddenly pulled out a blunt for, like, comedic effect, that's how big that blunt was.*

*So, Method Man, he's smoking this giant blunt and gets on the mic and tells the audience, "I want you to say, 'Fuck you, Method Man,' on three, one…two…" and the crowd does it. Twenty thousand people or whatever yelling, "Fuck you, Method Man," like it's their job. He does this, like, three or four times, and just about the time the crowd is wondering what's going on, he smiles real big and goes, "No. Fuck you." He's smiling like his mama just told him he could get ice cream and then gets off the stage still smoking his giant Bugs Bunny blunt. That was his entire encore.*

*The second he left the stage, I said to myself, "That's the secret to world peace." Imagine it—just everybody chill as fuck, not taking anything too seriously.*

*[ANGRY VOICE] I think there was massive voter fraud in the last election and anyone who disagrees with me should be shot for treason!*

*Cool. I disagree. [puff noise] Wanna get some nachos?*

*[ANGRY VOICE] [puff noise] Well…what kind of nachos?*

*As long as they're gooey with cheese, I don't give a fuck, my man.*

*[ANGRY VOICE] Okay. But no olives, or it's treason.*

*See? World peace.*

*[APPLAUSE]*

*That's a super power, man, and I wanted it, so I took up weed at the earliest opportunity and it was love at first sight. We're celebrating ten years next February. You can get us a card if you want. That'd be real sweet of you.*

*The thing is, I'm a monogamous weed smoker. I don't mess up our relationship with other shit, booze particularly. Booze, she's cheap, man. You can dress her up real nice, put her in a black slinky dress and cover her with diamonds and shit, but deep down you know she's going to end up screaming at the neighbors at three a.m.*

*It's like, I've had cheap weed and I've had cheap booze, and the cheap weed at least respects itself. Cheap weed is all, "I know I may not have washed my hair in a few weeks, but I'm at least gonna make you laugh." Cheap booze is a girl who punches your mamma. Cheap booze is a girl who shows her tits to get beads at Mardi Gras and then gets mad at you for looking.*

*And, like, you can go the other way and take harder drugs if you want, but if booze is your basic train wreck girl, then cocaine is like trying to stick your dick in a tornado made of sandpaper and regret. I tried it once and only once and went running back to weed like it was my only true love who was about to walk out the door. Come back, baby, I'm sorry I cheated. I mean, don't get me wrong, most of the incredible stories people tell me start with, "We were doing coke," but the snorting, man. I can't snort nothin'. The only thing that belongs up my nose is NOTHING! Nothing belongs up your fuckin' nose. If you disagree with me, I'd like to introduce you to gravity. Anyone who's been upside down in a swimming pool, you know what I'm talking about.*

*I used to not be able to talk about weed, man. There was a stigma attached to it. Now I go to my mom's house and she comes out smelling like Snoop Dog's rec room and she asks me if I'd drive her to get some nachos. It's everywhere, is what I'm saying.*

*But, for real, I think that's because there's been a shift. If people don't give a shit about something for long enough, the government eventually comes around to it. People ask me why I care about politics at all, and I tell them it's full of great little human dramas, but my favorite part is when the government says, "Oops, we fucked up." All the flag waving and Fourth of July fireworks and shit cannot erase the times the government was like, "Oops."*

*"Our Constitution now says booze is illegal. OOPS!"*

*"You, dude, you're only three fifths of a person. OOPS! Well, I*

guess our current Supreme Court has yet to weigh in on that one."

"Tax money is a representation of our values. OOPS!"

Folks don't even know that anymore, man. The budget, the way our nation spends its money, is supposed to represent our values. Ever seen a pie chart of where all your tax money goes? It's one sorry-ass pie. It's like sour cream and raisin pie. Seriously, if budgets are simply an expression of a society's values, then we place top dollar on blowing shit up. If budgets are expressions of our values and we pay so much for bombs and tanks and planes we don't need, then a good representation of our country is a fucking old guy sitting in his basement polishing a bayonet from 1945 surrounded by ammo that doesn't even go to his gun. That's who the fuck we are. That's what your government thinks you want, that's what your government spends your money on, and that's who you are until we tell our government to not fucking do that anymore!

Dug myself into a bit of a hole, didn't I? Yeah, I tend to do that. Hang on. [TAKES A HIT FROM A VAPE PEN] I like to get high and watch YouTube videos of white people punching each other in public...

# CHAPTER I

The good feelings hadn't lasted long.

It wasn't even closing time and Jaff was boiling with anger. He realized that much pretty early on in the night. Anger bled into impatience, nervousness, anxiety, then back to anger again with no space in between. He had yelled at his staff, he had yelled at the comics (had he hit one? It felt like maybe he had given one a good smack. It was hard to say.), and, to top it all off, with Calista rotting in the cleaning closet downstairs, he was shorthanded. One employee had called in sick and another, a new hire, had flaked completely. If she showed up for her check, she better hope Jaff wasn't around to answer the door.

Then Terry Stafford had come in and given him a temporary reprieve.

Being around famous people was always part of the gig, an enjoyable part, by and large. Jaff had hung out with some comics before they hit, but his favorite were comics who still came by to hang out after they were off the stage—comics who were so dedicated to their craft that they would do stand-up even if nobody paid them. Even though Jaff was about as cheap as they came when it came to paying comics, he always cut a small check and insisted they take it. It was weird, but some comics treasured that small check. It was like offering to pay for dinner by pulling out your wallet, knowing damn well someone else was picking up the check.

It wasn't like The Square was ever a spot that drew *lots* of famous people, but you could look out into the crowd on any given Saturday night and, if you were lucky, see folks with TV shows, talent scouts, and scattered industry types. Sometimes a famous comic would come in and ask to do a set, but most of the time they didn't, and Jaff was fine either way. When the big name did show up, they always made a point to talk to Jaff. These usually weren't deep conversations, but he got to hear about movie deals, divorces, financial issues, and some of the best stories he'd ever heard from the famous people who came to hang out. For some reason, the room seemed to act like a confessional, and Jaff was happy to play the priest.

He was convinced that's why Terry Stafford had shown up tonight—not to come grovel before an audience in a Manhattan comedy club, but to be around comics and get some of that energy back again. He had shown up when the opener took the stage, watched for a few minutes, realized it wasn't his cup of tea (drug humor didn't play to a Terry Stafford who was twelve years sober). and come to the back office to spill his guts.

In his prime, Terry was a beefy, handsome leading man type with sandy blond hair, a smile that made his eyes disappear, and a deep voice that made panties drop. He had such a reputation as a ladies' man at one point that some Hollywood executive got it in his head to turn Terry into a romantic lead. They tried three times with three separate movies, but the audiences never bought it, so Terry went back to stand-up and whatever other projects came his way, including a failed sitcom.

Now, twenty years after his heyday, he was fat, clearly tired, and was wearing a white suit with a big jacket that didn't do him any favors in terms of hiding his bulk.

"You know me, Jaff. I probably did everything they said and I don't remember it"

Terry's chair, a well-worn office chair with rollers and arm rests that dug into his sides, rolled over a red wet spot on the floor. The comic didn't notice.

By this time, Jaff's head was clearer, probably because this was one of his favorite parts of the job. He had been hearing the voice all night, but it was quiet now, which was fine.

"I thought you were clean and sober over a decade," Jaff said. "What are you talking about with that 'don't remember' bullshit?"

"Ahhh," Terry said, waving his hand. "I wasn't high, brother. That's not it. I used to have the chicks lining up out the door and down the hall to suck my dick, let me tell you."

He laughed, a deep, raunchy, wet chuckle, and Jaff followed suit, trying to be convincing.

"But the roles dried up and my belt got bigger and…you know, finding someone to fuck got harder and harder, so I had to get a system going."

"Not to be an asshole," Jaff said. "But weren't you married up until last year?"

Terry peered at Jaff over his thick glasses and they both understood.

"So, I had this system, right," Terry said. "And it ain't difficult. See, all you do is meet a lot of women and let them know you're looking to get in their pants. Sooner or later, one is going to either take pity on you or go, 'This is gonna be a great story." And then, boom, I get laid and it's a good day."

"How'd you let them know?"

"Sometimes I'm subtle about it, sometimes I'm all, 'Come on, let's fuck.' And that's where I think I got into trouble."

"How could you be any more clear than, Come on, let's fuck'?"

"I know!" Terry said. "But you tell a girl, 'Let's fuck,' and then having her come up to your hotel room, that isn't consent anymore. Or at least that's what I'm fucking learning these past few days."

The door to Jaff's office popped open, as he had forgotten to lock it, and Sammy Platter stuck his head in and saw Terry. In the second it took Sammy to assess the situation, Jaff was able to see recognition fade into an ugly expression that it had taken Jaff years to be able to identify.

Sammy Platter saw something that could advance his career. That piece of shit.

He had seen it in young comics with big dreams. He had seen it in veteran comics who heard a joke they could steal from an unknown. He had seen it in Calista's face when she realized he owned a comedy club. It was an ugly look and it brought violent thoughts into Jaff's head.

"Hey, Terry. How are ya? Jaff, what the hell?"

"Get the fuck out. I'm not asking."

"What you gonna do, break another glass?"

For a second, Jaff was a bit confused. What the hell was he talking about? Then he had a flash of earlier in the evening when he had overheard Sammy saying something. He couldn't remember what, but it had made him upset, as had everything this evening. But he did not remember breaking a glass. He had bandaged his hand up in his office shortly afterward, so it definitely happened, but he was feeling little to no pain. Slicing your hand open was something you think you'd remember.

But there was Sammy, with his smug demeanor and his unearned success and his hacky stand-up, wanting face time with

Terry, wanting to take away Jaff's favorite part of the job. His calculation was quick and unequivocal—nuke this bridge into a thousand flaming pieces and use them to create a splintery dildo that Sammy Platter could jam up his ass.

"Tell you what. Stay here another few seconds and I'll come over there and show you."

"I'm done with this club," Sammy said.

"You will be missed."

The door slammed shut, but it was a light-weight door and didn't make a dent in the wall of noise coming from Jackie's very funny set. Jerrod was done, apparently, though the applause hadn't filtered back. Jackie was a pro and Jaff liked her, but she was just the kind of woman who was making this business harder and harder and running legends like Terry out of town on a rail.

"Damn," Terry said. "Taking shit from no one tonight, are you, Jaff?"

"Nope. No shit, no lip, my way or get the fuck out."

They sat for a second, smiling, and Terry brought out a cigarette and lit it. Normally, Jaff was not a fan, but this was no ordinary night.

"Can I bum one of those?" Jaff asked.

"You smoke now?"

"Only when I'm taking no shit."

This made Terry laugh, a hearty rasp that was more than the line deserved. They both lit up, inhaling and enjoying the boys' club for a few seconds longer.

"Tell you what," Jaff said, finally breaking the silence. "Sammy can go fuck himself. I'm bumping him. How about you go up there and give 'em hell tonight?"

"Yeah, I was gonna ask. Not for you to bump anybody..."

"I'm closing up early tonight, so how about you go up there in about twenty minutes?"

Terry ran his hand through his salt-and-pepper hair.

"Yeah," he said. "I mean, I was planning on it. That's what you said on the phone. That's why I called."

"Now or never, man. If anyone can win them over, it's you."

"Yeah," Terry said. "Yeah, I got this. Thanks, brother."

With a loud, ugly creak and a grunt, Terry hoisted his frame off the chair and patted Jaff on the shoulder. He stubbed his cigarette out in an ash tray on Jaff's desk that he never used but learned early on was handy to have around.

"Who's out there now?"

"Jackie Carmichael."

"Shit," Terry said. "I might have hit on her few years ago."

"She's not going to jump off the stage and attack you. Go out there, I'll be out in a second and introduce you."

With a small nod, Terry was out of his office and Jaff took a deep, smoke-filled breath, the cigarette now burning in his hand. He needed to figure out what to do with Calista, he needed to get everyone out of his club, he needed to figure out what the fuck was going on with his brain and his body. It was a lot, but first he was going to go announce Terry. One problem at a time.

His brain drifted, ever so briefly, to the look on Calista's face when he had clocked her with the printer. It wasn't the shock or the pain, but the surprise that stuck, and he found himself smiling at the memory.

*She can't leave.*

The voice was pleasant, soothing, and brought good news, so he listened to it. Plus, it was right, Jaff thought. She couldn't leave and neither could he. It hadn't occurred to him before, but once everyone was out of the club, he'd probably find some way to kill himself and that would be that. It was a strangely comforting sensation, knowing he wouldn't have to deal with the bills piling up or comics calling for time ever again. He would die in The Square, his life's work. She couldn't leave and he wouldn't have to.

Jaff got up to introduce Terry and rambled a bit (which was uncharacteristic—he was a get on/get off sort of guy), but got through it and stood back, watching Terry do his thing. It wasn't what he envisioned. The big man was groveling and contrite, then did his old material, word for word. He was a legend and had been reduced to groveling at The Square. He wasn't even that funny.

A feeling of intense disgust flooded Jaff's guts for a moment and he had to fight the urge to throw something at the emasculation happening in front of him. It was definitely the worst thing he'd seen on stage in quite some time, and he'd seen comics run off the stage crying. One guy bombed so hard he went home and shot himself in the head. Jaff smiled at the story. It was a favorite among some of the comics with a darker sense of humor.

As Terry was finishing up, so was Jaff. He had shut down the bar, he had sent most of his employees home, their jobs not anywhere near done, and anyone who expected more comedy or a comfy place to hang out and drink could go pound sand. There were a thousand demons trying to jam their way through the doorway of Jaff's mind and the slightest bump in the wrong direction could send him...

*Where?*

The voice was back and much clearer than before. It cut through the noise in his head like a bulldozer through a crowd of people. It wasn't anyone he knew, but it was there, clear and forceful, talking to him outside of his internal monologue.

*Where will it send you?*

As he cleaned up the bar and as people filtered out, he had no problem talking, in a low voice, to whatever part of his brain he figured was talking to him. It was objectively weird, but it didn't feel that way. It felt right and it helped stabilize his emotions that had been swinging wildly. He wanted it to keep talking and he liked what it had to say.

"I've already killed one person," he said, his words easily drowned out by the chatter of the leaving crowd. "I don't want to kill anyone else."

This was true. He didn't want to kill anyone, but he did want them to go away. The voice was silent for a while, and Jaff could feel the enormity of that confession pierce him in a thousand places. Calista was dead, in the closet downstairs. His brain felt like a ping pong game between feeling good about his actions and realizing he had done something unforgivable, between wanting to end it all and not wanting to die, to fight whatever it was he was becoming. Grief came after the shock and his actions slowed until he was staring at the bar, eyes glazed over. His throat had closed and he started to fight back tears.

*You can't stop now.*

"Yes, I can," Jaff said to himself, weakness finally overtaking him. "I can because I'm tired and I'm sad and I can. I can stop."

His senses came back to him and he looked around the bar and he remembered. The place had been his passion for years, a place where he had sunk his young dreams and energy in search of a Bohemian life, a place where the hungry to hone their trade and some, more lofty, worked with the idea of making a positive dent in the world. One comic, who had never really made it but who stuck in Jaff's memory, had spent long nights at the bar extolling the art of stand-up and going on and on about how they were the "new philosophers" and his stage was the one that "launched a thousand ideas into the world."

He had bought it. Full on, all in, balls to the wall bought it. He had believed comedy could change the world, and then it didn't, and now legends of the game like Terry Stafford were old and fat and probably going to jail. The Square wasn't his passion anymore. It was his job and he hated his job.

*That doesn't mean you can leave.*

Terry Stafford, who had just performed a deeply weird set in front of an audience the same day he has been accused of multiple rapes, was in the corner by the stage meeting with folks and accepting well wishes. These people would go back home tonight and post photos and video, saying things like, "Met a rapist tonight," and, "One good show before he goes to jail." It was all so easy to see. All so predictable.

This place had been his sanctuary, and that was good, but the demons were well into the sanctuary now, waiting to suck everything he had. Demons like Terry. Demons like Calista. Demons like that fucking guy Sammy Platter, calling his club a piece of shit. Jaff's brain flitted from one idea to the next, no clarity on anything other than the idea that he needed everyone out of his club as soon as possible. He needed to figure out how to get rid of Calista. The end of Terry's story was clear, but he had no idea how his story was going to end.

Back in his office, Jaff collapsed in his office chair in front of his computer. His phone was already blowing up with the news that Stafford had been there, so he calmly took it out of his pocket and shut it off. Out of the corner of his eye, he spied a blood stain on the carpet, unmistakable but not obvious. You had to be looking for it, but it was there. It was everything he could do to not run down the stairs and check on her, straggling employees be damned.

"All right," he said to his empty office. "Here's what you're going to do. You're going to go out there, make nice with Terry, and kick his ass out. You're going to lock the gates, you're going to go to the store and buy a tarp. Then you are going to wrap her in it—"

*There's no way out. You can't leave.*

The voice was clear and wise. There was no way he was getting out of this. Even if he didn't kill himself, he was going to jail, more than likely. His life ended with hers.

In a moment of clarity, he remembered his safe, right there in his office. Inside he had a few valuable items, an emergency supply of cash, a few autographs, important papers, and the gun he had found when he moved into the place, all the way back in 1992. It was a revolver, six chambers, with a box of bullets. He hadn't touched the thing since he moved in, putting it in his safe and leaving it to rot, not sure what to do with it otherwise. Would it still work? Could he stand on the stage of The Square, take one last look, and blow his brains out? Maybe put Calista's body in one of the seats, sort of like an audience? He'd need to test it first, he thought, maybe in The F Pit where the sound was swallowed up by brick and concrete.

"Sounds like a plan," he said.

A peace settled over Jaff. He had a plan, sketchy as it was. He moved over to the safe, pulled out the gun, blew through the chambers, creating a cloud of dust, and loaded it with six bullets.

Just as he finished, outside his office he suddenly heard shouting, someone talking loud and fast. He was unable to make out the words but he heard his name, clear as a bell, and burst out of his office, stashing the gun in the front pocket of his jeans.

Braden, the young comic from earlier in the evening, was in the main room talking to Terry.

"You gotta call an ambulance right now. Calista's downstairs… someone's beaten her nearly to death."

Several thoughts went through Jaff's head in rapid succession, starting with, *How in the hell can she still be alive?* He had beaten her until she stopped breathing. This didn't make sense. Shortly thereafter, the implications of having someone downstairs started to sink in. Who the hell was down there? Did they find Calista? Would they leave him alone so he could deal with her and then himself? It looked pretty bad.

But was it really all that bad? He still had the gun. He could still use it at any time on himself. He wasn't trapped, things had just gotten slightly more complicated. If he could talk whoever was down there into leaving, then he could still go out the way he wanted. Things could still be terrible, but on his own terms.

*You need to kill them, too.*

*Yeah, if it comes to that,* Jaff thought. One step at a time. He put on a very concerned face. *Well, if this is how it was going to be, so be it. There's no way out.*

"Head downstairs," Jaff said. "I'll be right there."

# CHAPTER 2

Her plea for help used so much oxygen it loosened Calista's grip on the door and she fell half in and half out of the doorway, making a wet thump on the carpeted floor. Her right lung was already punctured and her breath came in rattling heaves, made worse by her mouth sucking in decades worth of filth from the floor of the green room.

For a moment, nobody moved, trying to process what it was they were seeing. The beat seemed long, and it was Jackie that broke it.

"Oh my God, Calista, honey, we've got you."

She ran and knelt by the woman's quivering body. Calista made a small, meager effort to reach out her hand to Jackie, but she didn't have enough strength to grab hold of her.

"What happened to you, sweetie?" she said, putting her face down close to Calista's face. "Who did this?"

Calista didn't answer, but groaned, tears falling from her eyes and mixing with blood and scabs on her face. Jackie had never seen a victim of such extreme violence before and was shocked by how deep her wounds were. Several wounds, in particular, were deep, almost endlessly so. They oozed blood and didn't stop, and it was enough to bring Jackie right up to the edge of panic.

"Call 9-1-1!" she yelled.

"I tried already," Jerrod said. "No reception down here."

"Someone head upstairs, then," Jackie said. "Get Jaff down here. Find out what the hell happened to her."

With his long legs and youthful drive, Braden was out the door and up the stairs before Jackie could finish her sentence, leaving Jerrod, Sammy, and Taylor all in various states of shock. Jackie was far past that point of hesitation, opting to take control instead.

"Okay, guys, I know basic first aid, so, Sammy, you look around for a first aid kit. Maybe in the bathroom back there. Taylor, are you comfortable holding her head up?"

"On it," Taylor said, taking off her jacket to reveal a turquoise tank top underneath.

"Tilt it up very carefully," Jackie said "What we're doing here is making sure she doesn't choke, okay?"

Taylor nodded, already a few tears of her own falling. She had never seen anything like this and the gravity of it hit her like a two-by-four to the skull.

"Give me something to do before I lose my shit."

Jerrod was wide eyed and visibly afraid, but was pushing through it.

"Our goal here is to keep her breathing and stop her from bleeding to death," Jackie said. "If Sammy can't find a first aid kit, we need the cleanest strips of cloth we can find. We're going to make wound dressings and do our best to keep her alive until the ambulance comes."

With a short nod, Jerrod started looking around The F Pit for thin cloth he could use to help with her wounds. When Sammy came out of the bathroom with a first aid kit, Jerrod breathed a little easier. He wasn't sure he'd have been able to tear strips of whatever cloth he could find with his hands shaking so badly.

While a bit more steady, Taylor was also having a rough time. She was holding Calista's head but her hands kept slipping from all the blood, causing the poor woman's head to bob, doing nothing to help her condition. While part of Taylor desperately wanted to put her head down and run as fast as she could, another part of her was concerned about getting some sort of infection. Still, she locked herself into place. Jackie immediately recognized her struggle.

"You're doing great there, kiddo," she said. "Just keep steady. You're helping keep a person alive right now."

Taylor gave a nod and quick smile and went back to looking at Calista's terribly battered face. It was worse than she imagined a face could be. One entire eye was swollen shut, but it was the deep cuts in her face, dark with blood and somehow smooth and jagged at the same time, that were threatening to freak her out. She felt a gag coming and successfully fought it.

It helped when Braden burst through the door, out of breath from running up and down the stairs.

"Jaff is calling an ambulance," he said. "How is she?"

"If we get an ambulance here soon, she'll be okay," Jackie said, kind of lying. Her first aid experience was limited but she knew there were several wounds here that a reasonable person might never recover from. If Calista died right there on the floor, it wouldn't surprise Jackie one bit.

"Okay," Braden said, out of breath. "Anything I can do?"

"Tell you what," Jackie said, tearing off strips of bandage from the first aid kit. "Do me a favor and get by her head and talk to her, okay?"

"What do I say?"

"I don't fucking care," Jackie said. "Do your set. Read a

95

shopping list. Just say something so she knows you're there and people are here helping her."

As the young comic moved from the doorway around Calista's body, Jackie could see his blood start to boil. From her various bruises, wound, and smears it was hard to make out what she looked like, and Braden was clearly having a hard time. By the time he got to her head and held it in his lap, Jackie could see his eyes narrow and he spoke in a low voice through clenched teeth.

"You're going to get through this," he said, his voice a low growl, but loud enough so Taylor could hear. "I know you are. It's going to be a long road but we're going to get you to a hospital, you're going to get the care you need, and whatever fucked up psychopath did this to you is going to go to jail for the rest of his life."

The room was suddenly full of the distinct noise of someone coming down the stairs and all talking stopped until Jaff turned the corner and stood just outside the entry to The F Pit. The sound dramatically changed from the concrete of the stairs to more of a shuffling sound when he got to the floor. There was a bit of a dusty echo as he stood the few steps from the stairs through the hall filled with old office supplies and Christmas decorations and to the door of The F Pit.

Calista's body was partially blocking his ability to come into the room as she had fallen forward into the room. It didn't help that Jaff reacted with something resembling disgust when he saw her. He could have come in but he leaned on the door that swung out from the room into the dingy hallway full of chairs, boxes, and an old filing cabinet.

"What happened?"

"She can't tell us," Jackie said. "But once the ambulance gets here, they'll get the story." It seemed more like a threat than an assessment, her words clipped and sharp.

"Okay," Jaff said, wiping his face and running his hand over the back of his neck. "They're on the way. I'll...uh, I'll take care of her from here."

Everyone stared, adrenaline still very much calling the shots. His performance was not convincing and he knew it.

"So why don't you all get out? Get out of my club."

He hadn't meant to put it so bluntly or to make himself so obvious, but there wasn't much else to say. Jackie wasn't stupid. Sammy was an asshole but he could put two and two together. These people were going to leave and bring the police, which would accelerate his time line, and he could live with that. What he couldn't live with was them telling him what to do, holding him back, stopping him from ending Calista and himself in a way that he saw fit. If a man couldn't plan his own end in a situation like this, what good was he?

To his surprise, it wasn't Jackie or Sammy who stood up. It was the new kid.

"We're not going anywhere," Braden said.

"Speak for yourself," Jerrod said from the back of the room. "I'm happy to walk away."

Jackie shot him a look, but Jerrod was dead serious.

"Did you do this to her?" Braden asked. Jackie realized not only did the kid have youth, but he was tall, lanky, and looked like a scrapper. Add adrenaline and anger and odds were pretty good he could take Jaff down by himself.

"I don't know what you're talking about," Jaff said, staring at Braden. No one believed him.

"Tell you what," Sammy chimed in. "Why don't we all just sit and wait for the ambulance? They'll get this all sorted out."

"Ambulance ain't coming," Jackie said, her voice shaking as realization dawned. "God dammit, Jaff, how could you?"

Their relationship was not deep but it was long. Jackie had been playing The Square since the early days of alt comedy and had seen the luminaries of the movement take the stage. Hell, Jackie was one of them, one of the first female comics to break with the Clean Carson 5 model of success and find it on her own terms, in her own voice. Jaff had been part of that, giving her time on stage, providing a place where she could make connections, being part of the structure that supported her art.

Seeing the guilt on his face stung her but he didn't deserve any sympathy, friendship, or consideration based on what he'd done to Calista. Not a sniff.

"Jesus Christ, man," Sammy blurted out. "What the fuck is wrong with you?"

Jaff held up his hands.

"You are all jumping to conclusions."

"Call the fucking ambulance, man," Jerrod jumped in. "Do it."

Everyone started talking at once, and before he knew it, Jaff's head was pounding, the headache that had tormented him days before now returning like a pissed off specter. He felt the weight of the gun in his pocket, pulling down on his pants, the metal still cool against his inner thigh.

Everyone's words were interrupted as Braden let out a loud, "HEY," to quiet the room. His ears were almost glowing red and his fists were balled.

"If you don't call an ambulance," he said, "I'm going through you and calling one myself."

Nobody in the room doubted Braden. He looked ready to throw down, ready to destroy Jaff if he needed to, and it caused everyone in the room to hold their breath.

\*\*\*

The room was deathly quiet after Braden laid it down, with

the exception of Calista's rattling breaths coming from the floor. All eyes were on Jaff, whose eyes were narrow as he tried to fight through the pain that had taken root in his skull.

*Use the gun.*

Again, the voice was clear and impossible to ignore, a heavy buoy to cling to as waters swirled and crashed around him.

"Good idea," Jaff said, exhaling deeply. "Let's make some magic."

"What's a good idea?" Jerrod said.

With one smooth motion Jaff pulled out the gun, pulled the hammer back, and fired a shot right into Braden's stomach. The gun worked perfectly, even after all this time. A mix of dust and smoke came from the barrel, but other than that, it was a fully functional hand gun. *Good to know*, Jaff thought.

Jackie full-on screamed, Jerrod dove behind one of the chairs, and Sammy pulled himself into a standing crouch, trying to put anything of mass they could between them and the comedy club owner with the gun. Taylor jumped, causing Calista's head to a flop a bit. She quickly regained her position, but screamed when she saw what the shot had accomplished.

Braden collapsed onto his ass, both hands going straight to his stomach and holding the wound. The shot knocked the breath out of him and he wasn't able to muster up much by way of a reaction other than a few grunts as he hit the ground. The pain was beyond what he had experienced before, extremely sharp and urgent, and he felt the blood already seeping through his shirt. Strangely, he did not feel a particular sense of surprise or betrayal. Just pain, a dropping sensation, and the urge to vomit as the anger and bluster drained out of him along with his blood.

Everyone's eyes went immediately to him, so Jaff took the opportunity to slam the door of The F Pit shut and throw a filing cabinet in front of it. That wouldn't hold, he thought, especially not with four able-bodied adults throwing their weight against it, so he grabbed a solid wooden chair from the hallway and tried to prop it against the door, but it didn't do much to ensure those assholes would stay in there. He looked around for other ways to block their escape.

"You know what?" Jaff said to himself, piling a few other things on top of the filing cabinet. "This is fine. This is okay. I've still got a plan. We can do this. Still got a plan."

***

Inside, Taylor set Calista's head down as softly as she could and ran to Braden, hoping it wasn't as bad as it looked. It was worse.

"Jesus..." Braden finally got out. "This hurts so fucking bad."

"I know, baby," Taylor said, holding his head up with the crook of her arm. "Let me see."

"Baby?" He grunted. "We back on—oh, God..."

The pain split his joke in half, and when Taylor pried his hands apart, she saw the bullet hole wasn't as big as she had anticipated, but the amount of blood was considerably more. From behind her, she heard Calista rasp and Jackie scream.

"Jesus Christ," Jackie yelled, her circuits finally overloaded. "Fucking Jaff. Jesus."

"Did he just lock us in," Sammy asked?

"I can't check," Jackie said. "I'm holding some pretty big wounds here. Go."

Sammy took a step and stopped. He was clearly scared Jaff might be on the other side of the door, waiting to shoot the first face that popped through the door. Braden continued to moan, obviously trying to hold in his cries of pain and obviously failing.

Jerrod started jumping up on the couch, holding his phone to the ceiling, trying desperately to get a signal. Nothing was coming through. The room was a digital dead spot.

"Come on," he said. "I pay a hundred and thirty-eight bucks a month for unlimited, you son of a bitch! Work!"

"Sammy!" Jackie yelled. "Nut up and go check the door."

It had been a while since Sammy had been anywhere near this afraid. The closest he could remember was when his cocaine dealer from the glory days of his drug use showed up at his front door, desperate for money to pay off some sort of debt. He had never overtly threatened him, and Sammy had been able to calm him down and give him a bit of money he had stashed. A few months later he was clean and sober, but he still remembered the feeling—helpless and heightened, his heart threatening to beat its way out of his chest in a bloody whirlwind.

This felt the same way, Sammy thought as he reached for the doorknob. He willed it not to turn and cursed quietly under his breath when it did.

"What if he's on the other side?" Sammy said to Jackie, who was just a few feet away with Calista.

"I've got two people who are going to be dead bodies soon if we don't get out of here," she said. "Open the fucking door."

Sammy took a deep breath, closed his eyes, and pushed.

# Chapter 3

Upstairs, Terry Stafford heard the shot clear as day and knew, beyond any doubt, what it was.

For years during his "imperial period" in the '80s and '90s, where everything he touched turned to gold, he hung out with a lot of heavy hitters from the entertainment and business world. All of them were men, all of them were insanely rich, and they had four things in common: they were incredibly confident, advancement was virtue, they all worked like dogs, and they all had guns. The reason they had guns varied, as some were paranoid self-protection nuts and others just liked the rush they got from firing them.

It took five or six invitations to the gun range before Terry went with one of them, and the second he squeezed the trigger, his brain released a flood of chemicals and he thought, *Yeah, I get it.* Since then, whenever he was invited, he went. He shot everything from small handguns to automatic rifles to shot guns loaded with a ball shot that blew his arm almost out of its socket. While he loved it, he never worked up the courage to go by himself. He always felt like he needed a guide.

So when Jaff shot Braden in the basement, Terry recognized the sound for what it was. It was a distinct sound and it triggered alarm bells in the comic's head. It was not a sound he had ever heard outside of a gun range and it made his guts squirm.

By this point all the customers were out of The Square and most of the staff had gone home or were on their way out the door. Most of them seemed to either have not noticed or deliberately weren't paying attention to the sound, with one exception, a short busboy who had been hanging around the comics earlier. Terry shared a glance with the kid, whose name he didn't know but who had run the lights and worked in the kitchen like a trooper, who wanted to be close to the action.

"That was a gunshot," Terry said, sounding definitive on the subject. "What the hell is going on down there?"

"Something might have fallen," the employee said. "Like a chair or something?"

"Nah, I don't think so," Terry said. "Gunshot."

The sound of Jaff throwing filing cabinets and chairs in front of the door made its way up the stairs and Terry, who was already exhausted, got a boost of adrenaline. There was some sort of fight or emergency or something happening downstairs. The employee, wearing a name tag that said "Raoul," furrowed his brow and Terry furrowed it right back at him.

He started walking over to the top of the stairway, but was met by Jaff, who was already in the middle of the staircase.

"What's going on?" Terry asked. "Is someone shooting a gun down there?"

"No," Jaff said. "Let me up. There's no cell signal down there."

Terry got out of the way and Jaff bolted up the stairs and pulled out his cell phone. Terry watched him dial, but something seemed off.

"What's going on, boss?" Raoul had come over and was trying to talk to Jaff. The owner held up his hand to keep him back and started talking into the phone.

"My name is Jaff Maul and my wife has been assaulted."

He gave out the address, his voiced panicked, but his actions and the way he was talking struck Terry as weird. Even though he hadn't been in a movie in upwards of eight years, he had learned a lot on those sets including how to spot a bad actor. Jaff couldn't pretend to have a conversation when he wasn't having one to save his life. His timing was all off. No one could have responded as fast as Jaff was talking, and the more he talked, the more uneasy Terry became. The comic was six foot five and towered over the five-foot-nine Jaff, so when he shifted while on the phone, Terry could see a dark screen. He wasn't talking to anyone.

"Hey, Jaff, let me talk," Terry said. "Seriously, I know people from the emergency center."

"No, I got this," Jaff said, holding up a hand.

Terry pulled out his own phone and started to dial.

"What are you doing?" Jaff said.

"Dialing 9-1-1, too. You know. Redundancy. Doesn't hurt anything."

Jaff nodded and retreated a few steps, taking a seat on the edge of the stage that was behind him. Just before Terry was about to hit send on his phone, Jaff charged him, hitting him hard in the stomach with his shoulder, knocking the wind clean out of him and sending the big man to the floor before he had a chance to react. Terry's knees, which were terrible to begin with, buckled hard, and the first thing he felt when his wind came back was intense pain radiating from his knees.

"Boss," Raoul said. "What the hell are you doing?"

In his earlier days, Terry would have kicked his ass and the ass of everyone in that room for good measure, but this was not the earlier days, and when Jaff got up, Terry stayed down, wheezing hard against the dirty carpet. He shut his eyes to cope with the pain, and when he opened them again, Jaff was pointing a gun in his face.

Terry recognized the gun. It was a Röhm RG-14, commonly referred to in the '80s as a Saturday Night Special. The guns were cheap, mass manufactured, and super easy to get once upon a time. The fact that he had one that was working was kind of amazing.

"Raoul, you know the gates?"

Jaff was talking about the security gates that locked from the inside, securing the front doors from the city, and making the side exit off Jaff's office the only way out, at least from the first floor.

"Boss…"

"Lock the gates, Raoul. Do it now or I shoot this fat fucker in the face. Got it?"

"Yes, boss," Raoul said, wide eyed.

With the speed of a busboy in a New York club, Raoul did exactly as he was told. The gates screeched a bit as he pulled them shut, grabbing the lock and clicking it into place. Terry took this in and felt a flash of fear and did what he always did when he was afraid—lashed out.

"I'm gonna stick that gun up your ass," Terry managed to croak out.

He saw Jaff's ears go redder than they already were and Terry knew what was coming before it came. With a swift motion, Jaff smacked Terry on the side of the head with the gun, causing a momentary loss of consciousness, but only just a second. The lasting effect was the pain and the nausea, and before he could say anything else, the big man turned his head and threw up his dinner onto the carpet at Jaff's feet.

Sensing his opportunity, Raoul took off through the kitchen where he knew there was a back door. His plan would have worked if he hadn't been a bit overzealous and tripped over his own feet in his desire to get away, trying to catch himself and failing. By the time he hit the ground, he had Jaff's full attention. His boss came up and kicked him, hard, in the side of his head.

Raoul felt his neck snap back, hard, accompanied by a lot of popping sounds and the taste of blood filling his mouth. He opened his eyes to see Jaff, inches from his face, red and twisted with rage.

"Is there anyone else in the kitchen?"

"No, boss."

"Why are you still here?"

His voice was a bit higher and more menacing than Raoul had ever remembered hearing it.

"I…Jesus Christ…"

"WHY!" Jaff yelled, pulling the gun and pointing it at the young man's head.

"I wanted…I wanted…"

"Yes?"

"I wanted to run my act by the emcee. I wanted some time on the stage, so I stayed late."

*Another bloodsucker. He deserves to die for that.*

For the first time, Jaff didn't a hundred percent agree with the voice, but he listened anyway. He wouldn't, after all, be much of a comedy club owner if he didn't have sympathy for a kid with a dream. He had seen hundreds of them in his day and some of them were absolutely tenacious, coming back again and again after he'd told them no, working the door or as a busboy just to be around the culture. The problem was he had seen so fucking many of them come through over the years, each with the same inflated sense of confidence, the same bumbling belief in their own inevitability. He got sick of it fast, and he wasn't the only one. Comics loved taking kids who knew they were the next big thing down a few pegs.

Maybe that's what he should do with Raoul, Jaff thought. Take him down a peg.

"You want some time?"

"I...I did," Raoul fumbled.

Jaff cocked the gun.

"Stay there," he said. "You run, I shoot you in the back."

The kid nodded while Jaff went over to Terry, still on the ground, recovering from the fierce vomiting and nausea that was still punching him in the gut and the throat.

"Get up," he said. "Go sit."

"Jaff, what the fuck?"

"You're the audience," he said, gesturing with the nose of the gun. "Go. Sit."

Terry gave him a long look that he hoped conveyed defiance, not that he had much of that left. His head was pounding from the blow and he had checked several times for blood, but didn't find any. Moreover, he was confused as to just what the fuck was happening. He wasn't good friends with Jaff, but a few minutes ago they had been sharing a few laughs and the guy had been generous with his time and his venue over the years. Now he was a full-on psychopath? What the fuck was happening here?

"Get up or I put a hole in you," Jaff said.

"Give me a sec," Terry sold. "You clocked me good."

He struggled to his feet, using the time to consider his options. None of them were rosy. There was a gun on him, he was old and fat, he'd get shot three times before he covered the distance between him and Jaff, and he wasn't sure he could take the guy anyway. One good kick to his soft underbelly and Terry was done for.

His only chance, he thought, was to cause a distraction which would give the kid some time to do something. That is, if the kid was the kind who would do something.

He snuck a look at Raoul, whose whole body was conveying panic. His eyes were huge, his hands shaking, and Terry thought he saw his bottom lip trembling a little. He was a kid in a bad situation and he was acting like it.

"Jaff," Terry said, finally on his feet. "This kid didn't do anything but work hard for you. Why don't you just tie him up and leave him alone, huh?"

"You heard him," Jaff said. "He wants some time. He asked me for some time."

"I don't need to, Mr. Maul," Raoul said, the words tumbling out his mouth fast. "I can just sit—"

"You can shut the fuck up, Raoul," Jaff said. He turned his attention back to Terry. "Now sit."

Terry took a few steps and did as he was told, picking a table near the front. Again, his mind frantically tried to figure out how to get the gun away from Jaff, because he was pretty sure he intended to shoot the kid regardless of how well his debut set went.

Jaff joined him at the table on the opposite side, well out of Terry's reach, keeping the gun on Raoul the entire time.

"All right," he yelled. "Please welcome to the stage, making his stand-up comedy debut, my busboy, Raoul."

The kid didn't move, frozen in place.

"Come on!" Jaff yelled. "You have the stage, you have a famous fucking comedian in the audience, what the hell else do you want? Tell us some jokes! Make us laugh."

Downstairs, there was a loud thud that momentarily got Jaff's attention. He listened for a second, didn't hear any follow up sounds, and nodded at Raoul to continue.

Terry flashed back to his first time on stage, and even though the circumstances couldn't have been more different, part of him felt like the pressure was the same. He remembered staring at the stage from the wings, his jokes memorized, prepared as he could be, but still feeling like standing on a spot on that stage was akin to taking your final place in front of a firing squad. That first step onto the stage was the bravest he had ever been, before or since, and he smiled at the memory, despite himself.

For his part, Raoul took those first few steps pretty easily and stared at their table. Terry saw something like defiance flash across the kid's face but he could have been wrong.

"Can I turn on the spotlight?"

"Sure," Jaff said. "If you would rather get shot than do your act."

Raoul swallowed hard and looked at the ground. He grabbed the mic anyway and the young man's demeanor immediately changed.

"Thank you," he said, his voice dying in the big, empty room.

"Turn the mic on," Jaff said.

"Huh?"

"The little button on the side. Flick it up."

He did and the room started buzzing with that slight anharmonic hum that comes with a live mic. To his credit, Raoul picked up the mic from the stand and took a step toward their table. He was going to do it, Terry thought, which meant the kid had at least some balls on him. Maybe if he could distract Jaff, the kid could make a move.

"You ever have a boss that's just, like, crazy?"

Terry let out a large "HA" despite himself and Jaff shot him a look. He was smiling, too.

"Look at the pair on this kid," he said.

Terry nodded as Raoul continued.

"I've got this boss, right, who, uh, seemed like a decent guy until just recently. I work at a comedy club and, uh, my boss pulled a gun on me. Talk about killing at the club, right?"

The kid's joke floated through the air and dived straight into the ground, killing any good will he had. Terry didn't even try to fake laugh. Jaff would have seen right through it.

"That's…that's not my act. I just thought it'd be funny."

"Tell you what," Jaff said. "Give me your best stuff. If it's funny, I'll tie you up. Deal?"

Raoul nodded and Terry got a dark feeling. If Jaff really was homicidal, if he'd beaten his lover nearly to death and stuffed her in a closet like that first kid said, he'd shoot this kid without warning, and Terry wasn't prepared to handle that. Not after the week he'd just had.

Raoul put his head down for a second, took a deep breath, and launched into his act.

"It's not that hard being a Hispanic kid in New York, it's just different," he started. "I get to see a world most of you all don't see. Like, you know the time your girlfriend got too drunk at brunch and threw up in the toilet. I saw that. I cleaned that up. It suuuuuucked."

As the word stretched out, Raoul opened his eyes very big and smiled in a way that he had clearly practiced in a mirror a hundred times. The joke wasn't solid and his material needed some work, but Terry found himself smiling anyway. The kid had good delivery, but not a lot of actual jokes at the moment. His problems were the sort that could be coached and improved, but Jaff didn't see it that way.

Without warning, the owner of the club opened fire, shooting three shots at the kid, hitting center mass each time. Raoul's face went from big and open to small and constricted as the pain hit him. He stayed on his feet for a few seconds, to his credit, but fell backward, hard, after the third shot, all the breath gone from his body.

Terry immediately stood up, but Jaff wasn't having it. He pointed the still smoking gun at Terry, who put his hands, palms up, right near his head.

"Don't shoot."

It was all Terry could think of to say. Given the occasion, it was woefully minimal, but at this point he was lucky to get anything out at all. On the stage, Raoul was gasping desperately for breath, unable to speak. If Terry wasn't mistaken, he had hit the kid's heart, which was both devastating and a blessing. He wouldn't suffer long.

For a second, it looked like Jaff was going to shoot Terry as well, but then he lowered his gun.

"Three bullets wouldn't be enough to kill you, you fat fuck," he said. "Besides, I need some help. And you're going to help me."

Normally, Terry would curse the guy out. Nobody presumed what Terry Stafford would or wouldn't do. He'd spent his entire childhood dealing with that shit and vowed his adulthood would never be dominated by people who bossed him around. Still, the man with the gun made a compelling case.

"Okay," Terry said, his voice surprising steady given he just saw a man shot in front of him. "What do you need, Jaff?"

"First thing," Jaff said. "Go through the kitchen. I'm pretty sure soon-to-be-dead Raoul up there was the last one, but make sure. I'm going to check to make sure he locked the gate in the meantime. Close up shop. No one's going anywhere."

Terry nodded and risked a glance toward the stage. The kid was still breathing, but Terry could see his breaths getting further and further apart. It was terrifying to watch, but Terry couldn't take his eyes off it as his breathing got more and more shallow. Before it stopped completely, the comic had headed into the kitchen to see who else remained. There was nothing to be done. The kid was beyond help. He briefly considered running through the kitchen door that led to the alley but decided against it. Jaff would hear and he'd have bullet holes in him before he made it to the end of the street.

When he got back in the main room, his heart sank a bit as Jaff yanked on the lock holding the metal gates shut. The main entrance was now not an option.

"You didn't run," Jaff said. "I expected you to."

"I ain't done a lot of running lately. And you would have shot me," Terry said.

"Fuckin A right I would have shot you," Jaff said. "Was kind of looking forward to it."

"The night is young," Terry said, and got another chuckle from Jaff. Terry ignored the gun for a second and snuck a look at the stage. Raoul had stopped breathing entirely. The kid was dead.

"What are you doing, Jaff?" Terry said. "This isn't you. You were a good guy."

Jaff smiled in a way that made Terry feel extremely uncomfortable.

"There's a dead guy over there who disagrees with you," he said, and walked into his office, leaving the door open and a legendary comic extremely confused, scared, and still a little nauseous from the head wound he'd sustained earlier. The reality of the dead body in front of him finally hit and he dry heaved, spewing more stringy, gelatinous stomach contents onto the already filthy floor.

# CHAPTER 4

When it came to muscles, Sammy was no slouch. He grew up in a family that valued fitness. He went to the gym upwards of four times a week and was a sinewy, veiny guy with the muscle to back up his mouth, which made it all the more surprising that he couldn't get the door of The F Pit to budge. Not even a little.

Even with Jerrod's help they were only able to get it open a few inches, certainly not enough for anyone to escape and get help.

"How is this not moving?" Jerrod said, throwing his full weight against the door. "Even a lock would have given a little bit by now."

"He's got something wedged against it," Sammy said. "Something big."

"Gaaaaaa!" Jerrod screamed, and kicked the door hard enough to make a little hole from the tip of his shoe. He tripped then staggered back, holding his foot.

"Fuck. I think I broke my foot."

Sammy rolled his eyes. He was panicked, sure, but he was trying to figure out what the next move was. He was coming up with a plan.

"Okay," he said, trying to get everyone's attention. "If the door isn't going to open, then we're stuck, right?"

"He's going to come back!" Taylor said. Panic had been rising in the room, quite understandably, since Jaff had shot Braden and disappeared into the club. As Sammy and Jerrod were trying to take down the door, a heated debate had been going on about how panicked they should be. Jackie was, in her own way, giving Jaff the benefit of the doubt, saying if he was truly murderous instead of disturbed, he would have emptied the revolver in the room. Braden, through gritted teeth, made a very convincing counterpoint that he was likely to kill all of them and they needed to get out as soon as possible. Sammy was sympathetic to his argument, given the hole in Braden's stomach.

All sympathies aside, Sammy wasn't so sure. He had heard of people in heightened states doing some pretty extreme things and wasn't entirely sure Jaff was going to barge in and murder them. Maybe a fight with Calista had gotten out of hand. He had done some terrible things, and before he could catch himself, he had beaten her almost to death. Then, the kid showed signs of aggression and he shot him, too. That's a far cry from murdering four more people in cold blood, and it wasn't a likely scenario in Sammy's mind. The more likely alternative was they were going to be trapped in that room until the cops came, which could be minutes, or hours.

If there was anything urging Sammy to curl up into a ball and start crying, it was the room they were trapped in. The F Pit was fine for a short amount of time, but after a while, it started to get under your skin, Sammy thought. The carpet color more and more resembled vomit, the lighting got worse and worse, and the smell of darkness and decay became more pronounced, not less. Something was off about the room and he wanted out. Even as everyone was yelling and grunting in pain, Sammy was sure he heard some sort of scratching coming from behind the walls and some sort of whispering coming from somewhere else.

Getting the door down and giving Jaff another reason to shoot might be just the sort of thing they should not be doing at this point. It was a pretty big gamble, but Sammy was pretty sure it wasn't as bad as it seemed.

"Take the door off the hinges."

Braden was still verbal despite his face going an ugly shade of white. He was sitting slumped on the floor, Taylor behind him, stroking his hair and whispering encouraging words to him as he held his stomach. The occasional moan aside, he was keeping it together pretty well. A brief pang of jealousy ran through Sammy. None of his exes would have cradled his head like that. They might have stuck their fingers in the bullet holes and wiggled them around.

"We'd need tools for that, man," Jerrod said. "We don't have tools."

"I've got a Swiss Army Knife in my purse," Jackie said. She was doing the hard work, watching after the ever-worsening Calista, who had lost consciousness when she hit the carpet but was still breathing.

"Not the kind of tools we need," Jerrod said. "I'm talking, like, a screwdriver and a hammer. Pretty sure none of y'all got that."

"Then find something to hit the door with," Braden said, his breathing heavy. "Fucking take it down and get us out of here."

Sammy could do it. He had noticed the big sign hanging on one of the walls, the one that said "F Pit" in small bright, naked bulbs, was outlined in some pretty solid-looking metal. He could take the sign down, take it apart, and likely use some of that metal as a chisel at the door. He could have a hole made in fifteen minutes, tops, but all that banging would cause a lot of noise and draw the sort of attention they didn't want.

Plus, staying in The F Pit was their best bet, not that Sammy was going to say that. He was emotionally intelligent enough to know not to tell the bleeding man to sit tight.

"Yeah," Jerrod said. "Yeah, there's, um…"

The doughy man flipped over one of the wooden chairs in the room and kicked it, hard, breaking off one of the legs. *So much for your broken foot*, Sammy thought.

"The door ain't solid or nothing," Jerrod said. "We can bust it open."

"Then what?"

The room turned and looked at Sammy. He understood everyone was heightened emotionally, but logic couldn't just be thrown out the window.

"Then," Jerrod said, pointing at the piece of chair and Sammy, "we go out the back exit and we call the fucking police. That's 'then what.'"

"What about Jaff?"

"Crazy motherfucker gets within striking distance, I'll bust him open, too."

*He can't leave.*

The voice was sweet, feminine, and loud. Sammy was used to living inside his own head, even though he talked a lot, and this voice was different from his normal internal monologue. To the contrary, it was sweet yet firm and he found himself wanting to listen for it, yearning for it to speak again. He paused for a second, and when nothing else came, he jumped right back in, trying to calm the situation.

"I get that," Sammy said, putting his hands up to show a little deference. "But it's not like Jaff is going to move whatever heavy-ass thing he has in front of the door and shoot us all."

"It's exactly like that," Jackie said.

"You don't know that."

"Well, I fucking do!" Braden said before the pain snapped him back. He had a brief Talking Heads moment when he realized he was yelling at a guy who he would have asked for his autograph a few hours earlier. *This is not your beautiful gut wound. Let the days go by, water flowing underground.*

"Look, I'm sorry you're hurting, man, but you don't know!" Sammy snapped back. "We don't know what the hell Jaff is doing. I don't think he knows. I know none of you want to hear this, but the best option is to sit here until the cops come, which could be any minute."

"What about her?" Jackie said, standing up for the first time in probably half an hour of caring for Calista. "I don't want to hear that, because it means you're willing to sacrifice her…"

She pointed at Calista, whose eyes fluttered but did not open.

"…and him…"

She pointed at Braden, with Taylor right behind him.

"…to avoid having actually do anything."

"That's not fair, and this isn't about me," Sammy said.

"It's always about you!" she said. "Ever since I've known you you've been one of the most self-centered guys I know. Your ego is so big—"

"How big is it?" Jerrod said.

"Shut the fuck up. I'm making a point here," Jackie snapped.

"You've made your point," Sammy said, again trying to calm things, but secretly smarting from Jackie's attack. "I'm not saying we let anyone die."

"Yes, you are," Jackie said, her eyes on fire. "That's exactly what you're saying."

She returned to Calista, applying pressure to the multiple

wounds with a rag they had found in the first aid kit. The woman let out a groan but did not wake up.

"I hear you," Sammy said, working hard to keep his voice calm. "But you're wrong."

"The fuck I am," Jackie said. "This woman here, she's been through more than you can possibly imagine and she's going to make it. She's going to fucking make it if I have to set fire to this place and make smoke signals to the cops."

Jackie looked at Braden, who had his eyes shut, dealing with the pain.

"You too," she said.

"I know," Braden said, opening his eyes. "I don't plan on dying here."

"All right, then," Jerrod said, and, completely out of character, got a running start and smacked the door as hard as he could with the substantial piece of wood. It made a satisfying *thunk* into the wood of the door, the first layer giving easily. The wood didn't stick into the door but it made a nice hole, allowing everyone to see the wood that made up the other side.

"Jesus!" Sammy yelled. "You're going to bring him down here!"

"Bring him!" Jackie yelled. "We can all take him."

"Yeah," Jerrod said, the adrenaline of the moment washing over him. "Bring it. There are four of us upright. He can't take us all down before one of us gets to him!"

The room was getting away from him. Any comic worth his salt knew that feeling and knew it well, when a joke not only didn't land but fundamentally offended a good cross section of the audience and they were unlikely to get back on your side. When he was on stage, Sammy had a go-to story that usually dug him out of that hole, but the older he got, the more he shied away from risky material that alienated his audience in the first place. His job was to make them laugh. Plus, there was no use in alienating folks who might potentially watch his show later on.

This crowd was different. He had to convince them not to like him, but to do what he said.

"Okay, how about this?" Sammy said. "You made a hole. Let's pull that wood apart as best we can. Jaff is more likely to ignore one loud noise than a bunch of them."

Jerrod, still holding the piece of wood, nodded.

"Makes sense," he said. "Then we can all crawl out through a little tiny hole in the door and run to freedom. Maybe we can run into a nice white cop at the end of the street and everything will be okay."

Sammy shook his head at Jerrod's sarcasm.

"You're not being rational."

"Well, sorry, Sammy, this ain't a rational situation."

*He can't leave.*

"No, it's not, but that doesn't mean we don't have to act rationally, asshole!"

He hadn't meant to attack Jerrod, but something inside his brain was making him angry, angrier than he'd been in a while. This wasn't a hard equation. Jaff was indisposed upstairs doing God knew what. If they made a hole and didn't draw his attention, they could get out. What part of this plan was he failing to convey? Anger flooded his brain and he had a momentary flash of Jerrod laying on the ground, blood gushing out of that giant bald head of his.

But if there's one thing Sammy Platter couldn't stand, it was letting a room get away from him.

"Sorry," Sammy said. "I didn't mean to say that, but I need you to tell me what part of this is throwing you? We take down the door. We do it quietly. In doing so, we run less of a risk because the crazy man with the gun is less likely to come down here. What am I missing?"

"You're missing the part where I'm fucking angry and want to hit something!" Jerrod said.

"I can't help that!"

"Jerrod."

Jackie was jumping into the conversation and had, through quirk of personality and age, established herself as the den mother, as much as it annoyed her. She was the one who was going to keep them all together and they all knew it.

"Man, I fucking know," she said to Jerrod. "There's blood and there's a crazy white guy upstairs and you're on the verge of breaking big—"

"I am, man," Jerrod said, putting his hand on his head and flouncing into one of the chairs.

"I know," she said. "No one's saying this isn't fucked up. Sammy's just trying to help."

She shot Sammy a quick glance and he nodded. They had never been friends, but if everyone got out of this alive, Sammy decided, he was going to change that. She was a hell of a comic and was keeping her head really well in an intense situation.

"Okay," Jerrod said. "Yeah, let's, um…let's get to work on the door, yeah?"

Sammy nodded again. With what seemed like monumental effort, Jerrod heaved himself out of the chair and they both got to work taking chunks out of the top of the door. The thing wasn't particularly solid and the wood tore away easily. The problem was there was another layer of cheap wood on the other side supported by beams of much stronger wood in between, meaning they could get the cheap stuff cleared away in short order but it wouldn't do any good. No one was fitting between the beams until they got a few of them clear, and to do that would require tools they didn't have.

Working together, Jerrod and Sammy punched through the second layer of cheap wood between them and the hallway using chair legs and their bare hands. Something resembling fresh air spilled into the room, accentuating the terrible stench of sweat and blood in The F Pit. In addition to the dank and decay, there was a pungent and strangely panicked smell, which was acrid and gave the room a nasty chemical undertone.

"We're through, but we can't fit yet," Sammy said.

"I can."

They all turned and looked at Taylor who had spoken up. Sammy did some quick math in his head. She was clearly the most petit in the group (Calista might have given her a run for her money but she didn't factor in to this equation in her current state) and might be able to squeeze through the beams.

"You sure, girl?" Jerrod said. "That puts you out there more exposed than I think is wise. And I usually love it when a woman is exposed."

"Really?" Jackie said. "That line doesn't even play."

"No, I can do it," Taylor's said, batting Jerrod's joke away. "We need to get help."

***

Taylor looked down at Braden. She couldn't help it. Since their tryst a while back she had been thinking about him a lot, agonizing over how she'd screwed it up. Truth of the matter was she had taken to hitting the clubs extra hard since he ghosted her, hoping to force some sort of contact. The time she had spent with his head in her lap as she stroked his hair and comforted him as best she could was the closest thing to intimacy she had experienced since their hookup. She was going to save him, she had decided. They were both getting out of there.

She leaned down and gave Braden a kiss, their heads upside down from one another. It was a kiss that was surprisingly wet and hot and Taylor instinctively put a little tongue into it, slipping slightly past the dying man's lips then quickly back.

"We'll get you help."

"All right," Sammy said. "Come on."

Jerrod very quietly took a few more jagged pieces of cheap wood away from the beams, creating a hole in the door he hoped was big enough for the petit Taylor to squeeze through. The hole was on the upper part of the door where the space was widest between the beams, meaning they'd have to pick her up to get her through the hole. "She'll fit," he said to himself. "No problem."

"Ready?" Sammy said.

Taylor nodded.

"Okay," Jackie said, still tending to Calista. "When you get into the hall, go upstairs as quietly as you can. I bet you Jaff has shut the gates by now so either go through the kitchen or there's an exit right off his office. Get the fuck away from here and call the cops, or, if you get up high enough, call 9-1-1. You got your phone?"

Taylor nodded and patted the hip pocket of her jeans. The pep talk was doing more to scare her than pump her up. A vision of Jaff, grinning widely as he pulled a trigger, wormed its way into her mind. She did her best to beat it back by focusing on the problem in front of her, which had lots of jagged pieces and sharp edges.

"Your job is to get help to come down here," Jackie said. "I know you can do it, sweetie. Go get help."

"What if she can open the door and let us all out?" Jerrod asked.

"Probably better to send one person at first," Sammy said. "We all want out of here, but four of us clomping around isn't going to help anything."

"What if he comes back and shoots us?" Jerrod said.

"Then he gets her first," Jackie said. "And we have some warning he's coming. Isn't that right, kiddo?"

She smiled at Taylor, who offered a weak smile back. Her big eyes gave away how terrified she was. It had occurred to her that Jaff might shoot her, but hearing it said aloud pulled the panic from the back of her brain to the front. She looked back at Braden and put on a brave face. Seeing him from this angle made her realize just how sickly he looked and how much of his blood was already on the ground.

"Yeah, that's right," Taylor said. "Let's do this."

"Okay," Sammy said. "Up you go."

Sammy and Jerrod both lifted and got her into a position reminiscent of a keg stand, only more horizontal, Jerrod on her right side, Sammy on her left. They moved her toward the hole and she put her hands out like she was flying.

That's when they heard the gunshots from upstairs.

Jerrod jerked forward, pushing Taylor toward Sammy, who, with his considerable strength, overcompensated, pushing Taylor's torso into the jagged side of the door. Taylor instinctively pulled her arms back to her sides, and before Jerrod could compensate, shards of cheap wood dug deep into Taylor's right arm, cutting into her skin and scraping along the top of her elbow.

She screamed in pain and Jerrod finally got his act together, matching Sammy's force from the other side. At this point, Taylor's head and shoulders were through the hole.

"Get her out," Sammy said.

"No!" Taylor yelled. "Keeping going. I'm okay."

She had no idea if she was okay. Her arm was on fire and she could feel projectiles sticking out of it from several angles. The pain was bad but didn't feel like anything major. Not yet.

"Keep pushing," she said. "I can make it."

Jerrod and Sammy complied, and soon Taylor was more than halfway through the door, her torso on the other side. They could hear her groping for anything to hold on to as she started to fall into the hallway. Her hands finally hit the filing cabinet that was wedged against the door, and she was able to catch herself before her face smashed into it. Her feet tumbled over her head and she landed in a heap.

"You okay?"

For a beat, Taylor took a second to contemplate the question. She was in the most fucked-up situation of her life, she was terrified, and, for the first time, she took a look at her arm. The amount of blood was alarming, with a stream already headed toward her hand, and there were chunks of wood protruding at odd angles. It would take an hour to pick out all the pieces, she thought. The good news was the pain was tolerable.

She pulled herself out of her head.

"Yeah," she whispered loudly. "Help is on the way."

# CHAPTER 5

Before Raoul, Jaff had never killed anyone. He had never even seriously considered it before trying and failing with Calista. As someone who swam in stand-up comedy all day, his sense of humor was considerably dark, but like a lot of comics, he was more apt to avoid conflict rather than embrace it. Still, he had seen his fair share of fights before he got smart enough to hire security. He had punched and been punched, but usually, the long-ago bad nights would end with a bag of ice and a stiff drink, not murderous grudges. He wasn't even sure he was the sort who could kill someone.

He was surprised at how goddamned easy it was.

Just a twitch of the finger three times and Raoul had bled and twitched and died, desperately trying to breath and eventually failing until the Raoul that was turned into a slab of meat on the stage ceased to be. It was an amazing feeling, to be honest, to take everything that kid ever had, but, more so, everything he ever would be. He'd never be a comic or a son or a lover or a person who rode the subway ever, ever again. To have that sort of power over anything, to decide if it could stop breathing because of a twitch of your finger, made Jaff feel more powerful than he ever had before. The voice had been right and he would listen to it more often, he decided.

Moreover, the gun, that had never left his hand since he fired it at Raoul, was starting to feel like part of his flesh, like a finger or a toe. When he fired, he hardly felt the recoil. When he smelled the barrel, he hardly caught the scent of the gunpowder. How had he gone this long without becoming a fan of these things? Even reloading it, which he did in his office, was nothing short of a joy. His fingers were able to naturally perform the motion like he'd been doing it his entire life, the slick bullets falling into the chambers effortlessly with a satisfying click.

It wasn't overstating it to say that Jaff was in hiselement, luxuriating in the first life he had ever actually taken, smiling at the idea of what was to come. Calista was still downstairs, apparently, breathing. That was about to change.

He and Terry were sitting in the club, like the old acquaintances they were, like they had dozens of nights before watching comics and audiences. The gun had changes their dynamic something fierce.

"Hey, Terry, wanna run an errand with me?"

He could see his words were terrifying to the big man. This request seemed to visibly raise Terry's blood pressure, which was probably a bad idea at this point. He was already of the cliff overlooking Cardiac Arrest Canyon.

"What's that, Jaff?" he finally said, trying to sound strong and failing.

"My old lady, she's downstairs," Jaff said, shutting the chamber of the revolver. Six shots, now ready to go. "I'm going to go downstairs and kill her, but I need crowd control."

"Crowd control?" Terry said, his face going a shade whiter

than it already was. "What do you mean? Who else is down there?"

"Couple of comics," Jaff said. "Nobody important. Well, Jackie. She's down there."

It was as if the mammoth fist of karma had donned brass knuckles and busted Terry's nose. Of course he knew Jackie. He remembered her as funny, smart, pretty in an earthy sort of way, and he remembered, vividly, exposing himself to her in a hotel in the late '80s. For years he had used the terminology "she rejected him" to describe the experience, telling himself a story to absolve any residual guilt. Recent events had made him think differently. Given they hadn't spoken since that night, he was pretty sure she was holding a grudge with both hands and that he had acted inappropriately.

Terry had done everything possible to not think about the fact that he was likely going to jail for the rest of his life, and rightfully so. The mere existence of Jackie Carmichael was enough to remind Terry of what a piece of shit he was, how far he had fallen, or that the bill had finally come due. Some part of him knew this was coming. A much bigger part had hoped it would never arrive. Now, here he was, with a gun in his face, the devil asking him for help.

"What do you need me to do?" he asked, stalling for time.

"Here's what I'm thinking," Jaff said. "You go down there, push all the shit out of the way so they can open the door, tell them the coast is clear, and then when they come out, I go in and empty six rounds into Calista's head. What do you think?"

This was the first time Terry was able to see what Jaff was after. Everyone trapped in The F Pit had nothing to do with his goal. Raoul, dead on the stage, had nothing to do with his goal. He had nothing to do with Jaff's goal. He wanted to kill his wife and everyone else was in the way. From the way Jaff's eyes gleamed when he mentioned shooting Calista, Terry had learned everything he needed to about the situation, and for Jaff, the situation was simple.

It was anything but simple for Terry. He turned the plan over and over in his mind, trying to find a way to get out of it, or, failing that, a way he could help get everyone away from Jaff. Maybe there was some good to be done if he could locate it.

"I'd be lying to you if I said I wanted you to kill anyone else," he said. "But it doesn't matter what I want, does it?"

"Nope," Jaff said, the gun casually held in his right hand. "Stand up, big guy."

Even though he didn't quite know where he was going with this, something inside Terry was urging him to stall.

"Before we go," he said. "Can you answer me a question?"

Jaff raised his arm and pointed the gun square at Terry's chest. He could see the chambers of the revolver, all of which were loaded.

"Shoot."

He let it sit a beat.

"Get it? Shoot," Jaff said, laughing to himself. "That's the best joke anyone told in here all night. It's a joke with some fucking stakes, you know."

"Yeah," Terry said, trying hard to smile. "Stakes. That's funny."

Jaff smiled, but did not lower the gun.

"You can ask," Jaff said. "Can't promise I'll answer."

"Fair enough," Terry said. "Why you doing this, Jaff? You don't seem like the kind of guy who'd go crazy and do something like this. Calista always seemed like a sweet girl. Hot, too."

Jaff got a smile Terry had seen a thousand times when he told dirty stories on the road, a smile that said "we're on the same page."

"Why'd you do that to her? Why'd you shoot that kid? What's going on?"

The smile across Jaff's face widened and Terry's stomach sank a little lower.

"You know, I never thought I was the type either," Jaff said. "You remember that movie *Seven*? The one with Brad Pitt."

"Yeah," Terry said. "One of my flicks opened opposite that movie. Killed it dead."

"There's this scene where good old Brad asks the killer, 'When you're crazy, do you know you're crazy?' I've been thinking about that, because, let's face it, I'm doing some crazy shit here. I'm off the reservation, but am I crazy? Like, really crazy?"

For a second, Jaff stared off into space and seemed to disappear inside his own head. It was a long enough pause and a deep enough stare to where Terry briefly considered making a move for the gun, but then Jaff snapped back to it.

"I think," he said, speaking slower, "my life ended a while ago. I think I gave up, you know? I stopped loving this place, I stopped loving that woman, I stopped moving forward and just kind of stayed where I've been, and I think when I did, that I died. Everything I wanted to do, all the dreams I had, all the things I thought I was, dead as a fucking doornail, Terry. Deader than your movie career."

The big man had to suppress the urge to flip the bird at Jaff, but he smiled at the dig. They were both likely at the end and here they were, busting each other's balls.

"Then, to be completely honest with you some more, I heard a voice."

"You heard a voice," Terry said. "Not to be disrespectful, there but that's crazy motherfucker one-oh-one right there."

"I know, I know," Jaff said. "I know it's crazy, objectively, but it doesn't feel that way. It feels like the most natural thing in the world, like, I know this is the end, and not only is it okay, but it's all been leading to this. This feels like where I was always going to end up. All my work here, every night mopping the floors and dealing with drunks and keeping you fuckin' comics happy, it wasn't pointless. It was leading here all along. There's some peace in that, I guess is what I'm saying."

"I can see that," Terry lied. "But if you're at peace, why kill anyone else? Why not let us all go and end things on your own terms?"

"Because fuck all of you, that's why."

The turn came so fast that it blindsided Terry and he flinched, waiting for the shot to come. It didn't, but the alternative wasn't much better. Jaff leapt out of his seat and ran at Terry, covering the distance so quickly he hardly had time to draw breath. Jaff smashed him with the gun, in the face this time, and the stinging pain was definitely worse than before. Blood immediately started running down Terry's cheek.

"Why do you think I died, asshole?" Jaff yelled. "Who sucked me dry all these years? Who got famous and rich while I slaved away in this shitty fucking club? All the comics who came on here to get shows, all the Netflix specials, all the talentless..."

Jaff pushed the gun barrel against Terry's temple so hard he cried out.

"Jaff, please..."

"...the talentless pieces of shit who had it all and pissed it away because everything wasn't enough. And you know what I got out of it? You know what piece of the pie I got? Shrinking margins, asshole. I can't sell enough booze to keep this place open, even if I upped the drink minimum. and if you go to jail. you got to live the golden life for a while. I never did, Terry. I never fucking did!"

He punctuated his final point by winding up and hitting Terry again in the temple, in the same spot he had before. Terry's head screamed again, but this time the pain was deeper and more hollow, the sense that something was going terribly wrong under his skin far more acute.

"I know we were buddy-buddy a second ago, but let me make one thing crystal fucking clear, my man," Jaff said. "You're coming downstairs with me and you're going to be the Judas goat leading Calista to slaughter. And if I feel like shooting anyone else, I'm going to fucking do it, and if you play nice and do everything I tell you, I still might put a bullet in that fat gut of yours."

The pain of the pistol whipping was not anything Terry could get used to, but as he came out of the white-hot part of being hit, he was becoming aware something was wrong. Phrases like "aneurism" and "stroke" floated across his mind, adding to his panic.

"Stand up," Jaff said, again holding the gun on Terry.

*Kill him now.*

The voice made sense. He was dead weight who was slowing him down and might turn on him at any moment. Terry was not fast, but if he got in a punch, it might be enough to put Jaff down. There was a lot of meat behind one of those swings, making him potentially dangerous. Plus, he was a big, fat asshole and the world would be a better place with him dead. He could feel his thumb start to pull the hammer back on the revolver.

Then the rational part of his brain took over. He needed Terry to make Calista dead.

In the very back of his brain, a voice was screaming that this wasn't right, that Terry was a colleague, that killing people was anathema to the way Jaff lived his life. He was not a monster, the voice yelled but it was so very far away in another room, another county, another state.

In the chair, Terry was trying hard to get up, but is equilibrium was all fucked up. He swayed one way, then the other before finally getting on his feet.

"You gonna puke again?"

"Maybe," he said, out of breath. "Probably."

"You won't if you know what's good for you. Let's go downstairs. You first."

Jaff waved a bit with the gun, urging Terry toward the back of the club. Closing his eyes and breathing deeply as he tried to stave off the nausea and panic, he eventually took a step forward and didn't fall over. The stars and black streaks were still swimming in and out of his vision. Another step was not guaranteed.

They made it to the top of the stairs and Jaff jabbed the small, snub nose of the pistol against Terry's back.

"Come on," he said. "You can do it."

"I don't know if I can," Terry said, wheezing. "The last thing you need is a passed out fat guy at the bottom of your stairs."

He heard the hammer of the pistol click behind him.

"How about a dead fat guy at the bottom of the stairs?"

"Hard to argue," Terry said, his voice interrupting between labored, heavy breathing.

He took a step down, his dress shoes finding the unforgiving concrete. He grabbed on to the hand rail, putting a lot of his weight on it, and it creaked and groaned.

"So," Terry puffed, "what's the plan? What happens when we get down there?"

"Quiet," Jaff said in a harsh whisper. "They can hear you."

The whisper voice made the situation extremely creepy, and for the first time, Terry was terrified to the point of paralysis. He was scared and hurt, but at no point did he feel like he needed to flee. Hearing Jaff's voice in his ear and feeling his breath on the back of his thick neck brought forth in Terry the urgent, all-consuming need to run, to get the hell out of there by any means necessary. It was almost more than he could control.

He took another step. Everything held together.

He took one more, stumbled a bit, and caught himself. The shock of almost falling took away some of his fear, clearing the way for the rest of his surroundings to come flooding in. The smell of sweat and mildew, the stains on the janitorial door at the bottom of the stairs before he got to the hallway leading to The F Pit—his senses were heightened to a wild degree.

It was on the third step that he saw her, the girl with dark hair who was in the club earlier in the night who was itching to talk to him but didn't work up the nerve. She was on top of what looked to be a filing cabinet and she immediately rolled off. Terry heard her roll, and increased the sound of his breathing, hoping it would cover it up.

It was an extremely exposed hiding place—all Jaff would have to do is stand on the filing cabinet to see her—but for the moment she was hidden from view.

At the bottom of the stairs was the cleaning closet, the door cracked. Beyond that was the hallway, maybe five or six solid steps to the door of The F Pit. The hallway continued back a ways and Jaff had that space jammed with boxes, Christmas decorations, broken machine parts, and several filing cabinets. One of them was on the ground, horizontal between the door and the wall, with the poor girl laying on the other side.

For the briefest of moments, their eyes met, and Terry was sure he had never seen such pure fear in all his life. Actually, he had, in the eyes of Bonnie West and Tisha Hamilton and several other women he had hurt over the years. And in Jackie Carmichael's face. He had seen it then, but he hadn't understood, and now she was on the other side of the door, probably taking care of Calista and hating him. She had a point, all things considered.

Terry continued moving slow, hoping to give her time to find somewhere else, anywhere else, to hide. But there was nowhere to go.

"You're stalling," Jaff said. "Move your ass."

Terry's shoes finally hit the floor of the basement and he immediately noticed the hole in the door. His bulk was blocking Jaff's view but it would only be seconds before he saw. Not thinking all that clearly, he turned around to face Jaff, the door still out of his view.

"What do you need me to do?"

Terry's voice was loud and confident and the look of rage that crossed Jaff's face was enough to convince Terry he was going to shoot him right then and there.

"Shut the fuck up," he half whispered, half spat.

"Buddy, they heard my fat ass coming down the stairs," he said. "You ain't real good at this killer maniac shit, are you?"

Terry let it sit for a second, then went for broke.

"ARE YOU?!" He yelled as loud as he could, his New York accent reverberating a bit off the walls. This was it.

Jaff's lip curled. It was the indignity that did it, Terry thought. He wasn't showing the man with the gun enough respect, and that pissed the man with the gun off something mighty. Terry didn't show him much respect as a club owner and he sure as hell wasn't showing him respect now that he had a gun on him.

He raised the gun and pointed it square at Terry's head.

"Wanna rethink that?"

"Nah," Terry said. "I think I'm good. You're gonna have to kill your girlfriend without me."

The gun jammed all that much harder in his back before Terry *really* went for broke, throwing his big meat hooks up and making a play for the gun. He got a hand on Jaff's wrist and had superior strength and mass, but not superior balance. The big man pitched and rolled as they fought for the gun, and, at one point, it looked like Terry was going to beat him, until Jaff kicked hard at Terry's bad knee and he went down onto the cold concrete stairs. Red-hot pain roared in Terry's leg as gravity kicked in and pulled the big man down onto the floor, his shoulders and back absorbing most of the damage.

When he hit the floor, Jaff was there, one step above him. Terry still had breath, much to his surprise, and he used it.

"Fuck," he said as he hit the ground. "That was fucking cheap."

Jaff responded by kicking him in the face, hard. He didn't pass out, exactly, but he definitely wasn't far away. He could still see the club owner standing over him, gun pointed down.

"You like to rape women, I hear," Jaff said. "Rapists, man. Are you even worth a bullet?"

In his haze, Terry chuckled.

"I'm worth over eighty million dollars," he said. "And I still came to your shitty club."

When the ringing in his ears stopped from the gunshot in the small, confined space, Terry both realized that he wasn't dead and that his pain had doubled, if that was even possible. The sound of screaming soon filled the hall and Terry realized it was coming from him. He managed to raise his head to see the smoking barrel of the gun pointed directly over his crotch, blood staining in a widening circle on his tan pants.

There were no quips, no jokes, nothing Terry could say if he wanted to. Not with all the screaming.

"Eighty million dollars won't buy you a new dick," Jaff said, but Terry didn't hear him. He had stopped screaming and passed out.

It was at that point Jaff saw the door with its large hole. He gave Terry one more kick to where his balls used to be and walked over, jumping on top of the filing cabinet in one smooth jump.

"Hey, everyone," Jaff said, poking his head through the door. "How's my little lady doing in there?"

# MIDDLE

**Jackie Carmichael [abridged]**
**Live From The Square in Manhattan**
**Friday, October 12**

*[crowd claps]*

*Thanks for the applause, but that was kind of weak. It's okay. I know why. Look at me. I'm a big, loud, opinionated Jewish woman with big hair from New York, but when I travel around, when I'm in the Midwest or the South or anywhere other than New York, I'm an attraction. "Holy shit, Carol, look! It's one of those frizzy screaming Jew ladies I've heard about on Law and Order. Let's see if she has anything interesting to say."*

*I tell them for thirty dollars and two drinks they can stare at me while I say things. Like you guys are now.*

*That's okay. I don't want to get all passive aggressive on ya. You're not every man I've ever dated.*

*You, sir, down there. Yeah,, you in the stripes. Didn't like that joke, did you? What are you gonna do, not talk to me for a day and a half and be a little whiny bitch about everything? Men do that! Men are supposed to be big and tough, but you hurt their feelings even a little bit and they turn into whiney little bitches. Do they think they've got such interesting things to say that being deprived of their wisdom and wit will suddenly have us women come running back, yelling, "Oh, please talk to me, oh please, I can't take it." If that's what they think, then men haven't listened to themselves. When was the last time a man said something interesting? Ladies, think hard. You might have to go back a ways. The reason men talk is so we know they're not dead or having a heart attack. Or if they have food in their mouth, I wanna know where they got it and if I can have some.*

*I complain, but I love men. I do. I've never been married, but I've been around this block and that block and that block over there and that neighborhood with all the black guys in it and what I can tell you, from my extensive travels around the blocks, is that I really like men. But I don't know why.*

*It isn't the dick. That lady, right there, she agrees with me. You're gonna love this bit. Have you ever taken a good, long look at one of those things?*

*It's functional, but you've gone hog wild on the veins to the point where it, frankly, grosses me out. I get what you were going for with the head, some sort of sexy mushroom, I guess. You all did your best, but at the end of the day, I feel about dicks the way Shakespeare feels about life, it's sound and fury signifying a lack of an orgasm. That might not be the full quote.*

*But it's not just the dick. It's what you fellas do with it that's so gross. Now, I'm about to say the most dreaded eight words in all of stand-up, but let me get serious here for a second.*

*Before I landed my gig on Dapper [crowd claps], thank you, I was a road dog. I did two hundred shows a year in cities other than New York, so I know from hotels and late-night gigs, and I hung out a lot with men who were not under the guiding influence of a benevolent woman, so I saw a lot of unsolicited dicks. A lot. You're in the green rooms, some guy whips it out, and party over. And if it wasn't that, you'd show a guy the slightest bit of encouragement, you bat your eyes too much or mention that you forgot your pepper spray at home and, BOOM, four inches in two seconds flat.*

*One time, right, there was this comic. I'm not gonna say his name, you know him. He gives me good career advice, he treats me like an equal, he even tells me how to squeeze more money out of the club owners and it works. That's a big deal. Getting more money out of a club owner is like getting a decent meal at Subway. It's not the normal run of things, but it can happen if you yell loud enough.*

*We're in the elevator to our hotel, we say good night, then he asks if I want to have a quick drink. It didn't seem pervy, didn't seem like a come on, so I say yeah, let me put my purse in my room and I'll be right over. I knock on the door not two minutes after I left him, he's put on a...ahem... "Terry" cloth bath robe, and guess what?*

*[crowd yells indistinctly].*

*That's right, ma'am. His dangler is in the breeze. His waggling wang was waving, saying, "Hey, I'm short and fat and am a disturbing number of different colors."*

*[addressing man in the crowd] His dick was out, sir. Sorry if I'm being too obtuse for you. That was a funny way of saying his dick was out.*

*And it hurt, you know? You think you make a connection with someone, a connection you are just so sure you feel, and it meant nothing to him but a warm hole. Everything he said, all the chemistry, all the kindness, it was all bullshit, and I decided, after that night, that I wasn't taking any more shit from guys like that. I'm single. I'll be with no man I don't trust and respect and who doesn't trust and respect me.*

*It's not bad being single, seriously. People go on and on about how lonely it is, and yeah, it's lonely, but it's easy. Being by yourself is easy. You ever do this, wake up in the morning and think, "Nope. Not today. I'm not dealing with anyone's shit, I'm not cooking, I'm not cleaning, I'm lucky if I can muster enough energy to get out of bed to use the bathroom. I will make myself a plate of saltines and butter and call that dinner"? That sort of day? I know this about myself and can prepare for it so when it happens, [snaps fingers] it's easy. Let's imagine this sort of day if I'm with a guy.*

*[Man's voice] Honey, get up. I need food and we need to go shopping and…oh my God, is this about me? This is about me, isn't it? Are you thinking of that ex-boyfriend, the one you told me had a big dick? Is that who you're thinking of! Oh my God, why are you thinking of that guy with the bigger dick than me? Why are you doing this to me?*

*You, down there in the front, you're not liking this bit at all, are you? Hitting a little close to home? Your girlfriend is laughing, I'm betting you've said something real close to that. It's okay. You don't have to lie to me. You already paid for the show. I'm gonna call you a dirt bag on my own time.*

*I could not be with women, either, if that makes you feel better. Believe me, I tried. But if a doctor with a degree from Sarah Lawrence didn't do it for me, nothing will. And I could ask her anything. What do you like? What don't you like? Is this mole pre-cancerous? Do I need to get that looked at? You have no idea how hard it was not being attracted to a woman who'll give you free medical advice.*

*Sex just complicates everything. One minute you're talking, having a good time, acting like two human beings who might conceivably care about each other, next thing you know you've got these two disgusting body parts slamming together and you become aware that you're really nothing more than ugly, wet, blood-filled bags banging around. Yeah, it feels good, I get it, but it's just this one disgusting thing we're drawn to do and I'd much rather have a nice dinner and watch a movie. Given the options, I'll take dim sum and Below Decks over dick and balls one hundred percent of the time.*

*I've lost some of you. Let me make more of you mad. Anybody else hate every single person on Earth who rides a bike?*

# CHAPTER I

When she was fifteen, Taylor and her family went to Tokyo for a vacation. Her father, who spent his life trying all sorts of different careers while her mother had a successful career as an attorney, was always looking for something different and unique to do with his family. So, that summer, it was Tokyo on the cheap.

Somehow, despite not speaking the language at all, Taylor's dad had managed to book the family in sleeping pods, where you could spend a small amount of money to climb into a tube that was about four feet tall, four feet wide, and ten feet deep and, in theory, fall asleep. The pods had doors that swung shut for privacy, and the second night in the tube, her door jammed. Fifteen-year-old Taylor had spent what felt like hours kicking at the door and screaming into the most perfectly soundproofed walls she had ever seen. Her mother eventually checked on her and, long story short, she had been claustrophobic ever since. The feeling of panic would arise fast and consume completely, as she learned later on when she broke her leg, had to get an MRI, and damn near did damage to the delicate medical instrument.

Even with those experiences, she didn't consider herself highly claustrophobic, just situationally so. She could use the subway on crowded days, for example. Lucky for her and everyone else stuck in The F Pit, she was two years into a meditation practice. Through mindfulness she had made that fear her bitch on more than one · occasion and thought she had it licked. That was, until she got stuck in the door of The F Pit.

The panic hit her unexpectedly since, technically, crawling through the door was the loosest definition of an enclosed space. Her feet were free, her head was free, and her arms only got trapped because she was stupid enough to pull them to her sides in a moment of panic when Sammy and Jerrod lost their grip for a second. That constricting toxin had risen from her gut to her head and panic all but consumed her. Just before it overtook her, she remembered her techniques, controlled her brain, and pulled it back in. People needed her and she could get this done. It didn't work and she started to panic.

That panic of being stuck in the door, complete with the pain of large pieces of wood sticking deeply into her skin, was nothing compared to the panic she felt when she realized Jaff was coming down the stairs. Once she landed with a thud through the door, her plan was to take a beat, breathe, gather herself, and then move. Turned out she didn't have time for at least two parts of that plan. The second her feet came through the top of the door she heard a unique shuffling and saw a pair of tan chinos with dress shoes struggling to make it down the stairs.

There was nowhere to go. In desperation, she rolled off the filing cabinet onto the floor and crawled into the corner furthest from the door. Her head was propped up against the concrete wall, her body mostly hidden by the cabinet. The space was barely enough to conceal an adult woman and there was no escape route if she was discovered. She pushed her body up against the filing cabinet, feeling the cold metal steal heat from her body. Her heart was beating hard enough that she feared she was going to pass out and her breathing was making way too much noise, but she was physically unable to stop it.

"Taylor!"

It was Jerrod from inside The F Pit. She held her breath and shut her eyes, willing the comic to stop talking, to hear the commotion down the stairs, anything to avoid giving away her position. He either took the hint or stopped yelling at her for his own reasons.

The panic was overwhelming, and curling into a ball against the cold stone floor was doing nothing to alleviate it. Taylor took a deep breath as quietly as she could, desperately trying to steady her nerves and, to her surprise, not vomit. She was not a puker in general, but she also didn't live the sort of lifestyle that put her at risk for being held at gunpoint. It was a unique day.

Her brain started working on the situation, intellect cutting through panic. It was a blessed relief and she had done nothing to will her faculties to start firing again, but she had experience in using her brain in intense situations. She had played girls volleyball back in high school and had been good at it, particularly the split-second stuff. When a ball was flying toward her face, she was the one who both reacted and thought where to put the ball. It wasn't a skill she developed, but one she had, and thank God, because, suddenly, she had a plan.

"Okay," she whispered to herself, her voice shaking. "One quick look. You can do this."

She needed to understand where everyone was, what they were doing, and their relationship to each other. Without that knowledge, she was doing nothing but sitting in a corner waiting to be shot by the madman who owned the club. She had to look. It was one of the only options open to her, even if she wasn't sure she could physically do it.

"So," she heard Terry say a little too loudly, "What's the plan? What happens when we get down there?"

She slowly poked her head over the top of the filing cabinet and locked eyes with Terry Stafford as he came down the stairs. He looked like shit, with blood on his shirt and the look of a man who might fall flat on his face at any given moment. His eyes, while tired, were burning with a panic she completely recognized.

She didn't see him but she knew Jaff was behind him and the gun was in his hand. It was obvious even before she heard Jaff hiss something from behind him. They were between her and the stairway and she couldn't go back.

Part of her wanted to jump up with her hands above her head and beg for mercy, beg and plead for her life at the feet of the man with the gun. She pushed it down, knowing mercy wasn't on the menu tonight.

"ARE YOU?!"

Terry was shouting, and before she could stop herself, Taylor stuck her head above the filing cabinet and saw the two in an all-out tussle. Terry had seen her and seconds later they were fighting. This wasn't a coincidence.

With speed as the priority, Taylor got into a crouching position and rolled over the filing cabinet. She was shaky, but determined, avoiding any terribly loud noises. The effect was exactly what she wanted and any sound she produced was completely drowned out by the two men fighting. As she landed on her feet, she froze for a second. Terry was at the bottom of the stairs, breathing hard, and Jaff was talking to him from above. There was no way she was going to make it up the stairs undetected, and the only option available to her was a broom closet immediately to her right. Even that left her far more exposed than she wanted, but she was out of options.

The door was cracked but not latched, so she quickly ducked in, pulling the door shut slowly in case Jaff had seen a blur or something. She let the latch bolt out slowly and quietly until it lightly clicked in its holder. The room was pitch dark musty and smelled of chemicals and something metallic. A faint whiff of something musty and sickly sweet also hit her nostrils and panic rose again like bile and she attempted to push it down, which was having less and less effect. She could hear Jaff's footsteps as he finally made his way to the bottom of the stairs. He was talking to Terry, his voice smooth with no sense of urgency. It didn't mean she was in the clear, but it was encouraging.

Muffled voices made their way through the door but all the hard consonants needed to make words were swallowed by the wood and stone. Taylor put her ear to the door to hear better, when Jaff fired the gun.

Taylor let out an audible scream and immediately cupped her hands over her mouth.

More mumbling from outside the door made its way in and the panic wouldn't be denied any longer. If Jaff had seen her run into the closet, if he suspected something was fishy, now would be the time he would find her, and no amount of breath control or reciting a mantra would stop him from putting bullets into her. She started to shake, her hand still over her mouth, tears starting to fall down her face.

He didn't come for her, but what she heard next was almost as bad.

Another shot rang out, this time from her left, in the direction of The F Pit. Even through the concrete walls she could hear everyone in the room screaming and yelling.

Taylor made several attempts to grab the handle of the door, not quite sure if she meant to open it and peer out to see what was

146

going on or bolt for the stairs. When her hand finally grabbed the round knob, she held on tight, took a deep breath, and opened the door just a bit to see what was happening. Immediately, sound came flooding in.

"Jackie, move. I'm not giving you another chance."

From her spot she could see the door and Jaff with his head all the way into the hole she, Jerrod, and Sammy had made and was punching at the cheap wood, trying to wedge his gun hand in as well.

*Don't be dumb*, Taylor told herself. *Dumb people end up dead.*

"I'm not going to let you kill her," she could hear Jackie yelling.

"I already killed her!" Jaff yelled. "She just isn't dead yet."

Jaff's back end was extremely animated, kicking and pushing off the filing cabinet in an attempt to get a better view of the room. She watched him kick off once, then twice.

The action part of her brain kicked in and she decided if Jaff kicked off again, she would try to bolt up the stairs. It would give her a few seconds' head start and maybe she could make it upstairs undetected. If she made it upstairs undetected, she could call the fucking police and get out of this club already.

It didn't take long for him to kick with his right foot, pushing his body up further into the hole. Taylor's brain told her body to go. Her body hesitated, shook, then complied. She pushed the door open as quietly as she could and quickly hit Terry, who was splayed out on the floor in front of the door.

It shouldn't have startled her. She should have accounted for him, but in the heat of the moment she had forgotten about him and let out a small scream. His crotch was now deep red with blood and the stain had spread all the way up to the midsection of his suit. He was breathing, but even in the split second she stopped to look at him, she could tell he wasn't doing well.

147

The combination of the dark blood on his tan chinos and almost tripping over him in her hurry to get out of the closet caused her to let out a scream. It wasn't a small one either, it was clear and loud and born of genuine surprise and fear.

And it was more than enough to get Jaff's attention.

Taylor took a quick look back and saw Jaff start to pull his head out of the door. She never saw his eyes before turning around and starting up the stairs, but she knew they were coming and she feared them almost as much as the gun. Feeling a small pang of guilt jumping over Terry's body, she hit the stairs and stumbled a bit, breaking her stride and forcing her hands down on the third step. She pushed off and was on her feet when she heard the gunshot.

The wall behind her spewed chunks of brick and dirt onto her exposed arms, stinging them. Taylor kept scrambling, now using the panic inside her to help propel her forward, hearing her deep, fast breathing in her ears.

The second shot missed her as well, and she was up the stairs when she heard Jaff scream, followed by a third gunshot. The need to climb the stairs superceded any higher brain function to figure out what the hell was happening. She needed to find a way out of the club.

Once she hit the top of the stairs, she pumped her legs hard and headed for the main entrance. The tables were still set up from the show and she weaved through a few before realizing Jaff had locked the metal gates used to keep burglars and the public out. The gates were the sort that folded into the wall at the beginning of the day, and she tugged on them hard to make sure he had locked them. They shook, but the lock didn't budge. That left the exit off the kitchen or the smaller exit off Jaff's office close to the stage, both of which she had never used but Jackie had insisted were there.

"I'm never getting out of this club," Taylor said through heavy breaths.

A voice, sweet but firm and not anything like her internal monologue, busted its way into her head, and it wasn't encouraging.

*No one leaves.*

The voice was smooth and not threatening, but still triggered the fear response in Taylor, which was already raging uncontrollably through her body. She stopped and shook her head, trying to deal with whatever had just happened, and it was at that point she saw Jaff's face coming toward her as he ran up the stairs.

\*\*\*

Even as he lay on the ground dying, even as his own warm blood soaked through his clothes and up near his chest, even as his life flashed before he eyes, Terry Stafford had to admit "eighty million dollars won't buy you a new dick" was a pretty boss line.

He had to come up with a better one before he clocked out.

Pain was part of what was happening to him, but, surprisingly, it wasn't the main thing. It was weird. He knew he was dying, losing a lot of blood through his dick (the irony was not lost on him), but the main sensation wasn't the pain but the sticky, wet blood soaking through his clothes. It was uncomfortable. Terry hated being dressed and wet, and this was the worst.

His mind flashed to the filming of one of his movies, a romantic comedy called *Love Tips*. The cast had called it *Just The Tip* on set, even though it was about as standard a romantic comedy as had ever existed—mistaken identities, lack of communication, a spunky love interest, and a big, long kiss at the end. In this particular flick, the kiss had been in the rain, and Terry, then much more fit and desirable, had spent what felt like days on set in the fake rain, getting more and more drenched in his costume. It was the worst, and from that point on he had his contracts adjusted to make sure he'd never have to do a scene in the water ever again.

That life seemed like it happened a million years ago and belonged to someone else, but his hatred for being wet endured.

He heard Taylor make it to the closet during his tussle with Jaff and he knew she would probably make a break for it at some point. In preparation, he worked his meaty hands into his pocket and pulled out his Jumbo Jack Knife.

The Jumbo Jack Knife was created by the United Machine Tool Company of Grand Rapids, Michigan in the 1950s and was purchased, likely second hand, by Terry's father, who gave it to him on Christmas morning of 1971. It was the only Christmas gift his father had ever given him and, of course, it was contraband. His mother took it from him, but Terry stole it back without her knowledge as a young boy and had carried it every day of his life. His therapist had once told him it was a bad idea from a healing standpoint. Maybe so, Terry thought, but it was sure going to come in handy in a couple seconds.

He saw Taylor make a break for it, clocked Jaff notice her, and pulled the knife out of his pocket. Summoning up every bit of strength he had left, he waited until Jaff got in range and plunged the knife into the crazy man's calf. It was surprisingly easy to get the knife into the flesh, easier than Terry would have thought. While he put everything he had into the stab, it wasn't that deep and served only to slow him down. That was kind of the point.

The surprise of the stab made Jaff cry out, then turn down toward Terry. His expression gave new meaning to the term "murder in his eyes."

"It's just a little prick, ya little prick," Terry said, smiling.

"Good line," Jaff answered, and shot him in the face.

# CHAPTER 2

For comics, bombing was a fact of the profession, an unavoidable, soul-sucking, sweat-drenched pain in the ass, as unavoidable as stubbing your toe or tweaking your back. To cope, most in the profession turned the experience of bombing into tales of battle, described with breathless intensity to other comics who understood just how painful the silence of a crowd could be. Some turned it into a game—who bombed the worst. It was a game without a winner.

Jerrod Seybourne had bombed plenty of times, but his "worst I ever bombed" story wasn't funny. Not even a little.

Being a black comic, he had certain advantages and disadvantages—the advantages being he could play black clubs that had an energy and community like nothing else on the planet, and the disadvantages being racist assholes came to comedy clubs as much as anyone else. The way he described it to other black comics was with the phrase "there's always that one guy," and his contemporaries would all nod in complete agreement.

When a white comic bombed, it could be humiliating, but the threat of physical violence was far less pronounced. For Jerrod, this was a professional risk, and it filled him with enough rage to power his car.

It was, in part, why he became a political comic. To be blunt, as hard as he tried, he couldn't separate politics from his comedy. Others had mastered that trick—Eddie Murphy, Bernie Mac, Kevin Hart—but others who were just as great wallowed in politics. He resigned himself early in his career that he would never fundamentally change the landscape the way Chris Rock had with *Bigger and Blacker* or, God forbid, change the way the world worked like Richard Pryor did. But that didn't mean he was going to let the hate he sometimes experienced on stage slide. No fucking way.

Which had led to the worst time he had ever bombed.

It had been one of his first showcases, one of those shows with other up-and-coming comics people in the industry watched closely. His laid-back style of comedy and tight, intelligent jokes had gotten him noticed, and he was the only black comic on the bill that night. This wasn't his one and only shot, but it was one of a handful of nights that could make a career.

But there's always that one guy.

Jerrod's guy got on his radar the second he took the stage. He was yelling just a bit too loud, clapping later after everyone else had stopped. Over the years, Jerrod had developed a pretty decent radar when it came to danger. He was not a fighter, and not much of a lover either, as his exes were fond of pointing out, but he knew when something was wrong, and from the second he took the stage, something was wrong. The guy was to Jerrod's left and started lobbing incomprehensible blather during the down time between jokes as soon as the first words had come out of Jerrod's mouth. The crowd noticed about two minutes in. As someone who had done standup for a while, Jerrod knew this guy would eventually have to be dealt with, and he was more than equipped to handle it.

His first try was a straight up appeal.

"Man, why don't you let everyone enjoy the show?"

"Fuck you!" the man yelled back.

"Well, that escalated fast," Jerrod said to a big laugh. By now security was on the way, but some combination of alcohol, rage, and being the butt of a joke by a black man had set the guy off. He screamed and yelled as he was being taken out of the room, ending with all sorts of threats of violence, some of them very specific. They guy might have thrown the N word around, too. It wouldn't have surprised him, but Jerrod didn't remember hearing it. Either way, the wind was sucked completely out of the room and there wasn't much he could do to get it back.

He tried, hard, but after someone threatens to hurt you for telling some jokes when your skin happened to be a different color than his, that's enough to throw off your rhythm. The audience wasn't into it either. They chuckled, applauded politely when he'd done his time, and everyone left feeling like shit. Jerrod had dwelled on that night for years, trying to figure out what he could have done to recover from that sort of heckler. He'd talked to other comics about it and there were lots of suggestions, but no one had that magic idea that could bring a crowd back from something like that. It haunted Jerrod to this day, and deep inside his brain, a glowing ember of rage had grown significantly on that night.

So, he was a political comic. The way he figured it, he had to be. But his anger never translated to the physical. He could throw down on the mic, but in an actual fight, he wasn't worth very much.

That fact was pissing him off even more now that two people were bleeding on the floor and some asshole with a gun was threatening to shoot him and everyone else in that room.

"How's my little lady doing in there?"

Jaff's sudden appearance had, understandably, freaked everyone out, and Jackie let out a surprised scream.

Sammy had let out a very understandable "oh fuck," not just because there was a guy poking through the door with a gun, but because chances were good he'd find Taylor very soon. She was their best chance of getting out of The F Pit without the benefit of a stretcher.

It was at that moment, seeing Jackie freaked out and Sammy scared, that the little ember of rage in the back of Jerrod's head caught fire. Even in the green room, there was always that one guy.

"Hey, Jaff," he yelled. "I'd get a bigger gun if I were you."

For a second, everyone turned and looked at him, even Braden, who was starting to look paler and paler. Even Jaff was taken aback. Given Jerrod had been ready to scramble out of The F Pit by any means necessary just a half hour ago, he even surprised himself.

"'Cause if you're trying to compensate for your tiny dick, you need more help than that, man."

Something about the comment short circuited whatever Jaff had planned and he shouted back.

"My dick is fine."

"Dude, if she says it's fine, it ain't fine."

"You want me to shoot you, Jerrod?"

"Yeah, hide behind a gun. Way to prove you don't have a small dick, JAFF."

Jerrod saw, out of the corner of his eye, Sammy giving him a "what are doing?" sort of look. Truth be told, he wasn't sure what he was doing. He was angry, he was scared, and he wanted out of The F Pit more than he'd wanted anything else in his life.

"Fuck you!" Jaff yelled, and made a little jump like he wanted to get in the hole in the door. There was no way, with his angle and lack of athletic ability, he was going to get anywhere close.

"Yeah, if you did, I bet you I wouldn't feel it. You look like the kind of guy who gets asked, 'Is it in yet?' a lot."

To his delight, Jackie smirked. A good line was a good line.

Jaff's face was now red with effort as he tried several times to hop through the door. He was nowhere close, and if he had been close, he could get stuck and everyone could have taken turns beating his head and shoulders with the nearest available blunt object. *Maybe that is my plan*, Jerrod thought to himself. Anything he could do to give Taylor a fighting chance was in his best interest.

As if the universe heard his slightly hopeful thought, Jaff's face disappeared from the hole and his hand reappeared holding the gun. He pulled the trigger and the gun made a loud popping sound that was amplified by the thick concrete walls of The F Pit. Jaff, in his haste and rage, had aimed the gun low and fired into the carpet about three feet away from Jerrod's feet, not hitting anything.

No damage was done, but the shot was more than enough to serve up a fresh wave of panic. Jackie started yelling, Sammy ducked behind one of the chairs, and Braden started coughing, a new development in his deteriorating state. For some reason, Jerrod didn't yell, but the *pop* certainly sent his blood pressure up, as did Jaff's face when it appeared back in the hole they'd made in the door.

"You like that, Jerrod?" Jaff yelled. "You like having a bullet in your ass?"

"You missed my ass by, like, six feet," Jerrod said, his inexplicable bravado still very much with him. "You need to learn to shoot that tiny dick gun of yours."

Jaff screamed into the hole and made more attempts to jump through the door. It occurred to Jerrod that he was completely out of his mind, acting only on rage and something else pushing him to violence.

"Jaff!" Sammy yelled. "Calm down, man. Just take a breath."

"Dude, if you want someone to calm down, the worst fucking thing you can do is tell them to calm down," Jerrod heard himself say.

For a few seconds, Jaff disappeared from the door, and when he reappeared, he had led with his shoulder, pointing the gun through the hole and his head following. It was comical to look at, but the practical effect was he could both see where everyone was and aim the gun to actually hit them. It occurred to Jerrod to count the bullets. He had shot once outside the room and once inside. He had four left.

"I'm going to kill her," Jaff said, pointing the gun in Calista's direction. She was still in rough shape but Jackie had done a good job of keeping pressure on the most severe of her wounds. The lady on the ground was tough as nails, Jerrod thought, fighting significantly harder than he would in this situation.

"No, you're fucking not, Jaff," Jackie said. "I'm taking care of her now."

"Jackie, move. I'm not giving you another chance."

"I'm not going to let you kill her," Jackie yelled.

"I already killed her!" Jaff yelled. "She just isn't dead yet."

Sammy and Jerrod looked at each other, panicked.

"Jackie," Sammy ventured. "It's okay. Why don't you leave Calista there and come back here with us?"

This sent Jaff off and he started again trying to feebly jump through the hole in the door. On the floor, Jackie had started to cry.

"You don't get it…" she said, the tears falling straight down from her eyes, not bothering with her cheeks. "She can still make it."

From outside the door, everyone heard a scream.

Jerrod saw Jaff turn his head sharply, then start wriggling out of the hole.

"Oh fuck," he said. The blood in Sammy's face had also started to drain as they both put two and two together. Taylor was now running for her life.

The shot from the gun made everyone jump, and Braden screamed, "NO!" before lapsing into another coughing fit. He made a valiant effort to stand, but didn't get halfway to his feet before the coughs and weakness threw him back to the carpet. Jerrod was ripped apart by the desire to run to the hole and see what the hell was going on and staying in the relative safety of the room. He willed his legs to move but they weren't giving him any help.

The second shot bolted him to attention and Jerrod ran to the hole and stuck his head out just in time to hear a shriek from Jaff as he was stabbed in the leg. The shriek cut through The F Pit, and when Jerrod saw Jaff aim the gun at Terry's head, he retreated. When the shot finally came, everyone understood what had happened and Jackie's cries moved from restrained crying to full-on sobbing.

There was a beat where there was no sound beyond Jackie's sobbing, and after it ended, Jerrod grabbed his table leg and started chipping away more of the door.

"Why didn't we make the goddamn hole bigger?" Jerrod asked.

"We were trying to be careful," Sammy said, sounding completely shaken, almost hollow in his delivery.

"It's because we're comics and we don't know what the fuck we're doing," Jackie said through her sobs. "That's why."

The door was not strong and gave way easily as Jerrod

pounded. The thought of Taylor up there by herself, possibly shot and bleeding, propelled him forward with a deep urgency, and before long, the hole was big enough for everyone to step over with a little difficulty. Jerrod was sweaty when he came away and looked into the hallway, scared but prepared.

For years, he had been a marijuana enthusiast, and for years it had kept him mellow and calm in the face of pretty steady waves of self-doubt and anger. The pot had helped with the anger considerably, stopping him from yelling at friends, freaking out on subways, and generally being a dick to those he had let into his life. He typically smoked a few times a day and it struck him, even after missing his post-show smoke, how easy it was to tap into his anger. It never went away, it was always there, at a slow boil just seconds away from blowing.

"You guys go. I'm staying with them," Jackie said.

"If you want," Sammy said, grabbing another of the chair legs they had destroyed earlier. "But I'd give it some serious thought."

"I have," Jackie said. "I'm not letting her die. Him either."

"I'm not planning on it," Braden said. His coughing fit had been pretty terrible, but he had gotten it under control. "But I'm starting to feel pretty bad over here."

"Get help," she said. "And kill that son of a bitch if you can."

Jerrod locked eyes with Jackie.

"Guess you needed more backup than you thought, huh?"

She responded with a smile that dripped exhaustion. Lit by the glow of the F Pit sign, she looked beautiful in a ragged sort of way.

Struck by inspiration and the lighting, Jerrod unplugged the big metal sign that was the main source of light in the room. Then took the large, metal "F Pit" off the wall and immediately stepped on it, pulling strips of thin metal from the sign. For a good minute he twisted and pulled and destroyed the sign, then wrapped those strips around his wooden table leg. The effect was a bit wicked, a bit comical, but it would definitely do some damage if he got close enough to use it. The bits of metal were very sharp and Jerrod was impressed that he hadn't cut himself while constructing his weapon.

"I'm going to kill him," Jerrod said. "And I can help Taylor while I'm at it."

"Please do," Braden said. "You'll be my favorite comic."

"I'm pretty good," Jerrod said, smiling, shouldering his new weapon.

While Jerrod was destroying the sign, Sammy had gone over to Jackie, knelt beside her, and whispered something in her ear. She responded by slapping him in the face, hard. The sound made Jerrod jump almost as much as the gunshot.

"I'm not letting her die," she said. "Get that through your skull."

For a second, Jerrod thought Sammy was going to grab Jackie and shake her, but he kept his hands to himself. Good thing, too. Jerrod was not beyond smacking a bitch down if he got handsy. Plus, that lady had more balls than both of them put together, he thought. Jackie was still doing the most basic of first aid, applying pressure, making sure no one swallowed their tongue, desperately holding out for help that may never come. After a few seconds, Sammy gave up.

Both men took a few seconds to get through the hole they had made in the door, but they managed prettily handily. In front of them was a short, narrow hallway and the stairs leading up to the club. Near the bottom off the stairs was a very dead, very blood Terry Stafford.

Jerrod smirked a bit. He couldn't help it. It was clear from the wounds to the man that Jaff had shot him in the crotch.

"That…" Sammy said, gesturing toward Terry. "That is no way

to go."

"He ain't going to have a chance to shoot off my dick," Jerrod said, psyching himself up, holding the makeshift club against his shoulder. "I promise you that."

They both stood in the low, fluorescent light, staring at the staircase that led up to the club. The hall stood in stark contrast to the dark coziness of the club upstairs, which had blacks and deep reds and tables full of candle light and a bar full of stained wood. This hallway was dingy, the light seeping into every chip and line in the decaying concrete stairway. They stood, sticks of wood in hand, briefly contemplating the trip up and the madman that was waiting for them.

In order to stop looking at Terry's body, they moved the filing cabinet out of the way. It was considerably heavier than they thought it would be and both men grunted, trying to keep their motions from making too much noise. The battered and destroyed door of The F Pit swung feebly, most of the wood and support beams destroyed, the thing damn near off its hinges. To Jerrod, it looked more like a failed construction project than anything that had once been a functional part of a room. Panting, Sammy stood up and readied himself.

"I'm getting the hell out of here," Sammy said. "I like you and all, but if you're still inside, I ain't waiting. If I see a chance to get out of here, I'm taking it."

Jerrod processed this information for a second.

"That might be the whitest thing I've ever heard in my life," Jerrod said.

Sammy gave a quick laugh and stepped over Terry's body on the way up the stairs.

# CHAPTER 3

The voice was stubbornly refusing to give him direction and it was pissing Jaff off.

If he had some ethereal force as his guide, something beyond himself and beyond his comprehension, it should not just be guiding him, but giving him direction when he needed it most. Right now, there was a loose comic upstairs threatening to pooch the whole deal, and Jaff was desperately looking for some direction or reassurance. Instead, the voice had decided to be quiet. It hadn't been very talkative since he shot Raoul, just encouraging him to kill Calista. That was already very much on his to-do list. He didn't need the voice to tell him to do that.

What he was unsure about was everything else. The voice had told him to kill Terry but he had resisted, taking him downstairs for "crowd control." Truth of the matter was that wasn't why he had done that. He liked Terry and wanted him on his side, or had up until a few minutes ago. Now most of the big man's brains were leaking onto the concrete floor downstairs. It was always going to end up that way, but instead he had let Terry get in a good shot with some knife he kept God knew where.

As if on cue, the voice returned. Jaff did not like what it had to say.

*I told you to kill him.*

"You did," Jaff said, stumbling up the stairs, glad to have the voice back but pissed off that it was criticizing him. The wound in his calf didn't hurt so much but it was making it moderately hard to put weight on. He could feel blood seeping through onto his jeans and it was only adding to his already overflowing well of anger, fueled as well by the fact that he had a girl on the loose upstairs, two unsecured exits, and Calista was STILL breathing below deck. He felt the whole thing starting to get away from him. Anger on top of anger boiled up from his stomach and made its way into his bloodstream.

*She can't leave.*

"I know she can't leave," Jaff said, reaching the top of the stairs. The gun was feeling lighter in his hands and he could feel heat from the barrel through the fabric of his jeans near where his hand was resting. It no longer felt like an extension of his hand and that worried him.

He took a quick look around to find the place but didn't see the girl. Working on instinct, he stopped all movement and listened for her breathing. Over his years in this space, at the bar, sweeping the stage, working the floor, he knew all the places a body could fit. He quietly muted his footsteps and breathing as much as he could as he searched for any sort of noise, anything, that would give away where Taylor was hiding.

*She's behind the bar.*

Of course she was behind the bar. She didn't have enough time to make it into the kitchen. She could have run for the exit off the office, but there would have been a draft or a clattering door or something that would have given her away. No, Jaff thought, she was here. She was here, she was scared, and she was hiding, and where she was hiding was behind the bar.

Jaff took long, deliberate strides as best he could with his new injury, making his shoes thud on the floor as he approached. The more he thought about it, the more he was right. There was nowhere else she could be and she wasn't going anywhere. He was coming for her and she had to know it, which caused him no small amount of delight.

He approached the edge of the bar and whipped his head around and there she was, curled up against one of the filthy, grooved mats that kept your feet from sliding all over, her head near the ice machine. She was there, amidst the spilled syrups and hard liquors, her phone in her hand, tears streaming down her face.

Her phone.

"Shit," Jaff said. "Did you...?"

She held up the phone so he could see.

"9-1-1, asshole," she said. "This place will be swarming with cops in ten minutes."

Taking a quick look to make sure she was right, Jaff saw the phone, its interface lit up, the word "emergency" displayed. Some voice, tinny and far away, was trying to get Taylor back on the line.

*She can't leave.*

"No, she can't," Jaff said. He raised his arm and took aim, the gun again feeling good against the grooves of his hand.

The shot was deadly accurate, the bullet exploding through the center of the phone, proceeding into Taylor's hand, along part of her arm, and exiting through the back of her elbow. She screamed, both out of shock and pain, and fell back to the ground, holding onto the remains of her left arm with her right. Before the blood started pouring out, Taylor saw one of her fingers bending at an odd and impossible angle, looking floppy and fake, yet oddly familiar, like a fun house version of her own flesh. When the blood came, it was in great gushes from the top of her hand and her elbow.

Jaff took a few steps and aimed the gun, this time at her face. Taylor saw him coming and her screams died into a whimper, even with the pain consuming her. She gathered herself as best she could.

"Fuck you," Taylor said, half crying. She had wanted to sound tough but it didn't come out that way.

Jaff smirked. He had heard that dozens of times from dozens of comics who didn't get the time they wanted, who didn't get the pay they wanted, who didn't get the respect they wanted. Over the years, Jaff had, on occasion, day dreamed about shooting them in the face. This was literally a dream come true.

He fired and the gun clicked.

Jaff did a quick count—one shot at Terry, one in The F Pit, two at the girl on her way up the stairs, another at Terry, and one that just blew apart her arm. He was empty, but she was down. Taylor tried to get on her feet, but the shock from her arm was keeping her feet from properly responding, which only put her into a worse state of fear. The tears came harder, trying to match the volume of blood pumping from her hand and arm.

For his part, Jaff was pretty calm about being out of bullets. Too calm, by Taylor's estimation.

"Don't move," he said, putting the gun in the back pocket of his pants. "I'll be right back."

When the gun didn't fire, Jaff's thoughts became very clear. She wasn't getting up any time soon and he had a chance to make sure she wasn't going to leave. He could go to the kitchen, block the exit, and grab a big knife on the way back. The voice wasn't talking, but it felt like it was leading. As for the 911 call, if he worked fast, there wouldn't be anyone to alert the police that something was wrong. She hadn't had enough time to say muchto the police, so they wouldn't come lights and sirens, more likely a patrol would come by to see if the call was a mistake or not. It was a small hiccup.

The whimpers from the girl were still strong as he made his way into the kitchen, a traditional industrial affair with a door that had a singular round window and fake leather upholstery on it. He had found the door at an auction years ago and it reminded him of clubs from the 1940s. Calista had loved it at the time, gushed over it, in fact. She was big on most things retro and even had a matching tiger print bra and panty set that she would dance around in when she was in a good mood. Inside Jaff's head, other memories of his partner started to worm their way in—the way her hair looked in the morning, the way her eyes always found him in a room, the way she would stretch and lean against him when he held her—

*You've got a job to do.*

He fought it a bit, tried to hang on to the memories, but they disappeared like a shot down the throat of someone at the bar. He was standing in the middle of his kitchen and he did have a job to do. The voice wasn't even that compelling. It was direct and Jaff listened to it.

His first stop was to block the exit. Even if she or anyone else tried to get out, throwing a refrigerator in front of the door would slow them down enough to put a bullet in their back. For his purposes, that was secure enough.

"I've got…" Jaff said to himself as he unplugged the refrigerator next to the door, "…another ten bullets in the office. If I need them."

The refrigerator, silver with an industrial finish,- was heavy and full of food, and for a second, Jaff wasn't sure he was up to the task. He gave it a hard kick on its side and the big machine rocked a bit. He was able to catch it from falling back to the floor completely, and got his hands underneath.

The sound of the refrigerator hitting the floor sounded more like a minor detonation. The floor rocked, windows rattled, and Taylor let out a little scream in the other room.

"There you go," Jaff said, admiring his handiwork. The refrigerator, on its side, blocked the door all the way up past the doorknob. To get out, you would have to move the entire thing a couple of feet, and that would take time and energy. If someone was being chased, this might as well be a dead end.

"Good luck moving that, assholes," Jaff chuckled to himself. "She's not going anywhere."

He eyed the dishwasher, which had a rack of sharp, gleaming knives, fresh from a soak.

"And since she's not going anywhere…"

He took his time picking out the knife. One of the butcher knives in particular was almost comically large and the handle looked to be cheap plastic. He picked it up and immediately tossed it into the dishwasher, where it made a cheap-sounding clang. A few more knives that looked like they might fit the bill also got chucked away, not up to the task. It was the serrated big boy that caught his attention—fourteen inches tip to tip, nine inches of blade with ridges that looked like shark teeth. He picked it up and things felt right.

Jaff delighted as images crossed his mind of the girl, whose name he honestly didn't know, screaming and begging him for her life, and he obliged by stabbing her slowly, then pulling the blade out, ripping her flesh anew. In his mind's eye, the look on her face as she realized she was being stabbed was so real he could almost smell her breath and her blood.

He could take his time with the girl (was she even a comic?) behind the bar or he could go downstairs and finish what he needed to finish. Calista had started all this, after all. She was the one who had pushed him, who had never loved him, who had only been in his life because of convenience.

*That's not true.*

This was a second voice, quieter and more distant, much more like the voice in his head that told him to order more Johnny Walker at the bar or pay that bill that was two months overdue. It had been there through the headaches and pain and violence, trying to talk sense to him, trying to get him to stop. It sounded a lot like Calista, which only made it worse. He didn't want to listen to this voice, but something about holding a knife in the empty din of his kitchen had shaken it loose and now it was hard to not hear it plea and beg.

*This isn't you. You are not a monster. You're just tired. You're tired.*

He wasn't a murderer, he wasn't a killer, or didn't think he was, but two bodies in his club now told a different story. Was he a tired guy who had made a life with a woman who loved him? What was he now? Possessed? Unhinged? Did crazy people not think they're crazy? How did they tell the difference?

It was as if Jaff's entire head space had tilted and he was looking at his crimes through the eyes of himself twenty-four hours ago, a week ago, a year ago. He had killed Terry Stafford. That, in and of itself, would put him in the pantheon of villains amidst entertainers, right up there with Phil Spector and Col. Tom Parker for time and eternity. His legacy wouldn't be The Square. It would be shooting Terry Stafford in the balls.

Anger had been the fuel on which he was running, and the voice, whatever the hell it was, had been the engine, but for a brief second, it disappeared. The voice or whatever it was tried to push back, but the flood was already on its way, and suddenly Jaff's chest felt tight and his leg started to throb and his splitting headache returned, threatening to tear his head open with meat hooks. Dizziness overtook him and he collapsed onto the dirty linoleum, his hands immediately covered in layers of grease and filth.

What the fuck was he doing? More importantly, what the fuck had he done? The flood of emotions he had been holding back spilled into his brain, choking him. He flashed to images of his lover, on the deck of a ship during their vacation, to the top of her head as they lay on the couch together, to her naked to the waist, asleep in their apartment.

*This isn't you.*

"Calista…" he said, spit starting to slide out of his mouth. "Why…why didn't you stop me?"

The quiet that greeted the question was deep and terrible. The pain in his head robbed him of much conscious thought, but when something finally did break through, it wasn't the voice, but the gruff baritone of George Carlin. Jaff's brain, functioning as it was, had started remembering a bit from the seminal *Back in Town* about prison reform. Instead of traditional prisons, George thought it would be fun to fence off large, rectangular states and throw certain types of criminals in each state. Then they could intermingle.

"Everyone would have guns, everyone will have drugs, and no one would be in charge…just like now," Carlin said inside Jaff's head. It was enough to bring a small smile to Jaff's face.

Out of the corner of his eye. through the tiny hole in the kitchen door, he saw a flash as two men came up the stairs, one with very timid body language, the other looking like he was ready to go to war.

*Get up.*

The voice was back and strong, wiping away all other thoughts, all other doubts, all other courses of action. In an instant, Jaff went from a man in pain on the filthy floor of his kitchen to a man with a clear purpose and unwavering focus. His headache evaporated and the grip on his knife tightened until his hand went white and the veins popped out. It was as if the last thirty seconds had never happened as the anger was back and roaring for blood.

"Motherfuckers," he said, more drool spilling from his mouth.

Calista didn't matter. He didn't matter. The club didn't matter. Only one thing mattered, and the voice, now clear as a bell, knew what that one thing was.

*They can't leave.*

"They won't."

All the pain was gone from the wound in Jaff's leg as he moved forward at a fast walk. He kept the knife down to his side but his instinct was to hold it up, show them what was coming for them. They didn't see him until he burst from the kitchen.

"Shit!"

Sammy saw him coming first and turned tail, going back down the stairs at a dead sprint. Before he fled, Jaff could see the panic completely consume him, wipe away any rational thoughts or plans he might have had. The look only fed Jaff's approach; having that sort of power to send someone running against their rational interest and right mind only propelled him forward.

Jerrod, on the other hand, seemed almost glad to see him. He held the wooden leg from a coffee table in The F Pit, wrapped in what looked to be sharp wire, down by his side, but looked ready to swing it at a moment's notice.

"What'd you do with Taylor?"

"Who the fuck is Taylor?" Jaff said, slowing a bit.

"Brown hair, tank top, cell phone she was going to use to throw your crazy ass in jail."

Jaff motioned with his head.

"She's behind the bar. Can't you hear her?"

Quick as could be, Jerrod yelled Taylor's name in his roaring baritone. It echoed off the bar and Jaff slowed his walk considerably, biding his time. Without consciously thinking about it, his fingers flicked and played with the serrated edges of the knife at his side.

"Taylor!" he yelled. "You alive back there?"

"Yes," she yelled. "I'm losing a lot of blood."

"There's a lot of that going around," Jaff said, a smile creeping across his face. He couldn't stop it if he wanted to, and he didn't want to.

"What'd he do to you?"

"Shot me in the hand and…the arm. I'm kinda fucked up. Called 9-1-1. Cops are coming."

"Good girl. Sit tight. Be there in a second, baby."

Jaff could see the rage continuing to build behind Jerrod's eyes. He didn't care. It would all end the same for him and for all of them. Through the anger, he saw the man's eyes go to Jaff's side where the knife was.

"Where's your gun, pussy?"

Where was his gun? The kitchen most likely. His little spell of emotion had thrown it off his radar, but Jaff remembered having it in the kitchen, where he had intended on reloading it. It was a small problem that didn't need his attention at the moment.

"Don't need it," Jaff said, the knife in his hand all the explanation he needed. "Come to think of it, don't want it."

Jaff's voice was crackly and raw, but his smile was big and his body coiled. Jerrod easily had fifty pounds on him and had a longer reach (and youth and strength, if Jaff wanted to be honest), but he didn't have the voice or a sense of purpose. He didn't have a purpose, and that's why he was about to die.

"Bring it, old man," Jerrod said. The two were easily within striking distance of each other, with no one wanting to take the first shot. Out of the corner of his vision, Jaff could see Sammy waiting at the bottom of the stairs, not sure what to do.

"There's an exit right behind you," Jaff said. "Why don't you take it?"

"I'll take it," Sammy yelled from the bottom of the stairs.

"Sammy, shut the fuck—"

The slight turn of the head was more than enough. In the moment Jerrod was distracted, Jaff had dropped into a crouch and stabbed Jerrod in the side. The knife penetrated with the tip and up through the third or fourth serrated edge, then Jaff pulled back, hard, pulling flesh and other bits of muscle and organ with it. Jerrod still held firm to his makeshift club, but he didn't swing, his other hand immediately going to the wound. Based on his expression, Jerrod was both in pain and extremely pissed off with himself.

"Told you I didn't need it," Jaff said, smiling.

Jerrod reared his right arm back, the club's heft telegraphing any move he was about to make. As easily as he'd made the first cut, Jaff went in on the other side, creating a wound on Jerrod's left side as he had on the right. This time, the knife was harder to get out, partially because Jaff hadn't completely avoided Jerrod's attack.

The club, with its sharp metal edges, clipped the back of Jaff's thigh as he lunged, the same leg that Terry had jabbed a few minutes earlier. The impact sent Jaff to his knees and he worked to get the serrated edges of the knife past the bone or muscle that was slowing it down. While it was painful, the club had been slowed and didn't pack much power behind it.

For understandable reasons, Jerrod started screaming and Jaff yanked the knife free, blood spilling onto the ground and splattering onto the carpeted floor.

Downstairs, Jaff saw Sammy disappear behind a concrete corner.

Jerrod, still screaming, dropped to his knees and dropped the club, both hands desperately trying to keep the blood and viscera from escaping out of his sides. Terry rolled, took a quick second to check out his scraped and bleeding leg, and again gingerly tested his weight on it. The leg was wobbly but it would hold.

Part of Jaff respected Jerrod for giving him a fight. It was a brave thing to do, no doubt, especially considering a coward had distracted him. Maybe a fighting chance was in order, Jaff thought. Pushing him toward the door seemed sporting and of little consequence. He'd bleed out before he saw anyone who could help him, even in New York.

*He can't leave.*

"Of course he can't," Jaff said. From behind the bar, he heard Taylor sobbing anew, likely aware of what was going down.

Noticing the club on the ground, Jaff walked over and picked it up over the slight protests of the bleeding man near the top of the stairs.

"You want to stand up?" Jaff said. "It doesn't seem right you die on your knees."

"Wanna suck my dick?" Jerrod asked. "It doesn't seem right… for you to…not…"

He was fading fast, and Jaff had been more than sporting. From behind the bar he heard Taylor yelling Jerrod's name and getting no response. Her despair must be all consuming, Jaff briefly thought.

"I was…" Jerrod said, his breath already failing. "I was going to get my own show…"

"Not today, you aren't," Jaff said, swinging the club hard, bashing in a good portion of Jerrod's skull.

# CHAPTER 4

Calista started seizing up just after Jerrod and Sammy left The F Pit. It was the most terrifying thing Braden had ever seen, partly because, if he didn't get out of there, he was looking square into his future.

He had been resting his eyes, trying to keep himself calm, when he heard Jackie start to yell, and came to in time to see the whites of Calista's eyes staring straight at him. They were completely rolled back into their sockets, her head flopping around, her body soon following.

"Calista, honey, come back to us," Jackie was saying as she moved up to the woman's head. "Honey, this isn't where you die. You're strong. You can pull through this."

Despite her comforting words, Braden could tell they she was both scared and resigned to the idea Calista wasn't going to pull through this. It was amazing she had made it as far as she had given the extent of her wounds. While he admired her strength, all the admiration in the world wasn't going to stop the terrible spectacle from playing out in front of him.

Jackie put both her hands on Calista's shoulders and pinned

her down. The room seemed much bigger and much emptier now that it was just the three of them and every grunt and thrash seemed to make an outsized noise. It was starting to get to Braden and he wasn't sure he was going to make it, mentally or physically.

Jackie looked up and saw him struggling to not lose his shit

"You're a goddamn hero, you know that, right? You're the reason she's still alive, you know that, right? Braden? You know that?"

He smiled but it felt like there was poison working its way from his guts to his bloodstream upward and from his brain to his spinal cord downward. He swallowed, hard.

"I don't know how much longer I can hold it together."

"Honey," Jackie said. "I have had three great loves in my life, men who could have held my heart forever if they wanted, and not one of them would have taken a bullet for me, I promise you that. If you can take a bullet for me, you can hold it together down here. I know you can."

Calista kicked, hard, and Jackie redoubled her efforts. The woman's blank, white eyeballs continued to catch his gaze every few seconds and he turned away.

"Thanks," Braden said, trying to keep his brain from seizing with fear and pain. He was able to refocus for a moment on Jackie and what she was doing.

"You're risking your life for that woman," he said between big gulps of air.

"We need to watch out for each other in this business," Jackie said, talking for the sake of talking. "If you were a female comic in the nineties, things tended to only go a couple of ways. You were either tough as nails or the men in this business would do everything they could to fuck you, literally and figuratively. I've seen, God, dozens of female comics just get fed into the meat grinder, and for years I never did anything. For years I watched it happen and said, 'Better them than me.'"

She looked down at Calista, whose thrashing was ramping down, as was her breathing. The woman's skin had taken on a grayish, clammy look. Jackie had tried to dress her wounds but there were too many, and many of them gaped like giant, open mouths waiting to suck you in.

"That doesn't work," she said. "We gotta take care of each other. If we don't…"

Jackie let it die. Calista had pulled out of the seizure but her breath was going more and more shallow.

"She's probably going to die," Jackie said. "And I'm going to be here when she does. She doesn't die alone. I'm gonna be here. Then things are going to get ugly. Believe me."

For a reason he couldn't put his finger on, Braden started to cry. He had been holding it back as hard as he could, but the combination of Jackie's words and feeling like a kid whose mom had just told him everything was going to be okay hit him with a combination he couldn't dodge. He sniffled hard and regained composure when he looked at Calista. She had been attacked by her partner, the person who she had made a life with. That was much harder to grasp then the loneliness and pain Braden was going through.

From upstairs, they heard the sound of Jerrod screaming and Sammy, who they hadn't heard come back down the stairs, started swearing from around the corner.

"Oh no," Braden said. "No, no, no."

Sammy appeared around the corner, his face drained of blood, looking sick and afraid.

"He stabbed him," Sammy said. "He's…"

Before he could finish, the sound of loud, sick banging came from upstairs as Jaff beat Jerrod to death a few feet above them. The sound was unlike anything Braden had heard, loud but thick, like someone was in the kitchen tenderizing meat.

Each impact from above seemed to hit Sammy down below as well. He stepped to the other side of the doorway and threw up on the filing cabinet, his vomit splattering on the slick metal. The act dropped him to his knees and he pulled himself up and stumbled through the doorway, using both hands for support.

"He's dead," Sammy said. "He shot Taylor but she's alive. She called 9-1-1. Cops should be here any second."

"Where is she shot?" Braden burst out.

"I'm not sure. Couldn't tell, but she sounded okay."

"And the cops are on the way?" Jackie asked.

Taking a second to shake off the cobwebs and gather his thoughts, Sammy steadied himself and launched into what he knew.

"All she said was she had called the cops. I don't think she was fucking with us."

"I wish we could close the door now that we know the cops are coming," Braden said.

There was motion coming from upstairs that culminated in a series of thick-sounding thuds on the stairs. Sammy held his fingers up to his lips and slowly peaked around the corner. What he saw forced him to take another step into The F Pit.

"It's Jerrod," Sammy said. "He threw his body down the stairs."

Jackie shut her eyes, on the verge of losing it. The F Pit was suddenly very still. Even Calista seemed to have gotten the memo in whatever state she was in, breathing shallow and quiet. It occurred to Braden he wasn't sure why he was being so quiet. Jaff knew exactly where they were, who was hurt and how. They were all but helpless.

Taylor's screams sliced through the silence.

"No," Braden said, sounding small and helpless. His back was against the wall and the screams spurred him to push with his legs and attempt to stand. He got about halfway up before a combination of fatigue, pain, and the trauma from the screaming took him back down. They heard Taylor fall down the stairs, tumbling on the unforgiving concrete, then sobbing as she hit the ground.

Sammy immediately ran over to her and helped her up, trying not to look at Jerrod's body or trip over Terry's body as he went. The tumble hadn't hurt her so much, but her arm was hemorrhaging and she was pale and scared.

"Goddamn," she said as Sammy threw her good arm around his neck and hoisted her up. "I usually…like having my hair pulled."

The desperate attempt at humor didn't land, and Sammy took a beat to stare at her.

"What?"

"He grabbed my hair and pulled me across the floor. Then… down."

Even though he tried to avoid it, his brain demanded a look, and Sammy shot a glance back at Jerrod's body. He immediately wished he hadn't. The comic's head was partially gone, not misshapen, just gone, skull and brain exposed. What little expression he had left wasn't anything Sammy could recognize—not fear or anger or pain, just nothing. It was that look of infinite, unending nothing that crawled into Sammy's brain and stayed there.

Taylor's voice was getting thinner and they had to step over Terry's body, and it occurred to Sammy, for the first time, they might not get out of this. If they couldn't signal the cops, if they couldn't fight Jaff off, if they couldn't get it together, they were all going to die in the basement of The Square and his face would have that expression of complete and total nothing. The fear was undercut by a job and a purpose—he had to get Taylor back to the group. Her legs were strong enough to help him significantly. Even with the short distance between the stairs and The F Pit, Taylor's blood stained the path they took.

"Why'd he throw you down the stairs?" Sammy asked. "Why didn't he kill you? I mean, I'm glad he didn't, but—"

"He said he needed to clean up for the cops," she said. "He said he'd deal with me later."

They tumbled into The F Pit, Sammy unable to keep it together. He made sure Taylor was on her feet and slumped against the wall, falling downward and sobbing as he went. The look on Jerrod's face was there when he shut his eyes, so he kept them open and stared at the dingy wall behind Jackie. Even when he tried to shut his eyes to avoid the horror, there was horror right in front of him.

"We're not going to make it," he said between huge gulps of air.

"Keep it together, Sammy," Jackie said. "You're not helping."

She had gone from tending to Calista's wounds to holding her hand, stroking it and occasionally whispering something in her ear. Across the room, Braden made another attempt to stand up, bracing his back against the wall. This time he was able to push himself up, even as Taylor asked him not to.

"Don't," she said. "You're not doing anyone any good."

Braden ignored her and stumbled over to Calista, kneeling down by her side with great effort.

"I've got her," he said, grabbing onto Calista's hand with more strength than he thought he had. "Go do what you can for Taylor, please."

The "please" struck Jackie. Even if they weren't fighting for their lives, that sort of politeness was not common in the bowels of a comedy club. Other comics were nice to each other, sure, but it was peppered with dick jokes and secret insecurities, hoping the others would fail at some point down the road. This kid was honest to God polite, Jackie thought, and in that moment, she loved him for it.

Jackie nodded and went to the first aid kit, already caked in blood and half its supplies used. She held out her hand to Taylor and forced a weak smile.

"Come on, honey, let me see."

Taylor held out her arm and briefly let go of the pressure she had been applying. Blood spurted out of the wound in her elbow and hand. Part of Taylor was surprised she had that much blood left given how much of it was already on her tank top and jeans. It reminded Jackie of a phrase she had heard once upon a time about blood leaving the body at a gallop, not a trot.

"Okay, we're going to have to wrap it really tight and apply a tourniquet," Jackie said. "It's going to really hurt but it'll keep you alive."

The spurt of blood had started to freak Taylor out, but Jackie's eyes drew her back to shore. She nodded and gritted her teeth.

"Let's do it," she said.

Braden smiled at her and she smiled back. Even in the midst of all the blood and bodies she still flashed back to her night with Braden, his body on hers, remembering how he smelled. He had been a jerk but she still wanted him. There was something there, and if they made it out of this, she was going to run headlong toward him and not look back. By the way he was looking at her, the feeling was mutual.

Pulling on the white tape and biting it off with her teeth, Jackie started wrapping big, long strips around Taylor's arm. It did hurt, but not as bad as she thought it would. The sound of the tape, separating itself from the roll, filled the room, drowning out Sammy's sobs, which were becoming more and more distant. Before Jackie was done moving up Taylor's arm with the tape, bright red spots were appearing, soaking through the slick material and spreading throughout her arm.

"Okay, this is the tough part," Jackie said. "Try not to scream."

"What are you going to do?" she asked.

"You're bleeding too much," Jackie said, holding up a piece of white cloth. "I'm going to apply a tourniquet. I took a bit off my shirt earlier."

She motioned to her midriff and Taylor smiled a little bit at her ingenuity. The bottom part of her shirt featured a fairly straight tear, exposing a very white stomach underneath. It sort of resembled pirate cosplay, and Taylor smiled a little more, then the word "tourniquet" passed through her brain like a dagger and her smile faded.

"Does that mean I'm going to lose my arm? Because I heard tourniquets are last resorts."

"Not if we get you out of here," Jackie said. "And I'm sorry, girlie, but there ain't a lot of resorts past this one. You ready?"

Taylor nodded, her lips pursed. She knew this was going to hurt and braced herself as best she could. She wasn't weak, but this was really going to hurt.

Jackie moved Taylor's arm away from her body and moved up high on her bicep. She tied the cloth on, looked Taylor in the eye, and pulled extremely hard. The pressure, coupled with the pain already in her arm, caused Taylor to gasp, but she held on to the scream, not letting it escape. When Jackie was finished, her arm felt both like it was going to explode and like it was going to die.

"That's the hard part," Jackie said.

"The hard part is getting the fuck out of here," Sammy said.

"Again, dude, you're not helping," Braden chimed in. "If you want out of here, we should be trying to figure out how to signal the cops."

"I've thought about it! You think I haven't fucking thought about it?" Sammy yelled, suddenly finding his feet and standing up. "There are no sprinklers down here. There are no cell phones, there are no landlines. Unless you got a sledge hammer and we can start beating on the walls, we're out of fucking options."

"Why do we have to signal the cops?" Jackie said. "Why don't Sammy and I go up there and just start screaming bloody murder? Hell, we could probably yell, 'There are a bunch of fuckin' dead bodies down here,' when the police come in and that's all she wrote."

"I'm not going back up there," Sammy said, back still pinned to the wall. "I'm not good in these sorts of situations."

It had taken a while to catch up with him but the guilt of distracting Jerrod and getting him killed was finally dawning. Remembering how the fear seized him and how, in the moment, he tried to reason with Jaff to get out of The Square was all but paralyzing. One of his seven keys to success was doing the hard thing, but another one was understanding, and planning around, your limitations.

Jackie wasn't having it.

"Jesus Christ, Sammy. If it's two on one, we can take him. Hike up your bra and let's get this done."

Sammy shook his head.

"You didn't see it," he said. "You didn't see him stab Jerrod…"

"Oh, you're right," Jackie said. "I've just been down here knee deep in blood and piss and dying people for the past hour or so. I haven't seen shit."

"Hey," Braden yelled back. "I can hear you."

Jackie was on a tear. She stood up and walked over to Sammy.

"I'm pretty sure that girl is going to die. That kid over there, he could go into shock at any minute with the amount of blood he's lost. That girl over there, she's gonna lose an arm if we're not out of here in half an hour. I don't care what you saw, I don't care how scared you are, he's one guy. One late middle-aged motherfucker with a knife, and when the cops show up, you and I are going to go up there and get help. You're Sammy Platter and you can do this. You hear me?"

Sammy had begun full-on shaking, the thought of going back up those stairs almost too much to bear. He didn't remember ever feeling this scared or desperate, ever feeling like the walls were closing in quite so tightly. He threw back his head and thought about his house. He had a beautiful split-level house in the valley, full of antiques and nerd stuff he'd collected over the years. He loved his house, he wanted to be in his house more than he'd ever wanted anything else.

"I'm not going to die for them," Sammy said. "Sorry, but I'm not. You either. I'm not going up there and nothing you say is going to change that."

"I'll go."

Jackie spun around to see Taylor on her feet. The tourniquet was holding but the tape on her arms had already soaked through with blood and her complexion was showing it.

"I've got some lungs on me. We can make some noise."

A smile crept over Jackie's face, even though this was a bad idea. Taylor was going to get herself killed. But maybe, together, they could get something done.

"Okay," Jackie said. "You and me, kid."

Jackie turned to look at Sammy, who has holding his arm out of nervousness and staring at the ground. She got it. Panic and shock here draped across him, filling every gap in his brain, and there was nothing to be done about that. Still, she felt anger swell inside her. Taylor had seen worse, had worse done to her, had been shot and was bleeding, for fuck's sake, and she was handling this infinitely better than high and mighty Sammy Platter.

"When we get out of here, you sack of shit, everyone's hearing about how you pussied out on us. Everyone."

To put a fine point on it, she rummaged through her purse, which had been on the ground since before Calista stumbled into The F Pit, found her cell phone, which still couldn't get a signal, and tucked it into one of the cups of her bra. She didn't like doing this, and the hunk of metal felt weird down there, but desperate times called for uncomfortable measures.

They left the room and Sammy started to cry, first silently and then in louder sobs. Braden smiled but tried not to laugh, as he had enough trauma going on near his midsection. Taylor smiled and accepted Jackie's help out through the door. It wasn't over yet, but Jackie felt like she had done all she could do in that room. It wasn't time to be the caregiver anymore. It was time to fight.

They both turned and faced the hallway and the staircase on the left leading up to the club. At the bottom of the stairs were the bodies of Terry Stafford and Jerrod Seybourne. Terry was a little closer to them than Jerrod, and they were both in pools of blood, wounds on full display.

The bodies grabbed Jackie's and Taylor's gazes. What was left of Jerrod's face stared back at them. Terry's head was tilted and staring right at them, the entry wound in his forehead a mix of deep reds and blacks. Blood had spilled from both bodies, which intermingled into one large pool underneath them on the floor.

Jackie didn't turn away, and though Taylor was tempted, she didn't turn away either. They took a few steps forward, unsure of what they were doing.

"Honey," Jackie said. "Get on my other side, please."

Doing as she was told, Taylor hugged the right side of the hallway, bumping into the closet where she had hidden before everything had been drenched in blood. The door swung outward and she was hit with the scent of industrial cleaners. She opened the door a little wider, peered in, and got an idea.

"Jackie," she said.

When she turned around, Jackie was on her knees, her hand on Terry's white, dead cheek.

"Lord, have mercy upon this man. Pardon all his transgressions, shelter his soul in the shadow of your wings and make known to him the path of life."

Taylor stood and watched as Jackie prayed over Terry, took a big step over him, and did the same for Jerrod. It was oddly touching, and for a moment the only real things in the world were Jackie administering last rights and the terrible pain in her arm that radiated with every heartbeat.

When she was done, she stood up, tears in her eyes.

"That was the mourner's Kaddish," she said, pausing before adding, "Terry Stafford assaulted me about fifteen years ago."

"I'm sorry," Taylor said. "You told us earlier before everything went to shit."

"The old noggin isn't what it used to be," Jackie said, smiling. Then, staring at Terry, "He was my friend. I thought he was my friend. He took me under his wing, taught me about the business, then, one night after a show, he dropped his pants and told me to suck it."

"And you still prayed over his body?" Taylor said. "I'd be more inclined to kick him in the balls…well…yeah…sorry. That was in bad taste."

"Honey, I'm a comic, don't worry about it." Jackie said. "He can't hurt me anymore. But I can still show kindness to him. I don't think that's weakness."

The flat, florescent lights flickered as the two women stood, taking a moment of silence neither of them had planned. There was blood on the floor, there were bodies in front of them, there was a killer above them, but taking a second made sense. Neither were sure why.

After a few seconds, Jackie got back to business.

"Jaff's still up there and he's probably going to kill us," Jackie said. "He's got that gun, he's got knives, and he's crazy as fuck."

Taylor smiled, a big toothy grin. Reaching into the front of her pocket, she pulled out Jaff's small revolver.

"You're mostly right," she said. "Plus, I've got a plan."

# CHAPTER 5

The first time Jaff had met Jerrod, years ago when he was just a kid begging for time on stage, he was kind of taken with the guy.

Here was smart, generous, and supremely laid back. He made the audiences laugh and never got a big head about it. He was ambitious, sure, but not pushy, which could be rare in a culture where comics thought they were owed time on your stage. In a world of people who were convinced they were going to become stars, make millions of dollars, and move straight from The Square to their own HBO comedy special, Jerrod's attitude was a refreshing change of pace. And he had the goods to go further than a lot of other comics he had seen.

*Who knew he had that kind of anger in him?* Jaff said to himself as he threw his body down the stairs.

Jerrod was heavier than he ought to be, or Jaff was weaker than he thought, one or the other. He was playing hurt, though his leg didn't hurt as bad as he thought it might, so that was a positive. One thing Jaff was starting to realize this evening was how both men and women tried to hide their elemental selves as much as possible. Hell, they tried to hide parts of themselves that were downright fine, as far as Jaff was concerned. Jerrod, for example, had a bit of a belly on him. Jaff would have never realized it to look at the guy standing up right (or crouching with a knife in his hand, for that matter), but his belly was round and hairy. Nothing wrong with it, but Jaff would have never seen it had he not grabbed Jerrod by the shirt to drag him to the top of the stairs. Funny.

He had a plan. It wasn't great, but none of his plans tonight had been great and everything had turned out pretty well so far. Having a plan made everything seem like it wasn't spiraling out of control even though Jaff could feel the force of the spin.

He walked over to the bar, not making any attempt to hide his approach. Peering around the side with a big, wicked smile, he found the girl right where he had left her.

"I don't suppose you'd just walk down the stairs, would you?"

He must have been a sight, blood (his and others) covering about forty percent of his shirt, his grin never really leaving his face. The girl was shaking, both from the wound and nerves, but probably because of how he looked as well. He was a scary son of a bitch right now and it only made him feel stronger. Her fear also fed Jaff's sense of purpose, and if she was too scared to put up a fight, all the better.

"Okay," he said. "Here we go."

She started screaming almost immediately, but it didn't change the plan one bit. Jaff had checked his watch and the cops weren't due for another five minutes or so, if they decided to show up at all. Being a club owner for years and years, he'd gotten to know his local patrol officers thanks to a constant array of angry drunks, violent drunks, mean drunks, drunk parties who wouldn't leave, drunk assholes, and other shades of the same theme. Even if he called 911, it was fifteen minutes before the cops showed up on a good night. He had plenty of time to clean up a bit.

The plan went like this: throw everyone down the stairs and

count on fear to keep them quiet. Don't forget the kid on the stage. Again, not the best plan, but he was deep into it now, and if things got messy, that was fine. He was already a mess. He'd reload his gun and keep it handy, stow the knife in his pocket, do his best not to limp, and get the cops out before they could snoop around. He briefly considered mopping up Jerrod's blood but decided it was a waste of time. He already had too much to do. What was coming was what was going to be.

But first, this girl, whoever she was, needed to get downstairs.

"Why are you doing this?" she yelled. It seemed out of character to Jaff. Moments before, she had been tough and defiant, holding the phone up and calling him an asshole. Now she was a child crying on the floor, but she wasn't a child. She was an adult and she didn't deserve his pity.

He grabbed her by the hair and started to pull, hard. When it became clear what was happening, she made a few half-hearted swipes at his arm with her good hand, but years of tending bar and hauling boxes had built Jaff's forearms to an impressive size and strength. Quickly, the pain hit her and she started using her legs to push off the floor to alleviate the pressure. Jaff sort of smiled. Her kicking made for sort of a pathetic plea, a "I'll go the way you want if you stop hurting me" sort of thing. He was getting a kick out of it.

They reached the top of the stairs in no time. The girl was in full-on hysterics.

*Kill her now.*

This time, Jaff completely disagreed with the voice. No, he wasn't going to kill her. She was losing a lot of blood, she was defenseless, and he was having fun. Plus, he had no way to do it, except with his bare hands.

*Strangle her.*

Jaff considered it. She had called the cops. She was wily and determined. She was defenseless and crying. No reason not to take one more item off his to-do list. At that moment he remembered a sick story, long buried, about a comic who turned out to be very mentally ill and was committed to a mental institution. Before that, he was a funny guy and could definitely do his job on stage, but backstage, he wasn't anyone you wanted to hang around with. He had once told Jaff a story about strangling a stray cat. Amongst his many vivid descriptions of the cat's reaction was just how long it took. The comic had said even with a cat who was small and defenseless, it took a good ten minutes to make sure it was dead, not like in the movies where it took thirty seconds, tops. He had time, but he didn't have that kind of time.

Still, Jaff pictured wrapping his hands around her neck and squeezing as she flailed. That was one of the details that had stuck with him from the comic's story. The flailing was all front loaded, then it's just long, consistent eye contact and life and breath disappeared.

"What was his name?" Jaff said out loud. "God, my memory is getting so bad."

Taylor stopped crying, confused.

"What?"

"Ah, fuck it," Jaff said.

He kicked Taylor in the chest, forcing her backward and down the unforgiving concrete staircase. Part of him was hoping she'd break her neck, but she rolled, landing initially on her shoulder and rolling on her side down the rest of the stairs. It must have hurt, given her arm having a bullet hole in it, Jaff thought.

She landed to the right of Jerrod, who didn't exactly break her fall but definitely cushioned it. She lay there, not moving very fast but definitely moving.

"Stay down there," Jaff said. "I see your face up here, I'm going to blow it off."

There was no door separating the stairway from the rest of the club and he briefly considered throwing something in front of the entrance—a bunch of chairs, a few tables, broken glass from the bar—but decided against it. No need. They were either going to stay down there or they weren't and they were either going to alert the cops or they weren't. All the more reason to head back to the office and reload his gun.

He took a few steps toward his office and reached into his front pocket. Part of him knew before his hand got there that the gun was gone. Before he thought maybe he had left it in the kitchen, but now he was sure he had put it in the front pocket of his pants, remembering the pleasant heat it generated against his thigh. Now it was gone.

"No," he said softly, quickly checking all his pockets. "No, no, no!"

*You should have killed her.*

The voice wasn't angry or mocking, but matter of fact. It had given advice, Jaff had elected to ignore that advice, and now he was suffering for it. His laziness had caught up with him and now the girl had taken away the one thing that would make sure he could end things properly, on the stage, like he wanted. He had messed up and now the plan wasn't the plan anymore and he was going to pay for it in pain and blood.

"FUCK!" Jaff yelled, and kicked a chair with his good leg. It went flying and crashed against the stage, leaving a little indentation on the base. Pain radiated up his leg and he spun into a sitting position on the floor.

*You deserve this pain.*

"I know," Jaff said. Even though he was pretty sure he had

broken a toe or two, the pain suddenly returned to his head and took all his attention. The throbbing started to make him dizzy and he started to cry.

"I will listen," he said. "I will listen, I promise."

He shut his eyes and tried to cope with the pain but it was all consuming, pushing his head to the ground and onto the carpet in front of the stage.

*You will listen. You will obey.*

For the first time, the voice wasn't just in his head but in his ears and in his heart. It was a soft, sweet voice of a woman and she had an accent Jaff couldn't place but it hit him like a cool wind on a hot day. The pain in his head dissipated as quickly as cotton candy in the rain, removing any trace of resistance he had left.

He would obey. He would sacrifice everything to obey.

The voice seemed to hear him and, his eyes still closed, he could have sworn he felt a hand on his brow near his hairline, comforting him and bringing him back to the waking world. He tried to focus on the hand, but just as he did, it disappeared, making him wonder if it had all been in his imagination.

The voice didn't speak again, but Jaff knew what he needed to do. Seconds later, he was on his feet, heading toward his office, where he found the box of ammunition still sitting on his desk. The safe was wide open and the office was in disarray, but the bullets were right where he left them. Jamming them in his pockets, he went back to where he had dropped the knife he had used to kill Jerrod.

"Right where I left you," he said, wiping blood onto the carpet and gripping the knife's marbled rubber handle with intensity. "We've got work to do."

That work was now clear, clearer than anything Jaff had ever done. Keep stabbing until they were all dead. That was the plan. If they took his gun, he'd plunge a knife into their face. If they were almost dead, he would quickly finish the job. If he had to strangle them with his bare hands, he would spend the ten minutes. If the cops showed up and didn't leave right away, he would lure them into The Square and kill them. He would kill them all. Then, when it was all done, he'd have the gun and he'd have the bullets and he could haul Calista's body onto the stage and have his death the way he wanted. He could stand before all he had created and all he had done and be satisfied.

As if on cue, there was a knock at the front door.

***

The 38th district was not a bad place to be a cop for Officer Mick Brunzell.

He was seven years out of the academy, and in those seven years had seen most major crime in his precinct drop. Not by much, but enough for folks to notice. His commanding officer had been enthusiastic about the NYPD's new Sector Policing Program, which designated officers to particular neighborhoods, and the result had been a lot more accountability on both sides. Going to work was still a slog, and he worked with more than a few complete assholes, but there was something to making progress than could cover up a lot of issues with a job.

Within the community, his first name had basically vanished. He wasn't Mick Brunzell, rather Officer Brunzell or just Brunzell. He embraced it. There was no reason not to, and he tried his best to give and show respect, especially with the business owners of the community. His partner, a former Marine named Jesse Ahrens, came at community policing from the opposite standpoint. Physical and anxious, she needed to be moving all the time, and while their styles didn't really click, they had solved the problem. When something like an alarm call came in, Brunzell would go and help solve the problem and Ahrens would walk around, waiting for him to finish, seeing if anyone else needed a cop.

It broke with policy of always having a partner back you up, but it worked for them. Plus, the neighborhood they worked in was pretty low in terms of risk, so they got away with it.

Officer Brunzell knew Jaff Maul as much as you can know a piece of white toast. They never had a connection, but like ninety-eight percent of the people he came across, they were friendly. That was all he ever needed to be until it was time to do some of the hard parts of his job. Then he could get unfriendly real quick. At six foot two and 235 pounds, he could handle those unfriendly tasks better than some, not as well as others.

But those moments were few and far between. Mainly, his job was checking 911 calls, responding to domestic calls and answering alarms. Most of the time they were nothing, and even when they were, that something was dealt with quickly. If something was wrong, he had been on the job long enough to develop an intuition.

Something about The Square tripped that intuition the second he pulled up.

It was nothing he could put his finger on, but by the time he rapped on the door, his internal alarm was blaring. He briefly considered getting Jesse on the radio, but resisted. Something was not right and he was going to figure out what.

Jaff answered the door with a big smile. And a limp.

"Hello, officer," he said. "Probably here about the 9-1-1 call?"

"Good evening, yes," Officer Brunzell said, one hand holding a flashlight. "Exactly. We had a 9-1-1 call from a phone we tracked to this address."

The owner looked sheepish and invited the officer into the club's main entryway. It wasn't very big but definitely big enough to have a conversation. Most of the lights were off and it was hard to see much past the bar at the back of the main show area. He noticed the sliding gate used to lock up had only been opened a very little bit and the rest of the club was dark, which didn't make total sense for this time of night.

"That call was one of my kitchen staff," Jaff said. "I had an accident with a knife earlier tonight…"

Jaff pulled his pant leg up and put his leg as high up on the wall as he could. The wound was nasty and deep, definitely the sort of thing one might call 911 about.

"He saw a lot of blood and panicked," Jaff said. "I was going to patch it up and hope for the best. To be honest with you, officer, I can't afford a ride in an ambulance at the moment. I don't have the best insurance right now."

"Sure," Officer Brunzell said, paying about three-quarters of his attention to Jaff. The other quarter was focused on a couple big stains on the carpet about a hundred feet away and a definite metallic twang in the air. It was the sort of smell he often got at crime scenes, but the big hole in the owner's leg might very well be the cause, he thought.

But the stains on the carpet, that was unusual. They were noticeable.

"Ouch. You should definitely get yourself to the hospital," Officer Brunzell said. "Don't take any chances with that. I understand about the ambulance, but what's…"

He shined his flashlight over by the stage. The beam of light passed just inches away from Raoul's feet as Jaff hadn't had time to move him.

"…what's with your carpet over there?"

Jaff's right hand went to his left back pocket of his pants where the serrated knife patiently waited.

"Not sure," Jaff said, squinting. "Want me to turn the lights on and have a look?"

The officer took a long beat, shining his light on the pooled blood.

"It looks like blood from here."

"Let me get the lights."

Before Officer Brunzell could turn around, Jaff had taken his leg off the wall and had disappeared into the club, behind the swinging metal gate. The cop took a few steps forward, the beam from his flashlight finally getting to the center of the pool where Taylor had bled not more than twenty minutes ago. The pattern was there and the color, even in the dark, was unmistakable. This was a lot of blood, and Officer Brunzell's gut was right—he was in danger.

Before he could pull out his radio, gun, or anything else, all the lights suddenly turned on, blaring white stage-quality light filling the club and temporarily blinding the officer. The sound system also kicked on and some heavy, guitar-centric rock music exploded over the speaker system, drowning out any chance of conversation. He didn't recognize the song, but at that volume very few people would.

Office Brunzell put his hands to his ears, instinctively, and dropped them a moment later when he saw the size of the blood spot. Someone had lost a lot of blood here and he was right in the middle of an active crime scene.

"Shit," he said, but the rock music swallowed the word, and everything else, entirely.

At that moment, two women came up from the basement and locked eyes with the officer. They were holding what looked like cleaning bottles stuffed with rags and one was holding a lighter. It was all a lot to take in, which was why, even at his advanced size, strength, and training, he never saw Jaff coming, eyes ablaze, knife in hand.

# Transcript

*The Silver Platter Podcast with Ted Silver and Sammy Platter*
Episode 291

[opening music]

TED: Welcome to the Silver Platter Podcast, I'm Ted Silver.

SAMMY: And I'm Sammy Platter.

TED: Tell them who we are and what we do here.

SAMMY: On this award-winning podcast, two veteran comics, that's you and me, talk to interesting people about what makes them interesting, but, unlike on my TV show, we do it with swear words and dick jokes. So…fuck. We also talk about getting motivated, getting it together, and getting what you want.

TED: I like your energy today, Sammy. You seem like you're in fine form.

SAMMY: It's all a front. I feel like crap.

TED: Ah, Sammy. Why do you feel like crap?

SAMMY: Did you read about Terry Stafford.

TED: Oh shit. We're getting right into it. Yeah, I read about Terry Stafford.

SAMMY: You're a comic, I'm a comic, and both of us have had that conversation a hundred times with a hundred comics when you just ask someone, 'Hey, who are your guys?' and they know what you're talking about.

TED: Damn right. I've had that conversation a bunch of times. Sometimes it's not who you think it would be but it makes a ton of sense. I once heard Sam Kinison was a giant Gene Wilder guy, and you think about it and it makes total sense. You know, the energy, the screaming. OHH! OOOOHHHHH!

SAMMY: Yeah, fix your levels, asshole. I need to get through this life with my hearing intact. But yeah. Comics milling around backstage, talking about their influences. For me, there are four guys, and they're all guys, sorry all you female comics out there, but they're all guys who just turned my brain into a different shape. They were, in order, Steve Martin, George Carlin, Bill Hicks, and Terry Stafford.

TED: That's a solid list. You want to get right into this?

SAMMY: You mind?

TED: Maybe we should mention who our guest is this week.

SAMMY: Yeah, okay. Today we're talking to Tracy Morgan. His new series on FX is back for its final season and we'll talk about his terrible, terrible car accident and how it turned him into a more motivated person. Okay, back to Terry Stafford, if that's okay with you.

TED: Go for it. I've got thoughts.

SAMMY: I bet, but he wasn't one of your guys, was he? He was one of my guys. That's part of why he's never been on the show before, because part of me is terrified to meet my idol. What if he's a disappointment? What if it's a terrible interview, you know? I couldn't take that. We never got to interview Hicks because he died so young; Steve Martin only wants to talk about his music anymore, sorry I don't wanna talk about the fuckin' banjo for ninety minutes; and Carlin died before the age of podcasts, so Stafford was the only one we could have had on and now there's so much more to reckon with, you know? Does what happened change how I view his comedy? And now, in case you haven't heard, he's been accused of not just sexual harassment, but rape. He's been charged with rape, Ted. Rape.

TED: That's just…monumental. He's done. He's fucking done. He's gotta be.

SAMMY: I don't want to be on record as defending a rapist. Not at all, and, of course, I feel for the victims, and that's not what I'm about, that's not what you're about. If he did one sixteenth of what he's being accused of, he belongs in jail. But when you're confronted with something like this, part of your mind goes back to the titan that he was and what he did for you, specifically, you know?

TED: How's the weather out there on that ledge, buddy?

SAMMY: Fuck you, I'm trying to make a point. Part of me is going to owe a debt, forever and ever, to Terry Stafford. You remember when it was a big deal if your car had a CD player in it?

TED: I remember.

SAMMY: I had an eighty-four...God, what was it...I don't remember the make and model but it was this little boxy Chevy that had no acceleration at all. I remember I picked up a date in it once and I'm driving around and she says, "God, I hope you have more balls than this car."

TED: I've seen photos of you in high school. That car had more balls than you.

SAMMY: Again, go fuck yourself. So this car was a piece of shit, but I saved a bunch of money and bought a CD player to put in it, and the first ten CDs I bought were comedy albums.

TED: Then you bought Green Day's *Dookie* and Pearl Jam's *Ten*, right?

SAMMY: You were issued those albums if you were white and of a certain age. They just came in the mail, no explanation.

Those ten albums, all of them were by my four guys. I had *Jammin' in New York* and *Back in Town* by Carlin, and *Let's Get Small* by Martin, and *The Final Rip Off* by Monty Python, and *Arizona Bay* and *Rant in E Minor* by Hicks, and I think I had a

Robert Schimmel in there, but I could be wrong, and then, I remember they were the first two in my CD carrier, were *I Pledge Allegiance* and *Fartknocker* by Terry Stafford. Do you remember when he put out *Fartknocker* and they had to put it in a fuckin' brown paper wrapper because no one could handle the word "fart" staring them in the face at their local Wal-Mart. Remember that?

TED: The early nineties were insane.

SAMMY: I could recite that album. The whole thing. There were nights when I couldn't sleep and I would lay in bed and have nothing better to think about so I'd just go over that album in my head until I drifted off. Sometimes, I swear, I'd fall asleep and know how long I'd been out because of what part of the album my brain was on. And this is before the internet when you could actually love something intensely instead of having everything that has ever happened hurled at your all at once.

TED: So, porn.

SAMMY: Yeah, Italian scat porn before breakfast. [LAUGHS]

TED: I know what you mean. The first Adam Sandler album was like that for me.

SAMMY: You and I have a long-standing disagreement on that album. I admire its purity, but, God, do I find it irritating.

TED: I find you irritating and you're wrong, but finish up here. You were getting to the point.

SAMMY: Yeah, here's my point. When you let someone into your brain like that, when you know their performances down to the pauses and their influence becomes part of what you *end up doing for a living*, then this sort of thing hurts. It hurts a lot and, as we've talked about in *Keys To Success*, you've got to let pain happen. So I don't mind telling you I'm hurting a little bit because Terry Stafford betrayed us all by probably being a rapist.

TED: Can I give you my thoughts?

SAMMY: Please do.

TED: I have two. First, Terry Stafford has always done stand-up and you can always find him performing somewhere, but he's not the guy he used to be and we can all see that. Second, if he did what they're accusing him of, then fuck that guy.

SAMMY: Listen, I hear you—

TED: I understand you're hurting, but I want you to hear me on this, because it has to do with this show, getting motivated, getting it together, and getting what you want. Breakups suck, whether it's with someone you're having horizontal fun time with or someone you lived with for a long time or someone in your family or someone who you invited into your brain. It sucks and I acknowledge that, but if there's a good reason to go through that pain, it's because that person is a fucking rapist.

SAMMY: Yeah.

TED: And holding on to whatever you had with that person,

no matter how deep it went, is stopping you from moving forward.

SAMMY: You're right. You're right, but, as with a lot of these "me too" style things, let's wait and see a bit. I mean, he's already tainted, but if it turns out he didn't do these things, then it's different, isn't it?

TED: I mean, sure it is, but you can't count on that happening into your reaction. You said it yourself, you believe the victims.

SAMMY: I do believe the victims.

TED: Then there you go.

SAMMY: But believing the victims doesn't change the fundamental way this guy changed my life, and I think I can keep that, you know? I think that's mine and if he cures cancer or was a serial rapist, that thing still exists for me. Sixteen-year-old me sitting in that boxy Chevrolet wouldn't have become the guy sitting in front of you if it wasn't for Terry Stafford and that's never going to change. It's personal and can't be applied to the larger narrative, but I think that's okay. But what you're saying is I need to break up with him.

TED: Yes, that is what I'm saying, because, already, some news outlet is going to pick up on this and say, "Sammy Platter defends Terry Stafford against rape charges," and there you go. You'll be the one guy on his side.
[pause]

SAMMY: Maybe we should cut this part of the conversation.

TED: You want to start the whole podcast over?

SAMMY: No, I don't, because I don't think I've said anything in support of his actions, have I? To recap for whoever decides to write that story, here's what I said—I admire Terry Stafford as an artist, he had a big impact on my life, I believe the victims and I'm publicly wrestling with the very complex question of what happens when one of your heroes is accused of one of the most terrible crimes you can be accused of. I don't condone what he did, not in the fucking slightest. That's not who I am.

TED: Totally, that's not who you are. You're an asshole, but you have a limit.

SAMMY: Thanks, pal.

TED: Anyone who's listened to this show knows I only speak the truth. But it's who you are. It's your truth.

SAMMY: And here's my bottom line. Here's what I mean to say. I think, in this day and age, it takes a bit of bravery to wrestle with this. It's one of the keys to success: nothing worth having is worth getting easy. If I'm going to condemn Terry Stafford and that's going to happen, I'm going to get there my own way. I don't think, as a Twitter army or as a group of people who want things a certain way, you can make me come to my truth through any means other than my own. That's what I'm saying.
TED: So stipulated.

SAMMMY: If Terry did these things, then he deserves to go to jail and his albums go off my playlist. That's the bottom line.

[PAUSE] I ever tell you I met him once?

TED: When did you meet him?

SAMMY: I don't want to go into it.

TED: We're deep into it, man. You've never told me this story.

SAMMY: I was the kid outside the club. I was the kid out there, CD and Sharpie in hand, waiting for him to come out so he could sign my CD cover.

TED: And he did.

SAMMY: And he did. And I told him a joke I was working on and he gave me some advice on the joke and on the profession itself that I've kept with me for a long time.

TED: What was the advice?

SAMMY: He said take care of yourself first, no one else is going to do it for you. Which is why that's always been the number one key to success.

# CHAPTER I

Calista died in Braden's arms. She did not go quietly.

She choked and gasped for air, her hands suddenly became alive and grabbed at anything they could touch—the carpet, the air, Braden's arms. Her eyes never came back from the back of her head but her mouth was open, and Braden was able to stare into her mouth as her tongue blocked her airway. He tried to help but the point of inevitability had been reached. She had fought hard but she had lost.

Her final kicks slowed and both Braden and Sammy were treated to her death rattle, the fluids building up in the back of her throat and her body unable to clear them. It was a terrible noise, both slight but terribly vivid. They would both remember the sound as long as they lived.

Through the terrible thrashing and panic Braden kept Jackie's words in mind, even though he wanted nothing more than to shut his eyes, plug his ears, and wish the dying woman away.

"She wasn't going to die alone," he heard Jackie say. Someone was going to be there with her even if that someone was starting to feel like he wasn't that far behind her. The blood loss from his stomach had dulled the pain, and while he was getting close to numb, he was also pretty sure he was going into shock, which meant if he wasn't treated soon, he would die just as Calista had— ugly and in the basement of a comedy club, the victim of an asshole with a gun and some sort of imagined grudge.

At least, upstairs, there were two women battling to help him. He couldn't ask for much more than that. Plus, he had a coward to keep him company.

Sammy hadn't stopped blubbering since Jackie and Taylor left the room, stopping only to watch Calista die. He watched with some sort of mix of terror and reverence. He shut up until he heard her choke on saliva and phlegm, and that set him off.

"Ah, Jesus," he said. "Jesus Christ, I need to get out of here. I can't be here. I can't."

He stood up, walked to the door and paused before going out. The reality of the situation had sliced through his panic and now it was a fight to see which was stronger—the panic of staying in the basement and dying or the panic of facing what was upstairs. Braden saw him push through, walk out the door, and then pause at something beyond his line of sight.

"What the hell are you doing? You're going to get us all killed."

The sound of the concrete walls muffled the sound and he couldn't make out what was happening, but Jackie and Taylor were clearly doing something just beyond the edge of the doorframe. In Braden's largely immobile condition, it might as well have been happening on Staten Island. After a few seconds of fevered murmuring, Sammy turned his head.

"He's not looking good."

Suddenly, Braden realized why he couldn't hear what was going on. The weight of his injuries and the stress of watching Calista die had done him in. He was passing out, though slowly and with full awareness of the fact. It was as weird a sensation as he'd ever experienced, and reality became thick and distant, wavering a bit around the edges.

Before the blackness came, he remembered, ever so briefly, an episode of *Alfred Hitchcock Presents* that had scared him to death when he was a child. In the episode, a bad man had become paralyzed but remained fully conscious of what was happening to him, complete with the ability to feel anxiety and pain. The man was mistaken for dead and then went through the motions of being a dead body—getting loaded up into the ambulance, being catalogued with a toe tag, and then was saved just before the autopsy. In the classic *Alfred Hitchcock Presents* twist, the attending physician was one of the man's enemies and cut him up alive anyway.

Braden's last thought before passing out was he hoped whatever was coming next happened without him knowing a damn thing about it.

***

As Braden passed out in the other room, Sammy had come around the corner to find Jackie stuffing a rag into a bottle of yellow liquid. It wasn't hard to figure out what was going on or how stupid what they were planning was.

"What the hell are you doing?" he said. "You're going to get us all killed."

"As opposed to what?" Jackie said, jamming a dirty rag into a bottle a finger length at a time. "Getting shot in the face?"

Just beyond her, Terry lay on the ground, proving her point and then some. Jerrod's body was facing them, the bulk of his torso behind Terry's significant girth. A small voice in the back of Sammy's head yelled at him for being responsible for getting Jerrod killed, but it was a small voice that he was good at ignoring.

It gave him a momentary pause, but Jackie's and Taylor's actions refocused him pretty quick.

"You can't just go lighting cleaners on fire," Sammy said. "You're going to create a toxic gas cloud or something. Instead of a fire, you'll be choking on poison."

This stopped both women, who had both been working on their improvise Molotov cocktails.

"I think you're not supposed to mix bleach and ammonia," Taylor said. "I don't remember anything about not setting them on fire except…to not set them on fire."

"What's a fire going to accomplish anyway?" Sammy said, more agitated.

"With any luck, we're going to light Jaff on fire and watch him burn," Jackie said. "And if you get in my way, I'll be happy to give your balls a good kick for you."

Taylor smiled at her distinctively New York way of speaking. She had tried out a few phrases when she first got to town, realizing quickly that personality didn't fit. She had the brassy attitude, but not the bulk or the gravitas to back it up.

"You won't be able to kick me in the balls when you're choking to death on toxic fucking vapors!" Sammy yelled.

"Shut the fuck up," Taylor said in a sharp whisper. "Something is happening upstairs."

Straining to hear, Sammy could hear voices coming down the stairs, but couldn't figure out what was being said. One voice, clearly Jaff's, was calm and the other one he couldn't put his finger on but it was definitely masculine.

Jackie's eyes were sparkling and a smile crept across her face.

"The cops," she said. "The cops are upstairs."

"That's great!" Sammy said. "What are we waiting for?"

"We can't just run up there."

Both Jackie and Sammy turned around to look at Taylor. Her face was pale but resolute.

"I want to get out of here worse than anything, but if we show up screaming bloody murder, the cop is going to be distracted and Jaff is going to stab him. If it even is a cop. Maybe it's a delivery guy or something. Either way just…give it a second."

"That's fucking crazy," Sammy said, his voice rising. "You're crazy."

"Says the guy who helped Jaff kill Jerrod."

Sammy's face went slack. With chaos surrounding him and panic consuming most of his head space, he had been able to put the last few seconds of Jerrod's life out of his mind. Besides, hadn't Taylor been behind the bar? His brain jumped for a second to the bar, trying to figure out where she could have seen it all go down.

"What are you talking about?" Jackie said.

"Jerrod was squaring off against that crazy assclown and he would have fucked him up if Sammy hadn't decided to beg for his life at the wrong moment."

Her curls flying around her head, Jackie turned to look at Sammy, whose face told the whole story.

"You asshole," Jackie said. "What the fuck did you do?"

The question was like a smack in the face, and nobody smacked Sammy Platter in the face.

"What the fuck did I do, what the fuck are you doing?" Sammy yelled, throwing caution to the wind. "I don't have to listen to your stupid ass, trying to save everyone. Fuck them and fuck you. I'm going upstairs."

Taking a large step over Terry's body and part of Jerrod's arm, Sammy ascended the first step and made it almost to the second before Jackie tackled him. She was bigger than Sammy, who was thin and muscular, so the simple act of throwing her weight against his legs was enough to knock him down. His upper half spilled onto the fourth step and he was able to get a forearm up to block his fall, but just barely.

For her part, Taylor picked up both of the cleaner bottles she and Jackie had been able to prepare, and tucked them under her bad arm with a grunt.

As soon as he hit the ground, Sammy rolled over and attempted to kick Jackie in the face, but missed, scoring a glancing blow off her right cheek and ear. It was enough to spin Jackie around, but she countered with punch aimed at Sammy's crotch. The shot went a little high and hit him in the bread basket, knocking the wind out of him temporarily. Sensing another kick was on the horizon, Jackie threw her weight onto her colleague and landed on him with a thud. The dull edges of the staircase jammed into Sammy's spine and he let out a scream that was music to Jackie's ears.

"Fuck me? No, Sammy. Fuck you."

She resisted hitting him further, though she wanted to. He was scared, she got that, but that didn't make him special.

"I might not get out of here, but if I die, I die fighting. I'm not laying down for Jaff or for you," she said, just inches from Sammy's twisted, strained face.

"You bitch," he finally spit.

"I'm a lot of things," she said, standing up, sweat dripping from her forehead. "I'm hurt, I'm scared, I'm pissed off. But I'm not stupid. We all have a better chance of getting out of here if we watch out for each other. Being selfish is gonna get you killed."

They were both breathing heavy and Jackie put one hand on Sammy's shoulder.

"You're better than this," she said. "I've known you for years, Sammy. You're better than this."

The moment was about to get sentimental, until the lights

went on and the music started blaring from upstairs. After several hours spent in low light and complete dark, the light burned for a moment and the music screamed from upstairs, cranked to the sound system's full volume. Jackie immediately recognized the song as the same one she had taken the stage to earlier that night. It was enough to take her mind completely off of Sammy. The fight had drained out of him anyway.

"Dammit, Jaff," Jackie said, pushing herself up the stairs. "You are not going to ruin 'Come Dancing' for me. You are not going to do that!"

"You ready?" Taylor yelled over the guitars. "We go now!"

Jackie reached into the pocket of her pants and pulled out a lighter. She hadn't smoked for twenty years but had found it on Jerrod's body. She had hoped he had one on him, and, like always, the guy hadn't disappointed.

"You and me!" Taylor yelled at Jackie, who smiled.

"You and me, kid. Let's go get help."

"What about me!" Sammy yelled. He was still supine on the stairs, his face pleading and expectant, like a little kid.

Taylor pulled out Jaff's gun. It was surprisingly old, now that she was able to hold it up in the light, and didn't look like it had ever been cleaned. She had grown up in the Midwest and knew how guns worked, more or less. Her grandfather was a hunter and ex-military, so she had helped him clean rifles and small fire arms, and this gun was in terrible shape. Plus, there were no bullets in it and she wanted Sammy out of their hair.

She tossed the gun to him and it landed on his chest.

"You said it, bud. Take care of yourself!" she yelled over the song.

He looked dumbstruck, but quickly grabbed the gun and rolled to the side to let the two women past.

The original plan had not involved a cop (or whoever it was), bright lights, or loud music, but the fundamentals were the same— charge up the stairs, light one of the bottles, and let chaos reign. If Jaff caught on fire, all the better. If it set off alarms, that worked, too. But one way or another, they were going to charge right at that son of a bitch and give him the fight of his life as they tried to find a way out.

As they charged up the stairs, Jackie flicked the lighter and the flame, hot and true, burned in her hands.

***

The second he had run from the cop to turn the lights on, the voice had welcomed him with open arms.

It was a woman, which he had always known. The spirit of the voice was feminine, though Jaff couldn't nail down exactly how he knew that. Something about a life spent largely among men telling dirty jokes and talking about their private parts might have had something to do with it. Either way, it was now clear that she was here and that she had been guiding him, helping him, telling him the best course of action, and now that he was near the end, she was here to make sure he finished the job properly.

While appearing only in his mind, it was as clear as if she had walked out of the audience of a show at The Square. She was thin and strong, her dress brown and old-fashioned, her hair flaming red and down past her shoulders, moving like it was underwater. While not young, she had a timeless beauty that Jaff could not shake and eyes that burned into him like fire consumed wood. She had revealed herself to him and he was both grateful and ready to be obedient. Jaff also understood he was nearly done with his job and that the end was coming.

*Kill them all.*

He hadn't nodded or made any sort of motion, but she knew

212

he understood. Their connection was complete. He had no choice, nor did he want one.

*Turn on the lights and kill them all.*

All within a matter of seconds, she showed him how he might do it. Bright lights. Loud music. Sharp knives. The policeman would go down easy if Jaff could surprise him. Even his hurt leg wouldn't factor into it if he shoved a knife into the officer's throat before he had a chance to put up a fight. Defensive tactics go out the window when you're bleeding from your jugular vein. From there it was downstairs, unless they decided to come up. He would cut and stab and they would scream and die and then he would finally have his moment with Calista, the moment he should have already had.

Unless she was already dead.

The thought floated across his mind but lingered, taking up more space than it should. What if she was dead? What if he had killed her but slowly? Would his end, on the stage, with the gun, be any less satisfying knowing she had died slowly in the goddamn green room while he was out here dealing with all manner of bullshit? Since the moment he knew she was alive he wanted to have that moment where she knew she was going to die and that he was the one who was going to kill her. He still wanted that.

*She was never important.*

The voice was less assured this time, but Jaff believed it anyway. Her. Believed her, because he had disobeyed her and look what had happened. This was not a time for doubt. This was a time to finish what he'd started, to end this bloody day the only way it could end. With more blood.

When he snapped to attention, he was hidden in the shadows of the tech room, a small alcove outside his office. He didn't remember walking there, but there he was, the officer shining his flashlight on the big pool of blood that had permanently stained the carpet near the entry to the basement. Where the rest of them were.

Jaff's eyes drifted to the board from which he ran the show. Once upon a time, in the late '80s, it had been nothing more than a simple mixer with a CD player in case anyone wanted to be introduced to music, which was a popular thing at the time. Now he had a four-thousand-dollar sound system, complete with mixing board, inputs for mics, and an iPad from which he controlled the lights. It wasn't state of the art, but he bought it because it symbolized this was his profession, what he had chosen to do with his life.

No one but Jackie had wanted music tonight, so the song cued up was still "Come Dancing" by The Kinks. Even though it was Jackie's song, he had to admit she had good taste.

"Works for me," Jaff said, and hit the lights and pushed the volume all the way up as he hit the music. "Let's make some magic."

# CHAPTER 2

Officer Brunzell had never been to a comedy club, but he had been in a firefight.

It was four years ago when he was still green around the gills, still trying to remember his training instead of it being second nature. He hadn't shot anyone but had discharged his weapon three times in the direction of a man who was trying to shoot his way out of a building. There were three other officers on the scene and the man was shot four times and didn't make it to the hospital. The official report showed that his bullets were not the ones that found their mark, which sort of bothered the young officer. He'd like to think if he was going to discharge his weapon, he was going to get the job done.

The situation had changed the way he trained. Instead of trying to get the proper score, he was now more careful with his actions and more decisive when action was needed. Training didn't feel like preparation for something that might happen, it felt like a dry run for something that was inevitable.

It was this mindset that stopped him from shooting Taylor and Jackie on site. A younger Mick Brunzell would have shot until they stopped moving forward.

The women came running up the stairs like they were charging toward an enemy, and only after he didn't pull the trigger did he realize they were armed with what looked like Molotov cocktails. Communication, at this distance, was impossible due to the loud music, so when the women saw him, he relied primarily on body language to assess whether or not they were a threat. From what he could tell, they were scared of his gun, but happy to see the uniform. After a certain amount of time on the job, he recognized that look.

One of the women was bleeding very badly from the arm and the other one was Jackie Carmichael, who was on a show that he and his wife had watched. It was weird to see a celebrity in this situation, and even weirder that she was pointing toward the stage. It took a second to realize what she was doing—trying to warn him.

Officer Brunzell turned just in time to see Jaff approach, leading with a nasty-looking knife, going straight for his throat. In the split second he had before impact, Brunzell thought to himself it was a smart move on Jaff's part. He wasn't rearing back to attack, leaving himself vulnerable. He was leading with the knife. Less power, more speed, more surprise. The man was almost on him, and getting his gun retrained wasn't an option. The cop flung his arms with as much force as he could toward the charging man and the knife, which was pointed toward his Adam's apple.

The blade, which was long and serrated, missed his center mass but cut deeply into Officer Brunzell's left shoulder, right between the thick fabric and Velcro that held his vest on, forcing him to drop his gun on the carpeted floor. It bounced under a table nearby. Amidst this sea of bad news, the good news was, while the knife penetrated a weak spot in the vest, he was wearing a thick uniform which absorbed some of the blade, making the wound not as bad as it could have been. That being said, the part of the blade that made it to his skin ripped and cut relentlessly, and the officer grunted but did not scream as he worked to overpower his attacker.

As they struggled, Brunzell got his first real good look at his assailant. The man, who had, moments before, been hanging out with Officer Brunzell in the entryway to his club, was now a full-on, drooling, dead-eyed attacker intent on murder and blood. Any experience Brunzell had had with these sorts of assailants was at a distance, and close up there was nothing but uncut ugliness. There was only one way to deal with this sort of ugliness.

Brunzell socked Jaff in the jaw with his right hand, creating good meaty *twack* that found its target and likely did some damage to the bones in his face. The first hit got Jaff to let go of his grip on the knife, but he recovered quickly, grabbed the knife still jammed into Brunzell's shoulder, twisting it as he went. The pain that had been dulled by adrenaline came roaring forward and the cop felt one of his knees start to buckle.

He had gotten all of Jaff with that punch and it should have dropped him, but the old bastard kept coming.

As he fell, stars starting to float into his vision, he saw a blur of flesh and hair as someone tackled his attacker from the side.

Jackie and Jaff both slammed into the side of the bar at the back of The Square, tumbling forward a little bit from the impact with the dense, solid wood. In the tussle she felt the cell phone in her bra come loose and go flying. Jaff was first to his feet and he managed to give Jackie a solid kick to the breadbasket before she was able to recover from the initial tackle, but the kick put him a little off balance. Even in the midst of the pain from the kick and the wind leaving her chest, she rolled her body enough to knock

Jaff off his feet again. There was a satisfying crashing noise as Jaff's head hit the bar, breaking glasses and sending coasters flying get, but it was a glancing blow.

Jaff rolled and ran toward the kitchen while Taylor ran up to both injured parties. The music drowned out the moans of pain from by the bar where Jackie lay curled up, the kick from Jaff firmly knocking the wind out of her.

"Thank God," she shouted to Officer Brunzell over the blaring music. "Jesus Christ, he's lost his fucking mind."

"Can you turn the music off?" he yelled back.

"I'll try."

"I can't call it in with the music going."

The cop pointed to his radio and Taylor nodded, understanding, but definitely not hearing every word.

Momentarily torn between wanting to help the bleeding and injured people and finding his gun, Officer Brunzell's training kicked in and he threw several chairs clear of the table to find his side arm. He spotted it on the other side of one of the tables and was just about to grab it when another man came up from the basement, an old revolver in his hand. The man made eye contact with Brunzell and started running toward him.

The music still blaring, Brunzell grabbed his gun and held it at the advancing man.

***

The reserve of energy had run dry. Any courage he had left was gone. It wasn't about being successful or being the best he could be or rising to the occasion or any of the other bullshit he spewed on his podcast or in his books. Sammy lay on the stairs, using everything he had left to take another breath.

He had moved the gun from his chest into his right hand. He had done that much but shuddered at the idea of doing more, as the gun felt like the forty-pound free weights he lifted every morning. Laying on the stairs feeling his heart threatening to beat out of his chest and end his misery, he did something he hadn't done in years. Sammy started to pray.

He wasn't entirely new to praying, just out of practice. He had been confirmed Methodist as a preteen, before the drinking and the drugs and the sex with girls in the backseats of cars had started. He remembered how, but realized there wouldn't be much oomph behind it. To be honest, if he had a religion, he believed in the power and ability of Sammy Platter, but the past half hour had taken his true faith out back to the shed and shot it between the eyes. So he prayed, for lack of other activity to engage in. If there was a higher power out there, he needed help, salvation, rescue.

"I need help," he said out loud. "I can't die here. I've got so much left to do. I need help."

Tears of fear and embarrassment started falling. He felt incredibly stupid, but, to his incalculable surprise, his panicked prayer for deliverance was answered.

*You need to fight.*

The voice was sweet and feminine and clear as a bell, so much so that he sat up and looked around for where it came from. He knew damn well it was in his head but it seemed to come from some physical place, both near to him and far away at the same time. It seemed like it had come from heaven, and while it didn't touch his soul or anything so cliche, it was a solid voice with solid advice he could grab with both hands.

*Go. Fight.*

Of course that's what had to be done. It was the one thing he hadn't tried. Since he first saw Calista's body on the floor, he had tried reasoning with the group and had tried advising the group, he had tried to run and he had tried to bargain, and he had kept a cool head and he had panicked and nothing had gotten him out of this goddamned basement. He was stuck there like he had been stuck in his alcoholism, like he had been stuck playing Xbox all day in his shitty apartment, lamenting his bad luck until he found the power of motivation and the success it brought.

He had to take this situation by the balls, not from a conversational standpoint or a leadership role. He had to actually go kick some ass. He had to get physical.

And he had a gun in his hand.

Sammy was not a gun guy by a long shot, but had been out shooting and enjoyed it well enough. He couldn't clean a gun, but he knew enough to see if it was loaded and cursed when he saw it wasn't.

"Fuck," he said, the music still blaring up above him. "What am I supposed to do without any bullets?"

*You can fight.*

He didn't like the idea, and fear started to creep back into his calculations. There was a madman up there with a knife who knew what he was doing with it. He couldn't scare Jaff, and the chances of him finding bullets were slim at best. Jaff might come for the gun, might know it was unloaded. Then what was Sammy going to do? Throw it at him?

On the other hand, he could get up there, fight if he needed, but make a run for the exit in the back of the building behind the stage. Fight if you had to, run if you can. Made sense, and the voice didn't seem to be objecting. Even without bullets, the gun felt really good in his hand and made him feel a little more powerful than he otherwise would have.

"Okay," he said to himself. "I got this. I can fight."

*Go. Fight.*

It sounded weird, even as the thought floated across Sammy's mind, but it was as if the voice wasn't just urging him on but giving him strength to move forward. His mind briefly flashed back to other situations in his life where he was afraid—bullies in school, more bullies in school, meeting boyfriends of women he was having sex with, fights in a bar—and realized his instinct had always been to run away. It was so clear. Running was his default, where he felt comfortable. On the fight or flight scale, he was all in on flight, but this situation was different. He was fighting for his life, and the voice, whatever it happened to be, was giving him strength. And he was taking it.

He felt a surge of energy and a lessening of panic now that he had a plan. Listen to the voice, he thought, and everything would turn out okay.

Rolling onto his side and getting his shaky legs under him (his balls still hurt like a motherfucker thanks to Jackie), Sammy took the stairs with increasing speed, the gun in his right hand up by his chest, and by the time he hit the main floor, he was at a solid jog.

He was greeted by a cop, a gun, and music too loud to cut through no matter how much he yelled.

***

No matter how loud The Kinks played, the shot from Officer Brunzell's gun was louder. The explosion from the barrel ripped through The Square, reaching the ears of every conscious person. For Jackie, who was just pulling herself together after tackling Jaff at the bar, it was a terrible sound that began a terrible sequence of events, and she had a front row seat for all of it.

First, she saw Officer Brunzell's back as he squared up and fired at Sammy. The bright light of the club spared her nothing as she saw the cop's stance react to the recoil and saw Sammy spin around to his left, as if pulled by an invisible string tied to his shoulder that had run completely out of slack. He spun faster than she'd ever seen anyone spin, hit the floor, and roll back down the stairs.

Second, she saw Jaff come out of the kitchen, a gleaming knife in his hands. This one did not have a serrated edge, but was just as long. It gleamed under the lights as Jaff ran, full speed, out the kitchen door and toward the man in the uniform.

Third, the music stopped and the lights went out completely. The only light remaining came from some foot lights leading up to the stage, from the open door to Jaff's office, and a bright, glowing exit sign on the other side of the stage. Other than that, the club was blacked out with only deep shadows and the sound of grunts replacing the light and the music.

She allowed herself a brief moment to enjoy the deep, Kinks-less silence before the panic grabbed her by the throat.

"Officer," she yelled. "Look out!"

She expected to hear a scuffle, bodies hitting and stabbing at each other, but nothing came. It was dead silent except for the sounds of Sammy screaming at the bottom of the stairs. He had probably landed on Jerrod and Terry, she thought, which would do nothing for his mood, but other than that there was just the sound of movement. The cop was moving around and she could vaguely make out his outline, gun drawn, legs apart. It could have been her imagination, but she could have sworn she saw the knife still sticking out of his shoulder.

Beyond that, nothing. She had completely lost Jaff and he wasn't about to show himself.

"Taylor!" Jackie yelled. "Turn the lights back on!"

"I can't," the darkness yelled back. "I don't know what I did."

"Keep trying," Jackie yelled, and proceeded to move along the bar, her hand outstretched, fingers splayed as she tried to find her way in the dark. She didn't want to be in the same place her voice had just come from, lest a madman with a knife track her voice and stab her in the throat. Even though it was dark, she had a feeling Jaff could find whatever body part he wanted to stab with relative ease.

She cursed leaving her purse downstairs, as there was a small mag light latched on to her ring of keys. Officer Brunzell was more prepared, and, shortly, a small beam of light cut through the darkness and right at Jackie.

"Who did I shoot?"

"There's one attacker," she said back. "And that wasn't him."

The cop let out a short little "shit" under his breath and started combing the room with his flashlight for Jaff.

"I saw him come out of the kitchen with another knife," Jackie said.

"Okay," he said, gun still out. "You go sit, keep your back to the bar. I'm calling this in."

Jackie gave a small nod and slowly started backing up. A few seconds later, she heard the cop cursing again.

"He got my radio," Brunzell said. "Caught the chord when he stabbed me. Does anyone have a phone?"

Panic was starting to get the better of Jackie. Why the hell couldn't they get out of this place? It's like every step that would save them was instantly thwarted—cell phones gone, cops without a radio, exit signs with murderers hiding in the shadows. She felt whatever calm she had left pouring out of her head and onto the floor. She had been brave and it hadn't been enough, and now the darkness that had gotten hold of Sammy, who was a prince under regular circumstances, was coming to swallow her whole.

"You gotta get me out of here," she said quietly. "I can't...I can't."

"You can't leave."

The voice boomed over the speakers in the club, just as loud as the music. In the darkness she saw Officer Brunzell spin around, trying to figure out where to point his gun. The voice was Jaff's and it cut her all the way to her heart and increased her dread to another level. The voice wasn't so much threatening but loud, as if its will was inevitable.

"None can leave."

The cop's flashlight started swinging around wildly and he was clearly having trouble working both the light and the gun with an injured arm. A hand suddenly grabbed Jackie's shoulder and she screamed. Out of the corner of her eye, Officer Brunzell swung his frame around but did not fire, but his light hit her square in the face.

It was Taylor, who had crept up to her soft as a cloud. She leaned over and whispered into Jackie's ear.

"I know where he is."

"Where?" she said, getting a grip on herself. Just Taylor's touch had pulled her out of her spiral and Jackie was breathing heavy and trying to keep her heart rate under control.

"He was in the hallway by the exit, waiting for us," she said. "I think he's by the stairs now."

She couldn't point because of the darkness, but Jackie was oriented enough to get a sense of where she meant. She squinted hard and, sure enough, saw one of the footlights blink off then on again as if something were moving across it. This meant Jaff was about one hundred feet away from her and about sixty feet away from the cop who was still trying to figure out where to aim.

"I think I know what he's going to do," Taylor continued.

"What?"

"He's going to go get the gun. He saw Sammy had it. I think he's going to go get it and then come up shooting."

Jackie thought for a second, and it definitely occurred to her to let Sammy get what was coming to him. He had said it himself, if there was a way out, he was going to take it and to hell with the rest of them. What was good for the goose, Jackie thought. Then it occurred to her why Taylor had seen Jaff sneaking around in the first place.

"Braden's still down there," she said. "I'm going to save him if I can."

"We will," Jackie said. "Do you think we can make it to the cop without drawing attention?"

"Wait until he goes down the stairs."

Their whispering was soft and intimate, but it still sounded like a bulldozer compared to the rest of the noises in the place. Jaff had noticed.

"What are you ladies whispering about over by the bar?" the booming voice asked through the microphone. "Not telling secrets, I hope."

"Can someone please turn on the fucking lights?" Officer Brunzell yelled. He was clearly starting to lose his cool as well. Jackie couldn't blame him.

"I'm gonna risk it," Jackie said, and stood up, moving toward the shape she prayed to God was Officer Brunzell. She whispered as she moved forward.

"I'm coming up on you, officer. I'm not going to hurt you. Please don't shoot me."

"I won't," he whispered back. He did not shine a light on her, though, as he was busy hunting the club for the man who had stabbed him. Jackie held her hands out and touched the soft, stiff fabric of his uniform. He was exactly where she had thought he was and she felt his fast breathing. Jackie wanted to hug him but fought the urge and got down to business.

"We think he's downstairs right now, but we aren't sure," she said.

"How many attackers are there?" Brunzell said, almost cutting Jackie off.

"Just the one," Jackie said. "The one who stabbed you. That's the one we have to worry about."

"He had a gun."

"The guy you shot is just trying to get out of here. But was acting like an asshole, if that helps."

He didn't laugh, but Officer Brunzell took Jackie's words to heart and started moving forward toward the door, gun drawn. The dim sources of light were not giving up the club's secrets and Jackie suddenly had a strong urge to run for the exit. The sign was bright by the standard of light in the club, red and suddenly very inviting.

Beyond the light, in the hallway, concealed by darkness, Jaff Maul stood, waiting.

# Chapter 3

He could have killed the cop in the dark. He could have cut the bleeding girl more, but wasn't sure he could have killed her. Because he knew the layout of his club like he knew the curves and imperfections of his own body, he could have quietly walked up and cut Jackie's throat as she lay, terrified, on the floor next to the bar. He could have done all these things, or whatever else he pleased, but Jaff hadn't. The voice had told him to wait and he was not disobeying again. He was listening and he was obeying.

*Wait*

That had been the only edict. The only instruction, but it was clear and unambiguous. When the cop had shot Sammy, Jaff had worked to stifle laughter. He couldn't think of anything more fitting. He had also chuckled inside when the cop said his radio was damaged by the knife, which Jaff still missed. He hadn't intended to do that and probably couldn't do it again if he tried. It was almost like someone was looking out for him, almost as if his victory was inevitable.

Part of him realized, for someone who had never perpetrated violence in his life, that he was getting very, very lucky, and he knew he owed his success thus far to the voice. It had to be. What else could have given him such a run of luck? It was not impossible to think that he'd have screwed up by now, taken a wrong step, made a mistake. Hell, in a one-on-one fight every other day of his life, he wasn't sure he could have killed Jerrod, much less done so in such a decisive manner.

But he was being protected. He was being guided. He disobeyed when he didn't kill the girl at the top of the stairs because he was enamored by his own success, high on his own supply, laughing at his own material. But his continued run of luck and the way the voice hadn't judged him but only guided him had won over his mind and spirit. He wasn't the one doing any of this. He was simply a vessel, and there, in the dark, knife in hand, he was happy to be so.

So, in the dark, he watched. And waited.

He had killed the lights a few seconds earlier with the simple tug of the main chord to the lighting system. A street light shown through some of the windows from the front of the club, giving him a better view looking toward the street. As such, he knew exactly where Office Brunzell was and even got a few thrilling glances of the knife still sticking out of his shoulder. His soft little grunts of pain were amusing as well. He was trying so hard to control his fear and failing spectacularly.

Speaking into the mic through the sound system (which was on a separate power source from the lights) had been another bit of fun. The idea had come to him in a flash, and with the cordless mic, he could have been anywhere. The voice hadn't objected.

He saw Jackie go over to the cop and heard her whisper everything. They thought he was downstairs. That didn't make sense to him, but it didn't need to. The only thing he had to worry about was protecting the one exit left and getting the gun away from that cop.

"Both of you stay up here," he heard Brunzell say. "If you hear me give the all clear, haul ass for that exit."

"Why don't we do that now if he's downstairs?" Jackie asked.

"Because we're not sure he's down there," the cop said.

"Then what happens to us if he's up here?" Jackie said in an angry whisper.

The cop let out a "shush" that almost echoed through the room.

They were trying so hard to be quiet and failing so badly, Jaff thought. But the cop was on his game. He was trying to protect them and he knew who the enemy was. He couldn't expect any more errant bullets flying through the air.

Jaff gripped his knife tighter. Once the cop was downstairs, those women were all his.

*Wait.*

Yes, he would wait. The plan was out of his hands. He was being controlled, but in an odd way, Jaff had never felt so free.

\*\*\*

Jackie made her way back to the bar, putting her back against the solid wood. In the dark, her hand found Taylor's and she grabbed it, squeezing it hard and feeling wet blood squish between her fingers.

"How you holding up?"

"I'm a bit woozy," Taylor said. "I'm not sure how much longer I've got left."

"You've done enough already," Jackie said, trying to reassure her. "If you have to pass out, that's totally cool."

"I've still got the bombs we made."

Smiling, Jackie heard the sound of liquid swishing as Taylor gently nudged the bottle with her foot. Jackie still had the lighter.

"Why don't we light them now?"

"Because they'll explode and get fire everywhere," Taylor said. "We'd be trading the dark for fire. Braden's still downstairs."

By this point, Officer Brunzell was at the top of the stairs and was moving slowly and deliberately. His outline was very clear against the lights on in the basement, and they could see the knife still sticking out of his shoulder. Jackie remembered movies she'd watched that said if you were stabbed and pulled the knife out, you'd have to deal with blood loss, which could be a bigger problem than having a knife stuck in you. She wondered if that was true or just Hollywood bullshit.

Now that he was in the light, there didn't seem much point in whispering.

"Jesus, there are dead bodies down here!"

"I told you he'd lost his fucking mind!" Taylor yelled back.

Quickly, the cop shined his flashlight to his left and right and, seeing nothing, proceeded down the stairs.

"Good luck," Jackie said, hopefully loud enough for him to hear.

Moving slowly, Officer Brunzell kept his gun trained in front of him. While she felt a swell of admiration for the cop's bravery, Jackie had to fight the urge, again, to run for the door. If Jaff was there, then he had the drop on Brunzell, and if that happened, maybe she could get to the door that led to the alley and away from The Square for ever and ever.

Taylor was having the same idea.

"Let's make a break for it."

"If he's hiding back there, we're fucked," Jackie said. "What about the lights? Why can't you get them back on?"

"I think he pulled the plug or something," Taylor said. "I wasn't even touching anything when the lights went out."

They watched the cop's head get lower and lower as he

descended the stairs.

"Come on," she said. "We can make it."

Jackie honestly considered it. Even the grim calculus that he couldn't get both of them entered her mind. If he was downstairs, there was nothing stopping them, and if he was lying in wait, maybe she'd make it, even if Taylor didn't. Terrible thoughts continued to bubble up. She didn't know this girl before tonight. She had already shown an immense amount of compassion. If anyone deserved a little luck right now, it was her.

Batting the thoughts away, she tried to keep a cool head despite the white-hot urge to charge the exit like a linebacker.

"Sit tight," she said. "I'm not going to lose anyone else. Not you, not Braden, not no one. We'll move when it's safe."

Even in the low light Jackie could see the despair cross Taylor's face. Jackie shared it. There was no reason there were already two dead bodies downstairs (that she knew about), no reason there were people bleeding out in the dark. This whole thing should not be happening. Yet the best way to serve herself and others, she told herself, was to keep a cool head and be as safe as possible.

"I know, honey," she said. "I want out of here, too. Just a little longer. I promise."

***

There was no sign of the man he shot.

There were two dead bodies piled in a heap at the bottom of the stairs.

Both these facts were surprising and distressing in their own ways. But the main problem, aside from the knife sticking out of his shoulder, was the attacker was nowhere to be seen. That fucker needed to show his face, Brunzell thought. This hide and seek shit was getting old and tapping into parts of himself he didn't like.

Like the fact, for example, that he really wanted to shoot the guy who stabbed him. A lot.

The two corpses at the bottom of the stairs didn't help that account any. His gun still aimed at the dank hallways (was that a tipped over filing cabinet? Why was it covered in vomit?), Brunzell bent down and felt for the pulse of the guy nearest him. He wasn't sure why he did it, given the bullet hole in his head was pretty definitive, but it seemed appropriate. Of course, he felt nothing.

It was only after pulling his hand back that he noticed the body was that of famous actor and comedian Terry Stafford and the pool of blood on the floor meant these two bodies had been sitting here a while and had both suffered violent deaths.

"Holy shit," he muttered. "What happened here?"

Small sobs floated down the hallway and he followed them. The hallways felt damp, smelled of blood, and, even with the aid of a gun, was terrifying for the cop. Following the noise, Brunzell noticed the destroyed door, jagged shards of wood and other materials all over the floor. When he finally turned the corner, he was confronted with more carnage.

He didn't know who was dead or who was alive, but the room was awash in injured or dead people and covered in blood. Against one wall was the man he had shot having a total breakdown, crying big tears as streams of blood leaked from his clavicle and down his right arm.

The man didn't acknowledge Brunzell but kept right on crying.

"Fuck," he kept saying. "Fuckin…goddamn…"

The man's left hand still gripped the revolver that had caused Brunzell to shoot in the first place. It was still relatively clean given how much blood was everywhere else. He looked a little closer and saw the entry wound had hit the space between the shoulder and clavicle. It was a bad wound and would bleed out if he wasn't treated soon.

"Drop the gun," Brunzell said. He was torn between watching for movement on the stairway and keeping an eye on the man with the gun.

Sammy tossed it at Brunzell's feet.

"Not even fucking loaded, man," he said. "Not even…"

Brunzell took a second to glance around. There were two people on the floor, one of whom was clearly dead. She was in yoga pants, which caught his attention for some reason, and had been badly beaten. The other guy was alive, if the rising and falling of his chest was any indication, but had been shot in the gut and was unconscious. It was a good call, given the conditions in the room.

Over his years as a cop, he had always heard a gut shot was one of the most painful experiences a human being can have, and given the amount of blood, he was inclined to believe it. The man with the gut shot was young and looked like he was hanging in there but needed some help.

"Are you going to stay down here?" he asked.

"I want to go home."

"Stay here. I'll send help."

"I wanna go home."

They both heard screaming upstairs and Officer Brunzell took off, running to provide aid per his training. Sammy sat, his eyes eventually landing on Braden. The young man was still breathing and writhing around in his unconscious state next to Calista who was now white and waxy looking, her skin already taking on a static quality of a body as opposed to a person. It was a grim before and after situation.

"Mom," he heard Braden said. "Mommy…it hurts…"

Sammy shut his eyes hard. He didn't want to. He really didn't want to. He had gone up there once and Jerrod had died. He had gone up there again and been shot in the soft part of his shoulder and neck. He didn't want to go up there again. Something bad was going to happen.

*Stay.*

He immediately recognized the voice as the one that had urged him to run upstairs.

"Yeah, fuck you," Sammy said to himself, his brain finally pushing out the pain and panic. "Key number six, never follow bad advice twice. I'm not listening to you anymore."

He pushed himself to his feet and followed the cop upstairs.

\*\*\*

When the voice told him to move, it was like a cool drink of water hitting his throat on a hot day. The cop had just found the bodies and Sammy was downstairs, nursing a nasty gunshot wound. It was time.

As quietly as he could, he crept in front of the stage, down past his office, and toward the bar. The office was well lit and shining into the seating area, so he took a bit of a circuitous route to avoid the bulk of the light, but eventually found his way behind the bar. Moving slow was not what he wanted to do. He wanted to cut across the dark room, see the fear in their eyes as they realized where he was and that he was coming for them, finally coming, but he kept it slow, steady, and quiet. From the conversation, it seemed like neither of the women had heard him or knew what was coming, and he approached, his footsteps muffled by the rubber pads along the bar floor.

"Where did Sammy get shot?"

"In the shoulder. Looks like he'll be okay if we get out of here."

"He'll have some great material for his podcast on Monday."

He stood up behind the bar, hidden by the dark, his replacement knife from the kitchen in his left hand. He'd need his dominant hand to get their attention.

Reaching over the bar, he grabbed a handful of Jackie's curly brown hair and yanked upward as hard as he could. She screamed out of shock and pain, but moved upward, her body reacting to the pain with compliance. Jaff's goal was to pick her up to bar level and have at her throat with the knife, getting in as many shots as he could so even if she didn't die right away, she would choke and die shortly thereafter.

What he hadn't counted on was that once Jackie got her feet under her, she would push up, hard, and hit the underside of is jaw with her head.

He reeled back, shocked by pain and the initiative shown, already pissed off that he hadn't gotten a good, clean shot at her throat. He had lost his grip on her hair and she pulled free, suddenly on the other side of the bar and ready to make a break for the exit.

Moving as fast as he could in the dark and using his knowledge of the club, he ran for the exit at the same time they did, beating them by a few seconds. Both of them sensed something was going on and stopped dead in their tracks. Everyone was breathing hard, so the game was up. They knew he was in front of them and the exit and he knew they were right in front of him, trying to get out.

"You missed your chance," Jackie said in Jaff's direction. "That's going to cost you."

At that moment, Taylor realized what she had tried to talk Jackie into was the exact opposite of what she wanted. Her legs were frozen in place and the fresh rush of adrenaline numbed the pain in her arm but exacerbated other symptoms—she felt weak and woozy, she worried she was going to throw up, and she was hyper aware of the blood running down her arm in the makeshift sling Jackie had made.

From behind them, Officer Brunzell came running up the

stairs, yelling something Taylor couldn't make out. The distraction was enough for Jaff to kick her in the stomach with enough force to knock her off her feet and force the contents of her stomach up and out. Not having any control over the way she landed, her weight crashed on top of her bad arm and she screamed, the adrenaline no match for the concrete brick of pain that hit her body.

Jackie's first instinct was to go to Taylor, but she fought it and kept her eyes on the dark outline of Jaff. Immediately after kicking Taylor, he lunged at Jackie with the knife and caught the very edge of her shirt on her left side. The force she used to miss Jaff's lunge sent her spinning to her right and she grabbed the edge of a chair around one of the tables, steadying herself before realizing she had her hands on a decent weapon.

Picking up the chair, she turned it, legs out, and pushed in Jaff's direction. The dark obscured her actions enough to where she caught him by surprise, jabbing him in the face and chest with two of the four legs and pushing him backward.

"Officer!" she yelled. "He's over here. I've got him!"

Almost before she finished speaking, Jaff, at what seemed like a running start, pushed the chair and Jackie backward. The back of her thighs hit a table and she tumbled on top of it.

"No one leaves!" Jaff yelled as he tumbled on top of the chair, pinning Jackie to the table.

She pushed back against the chair, waiting at any second for the steel from the knife to penetrate her skin, but it didn't happen. Jaff kept pushing down on the base of the chair in a rage, pinning her to the table, but not stabbing her. He continued to scream about leaving until his words stopped making sense to her. She started screaming back, fueled by adrenaline and rage.

Their screams were cut to ribbons by Officer Brunzell firing his gun into the air.

"Nobody move!" he yelled. "If you decide to move, I'm going to shoot you."

Jackie lay still on the table and felt Jaff stand up, his weight disappearing into the black.

"Can someone hit the lights, please?" Brunzell said.

"We don't know where they are," Taylor yelled.

"Get to the nearest exit," he yelled back.

Jackie did not need to be told twice. She spun the chair off her and ran to Taylor, kneeling beside her and immediately being hit with the smell of vomit.

"You alive?" she asked, reaching for her hand, fumbling around until she found it.

"Only dead inside," Taylor said.

"Jesus, did you just go for the joke?" Jackie said, helping her on her feet. Taylor let out a little grunt that told Jackie she was in a lot of pain.

Through the darkness, she thought she could see Taylor smile. There were a lot of things that sucked about their current situation, but one of them that came to the forefront of Jackie's mind was the lack of humor. This might have been the longest she'd been conscious without getting a laugh in a decade or so.

The exit sign was only about fifteen feet away from them when the lights came on and three things happened in rapid succession.

First, Jaff, standing behind Officer Brunzell, pulled the knife from his throat, fresh sprays of blood washing over the floor. The officer's eyes were big and terrified, his expression held surprise, pain, and a tinge of disappointment, his mouth and neck pouring blood. It was the first time Jackie had laid eyes on the cop in the light, and she mourned how young he was now that his life was ending. He had been stabbed from behind in the dark.

Second, part of the wall next to Taylor's head exploded as Jaff, now armed with the cop's Glock 17, fired a warning shot.

Third, the bloody mess that was Sammy Platter appeared behind Jaff, a lighter in one hand and one of their homemade Molotov cocktails in the other.

# CHAPTER 4

"No one leaves," Jaff repeated, the gun aimed right at Taylor.

She had no idea how he had managed to turn the lights on until she saw a light switch not far from where Jaff was standing. The light in the room wasn't the white-hot stage lights, just the overhead lights for everyday business, but they burned her eyes after minutes of straining to see in the dark. Something as simple as knowing where the light switches were had completely changed the game and now Jaff was in control, the only hope for salvation resting on the flick of a lighter.

Jaff hadn't noticed Sammy come up the stairs.

As Jackie and Taylor stood frozen, Sammy got the lighter to work and, quickly, a bright orange flame began danced up the rag they had stuffed in the top.

"Oh shit," Jackie muttered. Her exclamation brought a bigger smile to Jaff's face.

"You can't leave," he said, his grin almost supernaturally snide. "She won't let you."

When Taylor and Jackie were in the closet trying to figure out how to make use of the flammable liquid they'd found, there was one major design flaw they'd never been able to solve. In the normal run of a Molotov cocktail, the container is made of glass. This gives the thrower a chance to light the rag, throw the container, and when it breaks, fire spreads everywhere. They were stuck with a bottle made of thick, industrial grade plastic that would not shatter but that would definitely drip and melt.

The hope was when they lit and threw the plastic bottle, the fire would burn through the plastic quickly and start a smaller, more concentrated fire. Taylor had even reasoned this might give them an advantage—fire as a distraction, but controlled and not likely to spread. Turned out, she couldn't have been more wrong.

The second he got the bottle lit, Taylor could see it coming. This was not going to be controlled in any sense of the word.

It was going to be chaos.

The orange flame quickly danced up the rag stuffed in the top.

"Hey, Jaff, I fucking hate your club."

Jaff, his hand, still on the knife that had been in Officer Brunzell's throat, turned his head in time to see Sammy holding the lit bottle. The second the words were out of his mouth, a hole burned through the bottom of the bottle, spreading flaming liquid down Sammy's arm. His reaction was to ungracefully chuck the bottle toward Jaff, which was the best thing he could have done. As his right arm up went up in flames, the bottle flew through the air and hit Jaff in the leg.

His pants immediately caught fire below the knee and he let go of the knife to bat at the flames. Jaff's had to dance around Officer Brunzell, who was on the ground and still alive but not for long. The cop swatted the gun out of Jaff's hands on the way down, but in his death throws, it didn't go anywhere, weakly hitting the ground just before his body fell on it, effectively hiding it. He would bleed out on the floor in a matter of seconds, adding one more large pool of blood staining the carpet of The Square.

Jackie turned to Taylor, who was nearer the exit.

"GO!" she yelled. "Get help now!"

Taylor didn't hesitate. The fire and the smell of smoke mixed with some awful chemical overtone drove her down the hall and straight toward the door. Rushing toward it, salvation in sight, she hit the heavy metal door with a thud and pushed down on the long, rectangular handle. She pushed hard and the door budged, but did not open, slamming shut whenever she got even a glimpse of the streetlight from the ally beyond.

While she was trying to get the door to relent, Sammy had tried to stop, drop and roll, only to find out the age-old wisdom didn't apply when your arm was covered in flammable chemicals. Already, terrible things were happening to his skin, bubbles and blood and the smell of burnt hair hitting his nose, pain blocking out all but his most base of instincts. Panic set in and he started screaming.

Jaff was having a similar reaction. The flesh of his already wounded leg was getting eaten by the fire and he tried to beat out the flames with his hands. He had thrown the knife aside, near the door that led down to The F Pit.

Once Taylor was out of view down the dark hallway, Jackie had decided she would help Sammy if possible, and kill Jaff if it killed her. Her adrenaline was already spiked, fight or flight long ago tipped to the fight side. She had decided Jaff needed to die, and the killing of Officer Brunzell had only hardened her resolve.

Putting Sammy out was her first priority.

In front of her was a flaming Jaff, a huge pile of burning chemicals (the bottle was completely melted into the carpet), and beyond that, Sammy. There was a glint of metal on the floor as she saw the knife. Moving fast for a woman well into her forties, she grabbed the knife Jaff had dropped and, in a few more steps, grabbed Sammy and pulled the screaming man to the back of the bar. Sammy had still been on his feet and was full of hustle, not slowing her down but using his panic to fuel his legs. Finding what she was looking for on the near side, Jackie flipped open the lid of a long-outdated ice machine and jammed Sammy's arm inside. There was a hissing heard over Sammy's screams, and once his arm went out, the screams of panic died into sobs of pain.

Once she was sure it was out, she yanked on his shoulder and Sammy took the cue and pulled his arm out of the ice machine. While his screaming never stopped, it reached a higher pitch when large chunks of his skin stayed behind in the ice machine, his arm immediately bleeding and oozing once exposed to the air. Jackie was experienced enough to have seen gore make up before on movie sets, and none of them came close to capturing the horror of what she was seeing. Sammy was having a similar reaction.

"Oh God, fuck me," Sammy was saying.

Jackie got right in Sammy's face, forcing eye contact.

"Sammy, look at me."

It took him a few seconds, but his eyes stopped darting wildly around and he eventually focused on her. Even though their situation was dire and time was of the essence, Jackie couldn't help admiring how good he looked up close. His skin was great, arm excluded.

"Stay here," she said. "You're safe here. Don't move until help comes. You got it?"

Sammy started coughing and came away from one gasp of air with a smile.

"You still going to…ruin my reputation when we get out of here?"

"We get out of here, I'll make out with you on Colbert's couch."

"It's a date," he said, tears now falling liberally. "I really fucking hurt, Jackie."

"I know," she said. "Baby, I gotta go kill Jaff."

"Go, fucking kill him," Sammy said. "Please..."

His eyes rolled back like was starting to lose consciousness, which wasn't a bad play, Jackie thought. He was hidden behind the bar, well outside the field of play. If he had a chance to make it, Jackie decided, this was it, the fire raging in the center of The Square notwithstanding. She immediately scanned the bar for some sort of weapon and landed on a medium-sized knife, likely used to cut garnish for drinks. It wasn't huge and was one of several sharp-looking numbers on the bar, but it would do the trick. She would have to get close to Jaff anyway, and she was planning to.

Jackie picked up the knife and stood up, hoping to find Jaff on fire. No such luck. Instead, she saw him in the last stages of getting his pants off. The skin of one of his legs had blackened and fire was flicking at his arms. It took a few moments but she realized he'd also lost his underwear as well, his thick bush of pubic hair and penis now exposed to the flames and chemical stink. Her mind flashed for a second back to that night in Terry Stafford's hotel room. This was worse.

Even if she didn't kill him, the longer she could keep him occupied the more time Taylor would have to get help. As long as help wasn't too far away, she could do this.

"Hey, Jaff," she yelled, pointing the edge of the knife at him. "Shirt cocking it at your age, that's not a smart call."

He let out a guttural yell, now free of his burning cloths. The fire on his side cast a blazing, terrifying light into his face and Jackie understood, deep in her soul, that anything she had known as Jaff was gone. He was now just full of rage and murder and death. Jackie noticed the fire was also spreading, years of alcohol spills and cheap upkeep finally having their revenge. She would have to do this as fast as she could, as the smoke was already starting to sting her lungs.

"I hate to break this to ya, pal," Jackie said, leaning heavy on her New York accent. "But I ain't stopping until you're dead."

***

The cop had been easy to sneak up on. The dark had been an amazing ally and Jaff lamented that he had to turn the lights on, but the looks on their faces when they saw the cop go down was a hell of a consolation prize.

It also meant game over. He had a knife. He had a gun. They had nothing, and the voice had already told him they weren't going to leave. He had to stop calling it the voice. It was so much more than that, and he now knew, it was a woman. A woman who had always been here, long before Jaff had ever been born. But he didn't know what else to call her, not yet. So "the voice" it would remain.

*No one gets out.*

She had said it not as a command, but as a proclamation, an almost victorious one. No one was going to get out because of his hard work and obedience. None of these worthless people was going to stop him, and they would bleed and scream and die and there was nothing they could do about it.

The cop had been easy. Once, in one of his darker moments as the Internet was coming of age, Jaff had watched one of the beheading videos to be found online and was shocked at the amount of sawing and pulling involved. It wasn't a clean process to get the head off, but the initial cut, the one that had sent the poor victim into a state of panic and disbelief, had been remarkably clean. It was removing the knife where things might have gotten tricky.

So Jaff had stabbed from the back, trying as hard as he could to hit the windpipe to make sure the cop couldn't say anything. The cut had gone through tissue with surprising ease, just like he had hoped, and by the time Office Brunzell knew what was happening, the knife was out through the other side of his throat and the fat lady was taking the stage. Then he wiggled the knife a bit until he was sure he could get it back, then hit the lights.

He was so wrapped up in the reaction that he hadn't even thought about Sammy. The last time he'd seen that little shit, he'd been tumbling down the stairs, a well-earned bullet having taken a bite of his shoulder. Then that idiot motherfucker had set himself on fire.

The second Sammy made his presence known, the voice had been all but screaming. It wasn't giving him direction or screaming at him, it was just a generalized scream that let him know everything he'd worked toward and fought for was in danger. He was blowing it and he needed to bust his ass to make it right.

That started with not burning to death.

The contents of the bottle had burned through the plastic almost immediately and the fire spread at an alarming rate. His pants caught some of the cleaner and the burning sensation started to consume his right leg, the same one that had been stabbed earlier in the evening. He had beaten at it to no effect and the pain had gotten worse and worse, so he finally started stripping off his pants.

His fingers did not work quickly or efficiently, and by the time he had the button undone, the burning had intensified and Jaff started to scream. The flames licked up from high on his ankle, where the chemicals had landed, and were making it up past his knee. He had lost track of everyone, the voice continued to scream, and he might lose it all because he couldn't get his fucking pants off. When he was finally able to pull his leg out, his underwear went with and he didn't care, glad to be free, far beyond the horizon of not giving a fuck.

From across the bar, she called to him.

"Hey, Jaff."

He heard the rest, but it didn't make it far enough into his brain to turn into words. The voice was still screaming, but it now had a direction, and it was toward her. She had to die and she had to die right now.

"...I ain't stopping until you're dead."

*Bitch, you don't know the half of it*, he thought.

Weaponless, Jaff grabbed a chair and motioned for her to come out from behind the bar. She obliged, clutching the knife tightly in her hand, clearly scared shitless but focused and angry, a bad combination if there ever was one, but it was fine with Jaff. He couldn't wait to beat the spirit out of her and watch her anger bleed out as he cut into her skin.

She came at him surprisingly fast and hard, wanting to use her weight to her advantage now that Jaff didn't have an edged weapon. It worked, and even though he caught her solid in the shoulder with one of the chair legs, they both tumbled onto the floor. The whole time, Jaff kept his eye on the knife. It was the only thing that mattered and the only thing that could get him back in the voice's good graces.

Despite them both hitting the ground, Jackie held on to the knife and came up from the floor swinging. Jaff felt a dull pain in the side of his head and soon felt blood trickling town his right side of his face. She had cut him, but not badly. They both got back on their feet and it was Jaff's turn at being the aggressor. He picked up another chair and swung it at Jackie's head before she could get solidly back on her feet, and the connection made a dull thud that reverberated through the piece of furniture.

Jaff stood up, Jackie stunned and slow from the impact.

"Let's make some magic," Jaff said, his chest heaving. "You and me, Jackie. Magic."

The chair had hurt her seriously, but she was pissed off and not about to stop her attacks. From an off-balance position she made another jab with the knife, but wasn't nearly close enough to connect. This time, her punishment for missing was two legs of a wooden chair jabbed straight into her back.

This brought about the scream Jaff was hoping for and he pushed down on the chair, driving the legs deep into the muscles of Jackie's back. She wasn't pinned, but couldn't get to her feet, so she rolled to her right. Jaff was there to take a chair leg and bring it down onto her unprotected face.

Jackie's head snapped back onto the carpet and she spit blood into the air. It was a solid hit, Jaff thought, not strong enough to kill her but hard enough so that she'd never be the same. A tooth would be gone or a scar would be visible. Soon, it would be much worse than that. Either way, there was a lot of blood and he felt himself draw strength from her weakness, motivation from her suffering.

*Kill her.*

Of course that was the next step, and he looked around for the best way to do it. His eye landed on the fire still burning, throwing smoke and chemical stink into the air. It had grown, consuming the carpet at a heavy rate, his sprinklers not kicking on due to age and neglect. Maybe there was another reason, Jaff thought, grateful to the voice that was always protecting him, always providing.

Again using Jackie's curly hair against her, Jaff grabbed a handful and pulled the bleeding woman toward the fire. She screamed as he pulled her, sweating from the effort.

"You may be screaming now," Jaff said. "But just think of how you'll scream once you're on fire."

He was a few steps away when he felt it and immediately dropped Jackie's hair. His head spun around and was greeted to the sight of the knife, stabbed through his wrist. It was a full stab, the handle visible on the top of his wrist and the blade at the bottom. The pain was intense, but no more so than the fire a few minutes ago. The fire had been much worse, but being impaled through the wrist definitely wasn't fun. While this was one of the worst wounds he had endured in his life, at this point in the night it was a small thing.

Jackie was immediately moving away from the fire and tumbled behind the bar, the nearest refuge from everything happening in the club. She left a thin trail of blood behind her.

"Goddammit," he swore, leaving the knife in place for the time being. He could stand the pain. He could not stand letting her get away. Not again.

He tore off his shirt and tied it around the flesh of his arm just below his elbow. He then yanked the knife out. It hurt, but he now had the knife and that was the only important thing. Blood poured from his wrist but the tourniquet held firm.

"You were going to die anyway," he yelled at her. "But now I'm going to pull out your guts and make you fucking watch!"

At that moment, an incredibly cool wind blew through the club and the voice screamed so loud Jaff could hardly stand it.

\*\*\*

The second Taylor made contact with the door, she felt it. The door didn't open, but it wasn't because it was locked or because she was weak or because there was something on the other side. It was stuck because something inside the club didn't want her to leave.

She pushed on the door with everything she had and it gave and gave but didn't open, almost as if there was a seal keeping everything in, a mighty wind on the other side that wasn't about to yield. She almost saw the glow of the streetlight from outside, only to lose it with a terrible, final-sounding thud.

Desperate, Taylor shut her eyes and lowered her head onto the cool metal of the door.

"Let us out," she said. "God dammit, let us out."

*No.*

The voice was clear and loud in her mind, vaguely foreign but not of her imagination. It was there and it was talking to her. She was sure of that, and her anger overrode any rationality she had left.

"What did we do?" Taylor yelled. "What the fuck did we do to deserve this?! What do you want us to do?!"

*You should die.*

The answer wasn't nearly good enough. Taylor put her back against the door so she could see Jaff coming if he somehow broke free, and cleared her mind as best she could. Her arm had stopped throbbing, which was scary, but not as scary as what she was about to do. This idea was crazy, but no crazier than a door that wouldn't open or any of the other bullshit that had kept them from leaving The Square tonight.

"We don't have to die."

*Everyone has to die.*

"He doesn't have to kill us."

*Kill yourself.*

The ghost or spirit or whatever she was talking to was not being reasonable. This wasn't going anywhere, so she tired a different tack.

"Why can't we leave?" she said out loud, her voice echoing down the hall.

*Nobody leaves.*

In her mind's eye, it was suddenly clear. The voice belonged to a woman, dressed in an old style of dress, red hair spilling around her shoulders. Her eyes were terrible but her smile was worse as she grabbed hold of Taylor's mind, pulling at the edges of her sanity. The image was vivid and her goal absolutely unquestionable—she wanted to kill Taylor and everyone else in the bar. She didn't say why. She didn't have to. Her terrible visage gave away her intent, her resolve, her reason for existing.

For a second, fear completely overtook Taylor, melting her muscles and bringing her to a dead stop. She had never wanted to give up so badly in her life, sink into the floor and wait for the inevitable. Braden would die and Jackie would die and she would die and she was too tired and bloody and scared and completely terrified to do anything about it.

Then, a thought floated through her mind, unimpeded by the voice or Taylor's fear, and landed squarely in the center of her mind.

"Seriously? A ghost? Do you know how fucking stupid that is?"

The words had come out of her mouth, which brought her back into her body and all the pain that entailed. Once the words started, they didn't stop. Taylor had always been a talker.

"This is New York, you stupid piece of shit, you could be haunting a gay bathhouse four blocks from here or a police station or a fucking Subway. Any of them would be more interesting than The Square. Have you ever seen an open mic night? I have! Lots of them. I hosted open mics, which is the equivalent of punching myself in the face, for a free beer at the end of the night. It's nothing but people desperate to check something off their bucket list or to have an adventure telling jokes they heard on Conan three years ago in front of their drunk, stupid friends, while the veterans and the freaks and the comics are here because we have to be! We fucking have to. If we didn't do this, we would have nothing. No validation, no relationships, certainly no fucking money."

Taylor felt like the voice was trying to get a word in edgewise, but she wasn't having it. She kept going, her mouth working almost independent of her brain, which was something she had experienced on stage several times and always led to great material.

"No, no, if we're going to die here, you're going to listen to who it is you're killing. I have the mic, Casper, you don't get to talk when I have the mic, and if you try, one of the only things I'm good at in this life is ripping hecklers to fucking shreds. I eat hecklers. Drunk bachelorette parties, those are my favorite shows because I get to make someone cry! You decided to haunt the only place in the entire city where people come to laugh and the comics come because if they didn't, they'd slide into crippling depression."

Taylor wasn't even sure what her point was, but she kept going. Aside from the obvious catharsis, the rant spilling out of her seemed to be doing something. It was hard to identify, but she thought she sensed a low hum that was starting to build the more she screamed. Something was building in her and whatever was stopping her from getting out of the club was starting to give.

"You want to keep us here? You sure about that? Because once, I saw a comic jump off stage and punch a woman in the face who was on an anniversary date with her husband. I once saw Dave Attell get into a cursing match with a nun. You want to talk spiritual energy? How about a group of people with a healthy fear of death and people and life but no fear of an audience? How about people who will talk about their sex life to total strangers so that they'll fucking laugh at you? How about people who will take a bullet for someone they broke up with?"

She realized the low hum wasn't a hum at all. It was a scream.

It had started small but had grown into a torrent and now Taylor's head was full of nothing but screams from the voice and rage from her own mind. She pounded her fist on the door and it gave slightly, but she wasn't done.

"I'm not going to get killed by a fucking ghost," she said. "And Braden, he's not going to die. But if we do, you'd better fucking run for the deepest level of hell that will take you because we are not scared to find you in the afterlife, tear you apart, and haul you in front of all the other ghosts of New York and make fun of you until the end of fucking time."

She felt her strength growing and her arm started hurting much worse than before as her body vibrated with rage.

"You can't keep me here," she finished, her voice deep and resolute. "My set's over. I'm done."

Taylor kicked the metal handle of the door, connecting solidly, and it flew open. Light flooded into the dark hallway, a breeze hit her face and she smelled water and urine and garbage and it was the most amazing smell she'd ever experienced in her life.

"HELP!" she yelled, running out of the club and down the alley. "Somebody please help me!"

# CHAPTER 5

The pain returned to Jaff's head, intense and raw and bloody. He stumbled, grabbing the side of his temple, but kept making his way to the back of the bar.

*KILL THEM!*

The voice was incredibly loud and strong and he swore he heard an echo off the walls of The Square. Behind him, the fire raged, now having reached the kitchen on one side and the stairway leading to The F Pit on the other. He could tell the door was open and someone had gotten away, that he had failed and that he would pay. In a flash, as if spliced frame by frame into the fabric of reality, Jaff saw the woman from his mind with the old dress and the flowing red hair. She was screaming, her mouth a horrifyingly long oval from which no light could escape, and he felt himself tumbling toward it, unable to stop himself.

*KILL THEM ALL!*

Jaff could hear the voice in the breeze coming in off the street and in the crackle of the fire behind him. His strength surged and the headache disappeared, just as it had before.

Those two pieces of shit behind the bar were not going to get anything resembling mercy.

When he rounded the corner of the bar, a glass tumbler smashed into the side of his head, shattering and spewing glass all over the bar and floor. The thick glass had hit on the same side that Jackie had stabbed him, and now the blood was really flowing down Jaff's head and onto his bare chest, arms, and rest of his naked body. The shot knocked him onto one knee and his recently stabbed hand as he hit the floor.

When he was able to sit up, he saw Jackie and Sammy, both loaded for bear, a full regiment of glass tumblers around their legs, waiting to be thrown. Another one went whizzing by but it was badly overthrown, and Jaff got on his hands and knees and continued moving forward. The voice continued to scream and, for the moment, his body continued to surge with strength.

"There's no tomorrow," he said as he crawled toward them, another tumbler flying over his head. "There's no tomorrow and there's nothing left but her and me. Her and me!"

He said it as much for himself as for them and didn't give a shit if they understood or not. It didn't matter how much he bled or burned or hurt, this was the end, and as long as his body continued to work, he would kill them. He would split them in two while his club burned around him and the voice would give him all the strength he needed to finish what had been started.

Another glass hit Jaff in the shoulder, momentarily knocking him off balance, but it wasn't enough to stop him. He was ten feet away, the knife that had been in his wrist now in his hand, getting closer. Now that he was so near, he could see what he had done to Jackie with the chair. She was missing teeth and part of her left eye was close to gone. Another of the legs must have scraped down her right eye and the socket was either empty or completely covered in blood. Either way, it was messing with her depth perception because the glasses she threw were wild and weak.

Sammy, for his part, was using his left arm to throw the glasses and doing a poor job of it. He had thrown a couple that didn't have the speed to get to Jaff in the first place and Jackie's first shot that had smashed into his head seemed to have been beginner's luck. As he got closer, her throws were more and more wild and desperate. They both coughed as the flames which belched chemical smoke continued to grow.

Jaff felt the knife in his hand, not flashing it but not hiding it, either. They knew he had it and neither of them was in any condition to get away, their backs literally against a wall. Sammy tried to scramble first, getting to his feet but immediately falling again, downed by dizziness or pain, and Jaff stabbed him in the back of the calf as he went down. Sammy screamed and Jackie was able to give him a good punch to the side of the head with one of the heavy glasses.

"You killed that cop, I'm gonna kill you," Jackie said, panting. "An eye for an eye."

She chuckled to herself and pulled her arm back to take another desperate swing. With dexterity and an odd sort of grace, Jaff pulled the knife out of Sammy's calf and made a play to stab Jackie in the throat. She saw it coming and moved her head, deflecting the knife and catching the blade in her upper chest. It wasn't in her heart but it was damn close, and Jaff could feel the blood pour from the wound onto her shirt and onto his warm fist.

Close up, Jaff could see that her eyeball was, indeed, gone, the membrane broken and soupy insides washed away amidst the blood and sweat. With her good eye, she stared at him, clearly in immense pain, trying hard not to give up. But she would, Jaff told himself. She would give up her will, then her flesh, and then he'd throw her into the fire and it would be like she never existed. He smiled at the thought while staring at her and she understood.

Without warning, something on Jaff's back exploded and he turned his head to see Sammy, hacking away at his back with a small paring knife. It was one of many small, sharp knives behind the bar, and by the time Jaff realized what was going on, Sammy brought the blade down a second time, stabbing into the meat of his back just below his shoulder blade.

Jaff pulled the knife out of Jackie's chest and spun around, throwing his weight against Sammy and knocking him off balance and sending him a few feet down the bar floor. The knife Sammy had been using was still lodged in his back as he turned his full attention to his attacker, straddling him and forcing a scream from his lips as he sat on his burned arm. His body still hurt and the voice still screamed as he brought his own knife down. Sammy put his one arm up to stop him but it was no contest.

"You…should…have…" Jaff said, driving the knife down into Sammy's face, "…stayed…"

The knife went straight into Sammy's left eye, and at the last second, Jaff pulled upward, forcing the blade up through the orbital cavity and into his brain. Sammy continued to scream and kick, but he was done. Jaff continued to apply pressure, the blade continuing to cut, relishing the sensation of warm blood running down the knife's handle and onto his bare skin.

"…downstairs," Jaff finished.

As Sammy screamed, he pulled the knife out and jammed it into Sammy's throat. The knife went through flesh and stuck into the rubber matting on the floor of the bar and Jaff left it there, leaving Sammy to kick and choke. Even in the glory of the kill, he searched for approval from the voice and didn't hear anything other than Jackie screaming and trying to get toward him, her hand outstretched, blood pouring down her face.

It was beautiful.

\*\*\*

The panic Taylor was feeling as she ran down the alley and into the street was a completely different variety from the kind she felt inside The Square. There was an urge to flee, to get away. Now, the pace of normal life was far too slow to get her friends the help they needed and it was driving her to hysterics.

The first few people she encountered on the street stared at her bloody clothes and taped, gory arm. The site of her was enough to make them run the other direction. Her screams of "help me" were not going over well, either.

Finally, after what seemed like a week of looking at people, trying to get their attention, only for them to avoid eye contact, a chubby kid with his headphones in came into her view. He was engrossed, unaware that she was even there, but he had his phone in his hands and she was on him in a second.

"Hey," she yelled. "I need this."

"The fuck?" the kid said, then took her in. She was dripping blood, had been crying, and smelled strongly of smoke and chemicals. As the kid took her in, something clicked and he quickly whipped his headphones to the ground and grabbed the phone back from Taylor.

"There's a pass code," he said, punching in some digits, then handing the phone back to her. "There, go. Call 9-1-1."

For a second, she locked eyes with the kid. He wasn't out of high school yet and had the look of a kid who had grown up in the city. She gave him a small nod and he took a step back. The emergency responder picked up on the second ring.

"9-1-1, what's your emergency?"

"Jesus," Taylor said. "I don't know where to start."

\*\*\*

Sammy was still kicking and gasping for breath that would never come when Jaff turned his attention to Jackie. Only a short time ago, though it seemed like a lifetime had passed, he had considered strangling Taylor at the top of the doorway but hadn't. It would have taken too long, but now, at the end, he was thinking he wanted to give it a try.

*Kill her.*

That was definitely the plan. He could have gotten the knife out of Sammy's neck (he would bleed to death faster than he would suffocate), but he had come to realize this was the end. Whatever happened from here on out, he would bleed or burn or suffocate, too. He wouldn't get his ending with Calista on the stage like he wanted. He would die behind the bar, and, in some ways, it was more fitting this way. It was basically where he had lived, his life and work nothing more than slinging drinks for the mildly amused.

Jaff had long ago given up dreams of the stage, and even those dreams were never really his. They were formed by others who asked him, "When are you going to get up there?" and, "Ever get sick of not telling jokes yourself?" The truth of the matter was, no. He never wanted to be a stand-up. The furthest his ambition ever went was never wanting to wear a tie to work and to do something to recapture that joy he felt first hearing George Carlin in his dad's car. He wanted to be a rebel, an outsider, someone who trafficked in art and joy instead of money and greed. And, to that end, he had succeeded and found the prize painfully hollow and empty and littered with the mundane.

Instead of telling jokes and writing material, he ordered the booze and scheduled the workers and dealt with the artists who ran the gamete of mental illness. He never wanted the spotlight, but the darkness was no fun, either.

If his life had been behind the bar, he was going to go out his way.

*Kill her.*

He would. But the voice would have to give him some time with this one.

By the time he got his hands around her throat, Jackie had all but checked out. Her hand, which had reached out to Sammy, fell to her side and she had put her head down, utterly and totally defeated. As Sammy's motions got smaller and smaller and his body continued to die, all she could do was hang her head. It was an incredibly intimate moment, Jaff thought, watching the last bit of hope she had left leak out of her.

Softly, he raised her head with his hands and wrapped his hands around her throat. At first, he didn't squeeze, the anticipation on both their parts too delicious to waste. Then he gave it all he had. The hole in his arm where the knife had been immediately sprung fresh blood and pain, but the muscles still worked. It would be enough.

The fire was now going up the walls and was starting to lick the ceiling.. It was beautiful, he thought, as he squeezed, beautiful that the fire was consuming his life's work. At the end, after Jackie was dead, he would stand on the bar and let it all burn around him until he burned, too. It was a good plan.

Jackie's one remaining eye was starting to bug out when the strangest thing happened—she began to smile.

Jaff furrowed his brow. Surely she wasn't enjoying this.

"What?"

Of course, Jackie couldn't answer, but her smile only grew. The very little air left in her lungs began to heave, almost like a chuckle.

*KILL HER.*

The voice was insistent and loud, the screaming now at a fever pitch. Jaff could feel his heart beating faster, everything reaching a fever pitch, and there she was. Smiling.

He couldn't stand it. The smile was ruining the moment. He had fought and bled and been smarter, stronger, and more determined than every piece of shit he'd killed tonight. He was the one who deserved the ending he wanted. He was the one who deserved to make some magic, and there was that fucking smile, ruining everything.

Jaff let go of her throat.

"WHAT IS IT?"

Jackie didn't say a word, but reached above Jaff, grabbed the paring knife stuck in his shoulder. With one move she pulled it free, twisted her hand, and stabbed Jaff through the side of his head.

The knife entered, smooth and clean, through his scalp, skull, and into the brain matter beyond. Jackie put all her weight into her right arm, twisting the blade backward and taking Jaff's entire body with her. He landed with a thud on Sammy's legs, which were still twitching, and Jackie straddled Jaff, extracted the knife, and didn't even give him the courtesy of one last look.

"DIE!" she screamed, plunging the knife into his face, head, and chest, over and over and over. The knife was wicked sharp and gave her no resistance, either in or out. She stabbed until she lost count, and when she felt her muscles starting to fail, gathered her remaining strength and went for the throat.

"All right, you murderous piece of shit," Jackie said, breathing hard, brandishing the knife so he could see. "Let's make some magic."

Instead of stabbing, she had at his throat horizontally, sawing until she saw the flesh start to give, then moving faster. The wound started small but opened fast, spilling what blood he had left onto the filthy floor. Through it all, Jaff flailed a bit and kicked his feet, but there was nothing left. His wounds had overtaken him, his will was gone, and as he felt consciousness leaving him, he realized the voice had abandoned him as well.

In the moment before everything went black, in the deafening silence broken only by Jackie's grunts as she had at his neck, a small voice, way in the back, made itself heard.

"You deserve worse than this," it said.

He supposed it was right, this second voice. He had gotten some bad advice, had listened to something he shouldn't have listened to. He had done some terrible things, he thought, and while he wasn't ashamed of it, one of Jaff Maul's last thoughts was, *That didn't seem like me.*

The last thing he smelled before his brain shut the whole thing down was his club, his life's work, burning around him.

\*\*\*

The 911 operator begged Taylor to stay on the line, but she was having none of it. Instead of exhaustion and pain, her body was full of nervous energy as she waited for the police to arrive, and staying on the phone was the last thing she wanted to do. What she really wanted was to run in and help, maybe rescue Braden while she was at it, but the horrors inside The Square kept her far away from the door.

That, and some sparkling conversation.

"Damn, what happened to you?"

The kid whose phone she had taken was genuinely in shock and a small crowd had started to gather to try to figure out what had happened to the woman who was covered in blood. Flames were also visible inside The Square and some of the crowd was bouncing back and forth between looking in the windows and trying to hear what Taylor was saying.

She only felt allegiance to the kid whose phone she had borrowed and handed back to him with a considerable amount of blood on the screen. He hadn't seemed to notice and put it right back up to his ear to hear the 911 operator still talking.

The sound of sirens wound their way through the block and before long she saw the lights.

"Come on, come on," she said. "Get over here, you bastards."

"Are there still people in there?" someone asked, but Taylor was already in the middle of the street, waving her one arm that still worked.

"Guy in there…" she said, still breathing heavy, "…he went crazy. Killed some people."

"Did you fight him?"

"Yeah," Taylor said. "I fought him."

***

Having no experience in the subject, Jackie wasn't sure Jaff was dead. That's what she told herself. His breathing had stopped, there were more than a dozen holes in his head and neck (plus one really big one that was hard to miss), and there was blood everywhere, but part of her was convinced he had another jump left in him, one more horror to inflict, so she sat and watched.

In reality, she was in mental shock and creeping up on the physical kind as well. She could get up and run but it would mean both effort and turning her back on both Sammy and Jaff. Blessedly, Sammy had quit thrashing around and settled into his new role as dead body, and Jaff, while considerably whiter and more dead looking, she still didn't buy.

*Stay.*

"I'm talking to myself now," Jackie half sang, exhaustion and pain finally getting the better of her. "I always thought I'd end up… talking to myself…"

Her voice and the crackling of fire spreading through the joint were the only sounds, and for some reason, it made her laugh. The voice that had bewitched Jaff and pissed off Taylor just glanced off Jackie's damaged brain, not penetrating in any meaningful sense. Jackie continued to sing, this time something a bit more recognizable.

"Come dancin'…all her boyfriends used to come and call."

The chemical smoke was now too much to ignore and it filled her lungs, causing her to cough, which hurt unlike any cough had hurt before. It wracked her entire body, causing more blood and more pain, just when she thought she could bear no more. She felt her body start to slump and realized, on some level, she had to get up.

"Come dancin'…" she said between coughs. "It's only nat—"

Her brain filled in the final line, but she couldn't get her mouth to say the words before she started to feel her eye shut. It felt good, but she continued to cough, which kept her eyes from closing. She was stuck being awake and in misery.

*Stay.*

"Don't have much of a fucking choice, do I?" Jackie said aloud. Her head was full of a violent noise that she soon realized was her own coughs as the smoke started to eat into her lungs.

*Stay.*

It was strange, this voice. On one hand, it was quite clearly a woman's voice, inviting in a maternal sort of way. It struck her as certainly not safe, but more than welcome, like the sound of cicadas on a suffocatingly muggy summer night.

*You can rest here. Stay.*

Jackie had nothing left. The rhythm of her coughs was almost a lullaby as she shut her one good eye and let her in, gave herself over, listened to the voice. It took no time at all until the woman was there, in her brain, taking away the pain and smiling at her with a large grin. Her hair was red and her teeth had visible signs of black rot and decay and there was blood on parts of her dress and her hands were weathered from years of work and Jackie had no fight left to give.

The woman reached out for her, her arms long and getting longer as Jackie suddenly floated, just beyond her reach. In her battered, weary mind's eye, it seemed like the woman's arms kept getting longer and longer, and her rotten, terrible smile turned into something else entirely. She reached and grabbed at Jackie, her fingers curling and mouth extending into a scream, the black of her teeth consuming her entire mouth and then her eyes until here was nothing left but a screaming, blank void.

Something kept the woman at bay, a distance that she couldn't cross no matter how long and terrible her arms became. Like a train horn miles away, Jackie heard her own coughs continuing, racking through her chest. She always thought drowning and asphyxiation would be the worst ways to die because they involved panic and realization that death was coming. Seeing death come at you like a punch used to scare her worse than anything, but as her mind slowly crept back into her body, it didn't seem so bad.

Not that it meant she wasn't going to die.

The coughs were nonstop now as she faded in and out, very much inside her body but also floating up and out from behind the bar, past the seating area of The Square, leading up to the stage. A sudden pain in her chest rocketed her back into her body fully, aware, awake, and realizing she was being carried. Part of Jackie's brain went into panic mode, not only due to the strange sensation but because she felt the women's arms still reaching, still clawing at her from somewhere in the dark, still close and hungry and sweaty and pissed.

"No!" she said, batting her arms between coughs. "NO!"

The two fire fighters carrying her out on a stretcher were not taking no for an answer.

***

Taylor was in an ambulance, still awake, still jacked up and pissed off when two firefighters came out with Jackie. EMTs immediately ran over to her, crowding around, so Taylor couldn't get a good look at her friend. There was no sign of Braden or Sammy yet, but the firefighters knew they were in the club and were making every effort to rescue them. She had also told them about the knife-wielding maniac and cop, but she wasn't sure how much had gotten through.

The conversation had been infuriating. There was so much to get out and such a small amount of time. There were fundamentals—shot guy in the basement, two comics fighting the guy who started the fire, knife wielding maniac, stabbed cop. The phrase "stabbed cop" had really sent everyone into overdrive and there wasn't much she could say after that.

"I need to go over there," she told the EMT working on her. The EMT was a no-nonsense New York native with wild hair and some really great skin who was not about to put up with anything resembling bullshit.

"Stay down," the EMT responded. "I don't even want to see your head up."

"What's your name?"

The EMT rolled her eyes a bit and kept working on Taylor's arm. It hurt, a lot, but she wasn't focused on the pain. That would come later.

"Angelica," the woman said.

"Angelica, I just went through a night of living hell with that woman and I'm not going anywhere until I find out about her. Can you please find out if she's okay for me? Please?"

For some reason, Taylor added another plea, one she hadn't anticipated but that made her tear up all over again.

"She's so fucking brave."

Angelica seemed unmoved, continuing her work, but whispered to another EMT who was running between her ambulance and the building. Taylor leaned back and listened, partially for the voice, but mostly to see if she could pick up any little pieces of information. It was all a cacophonous blur of sound with the sirens serving as the base and everything else congealing around it. The voice did not make an appearance. If it did, she would have told it to fuck off.

"Whoever wrapped your arm probably saved your life," Angelica said out of nowhere. "You could be in much worse shape."

"It really hurts."

"You'll have to tough it out. We should be on the way to the hospital right now but I'm holding it for a second."

Taylor smiled and after a few minutes, the EMT came back and whispered something into Angelica's ear.

"Your friend is in real bad shape," she said. "She's alive but…"

An ambulance whizzed by them, full lights and sirens engaged. Taylor felt her breath catch in her throat for a second. Whatever Jaff had done to her hadn't killed her, and that was enough for now, but she felt herself crying again. She fought it.

"The best thing you can do," she heard Angelica say, "is to stay as calm as you can."

Fighting the tears, she kept her eyes glued to the front door of The Square, which the firefighters had busted open. Smoke was pouring out of one side and men and women in yellow gear were yelling at each other. She focused all her attention on the door, desperate to see any hint of Sammy or Braden and, strangely, ready to fight if Jaff came running, knife in hand. But nothing happened.

"We need to get you to the hospital," Angelica said. "This bus ain't waiting any longer."

Nodding, Taylor laid back on the gurney. As the doors shut, she put her head up and got one last look out the window to see Braden being brought out on a stretcher by two men in gas masks. She considered jumping out of her bed, banging on the window, making a big scene, but exhaustion had finally started to creep in around the edges and she knew she wasn't going to be awake much longer.

"If you ghost me this time," she said quietly, "I'm going to fucking kill you."

"What'd you say?" Angelica asked.

"If you have some of those painkillers now, I'd take them," Taylor answered, and smiled to herself as the ambulance cut through city traffic, taking her to safety.

## HBO Comedy Special Special Guest Appearance

**Taylor Tracks: Five Finger Death Punch**
**The Beacon Theater, New York City**
**March 18**

*Hello New York!*

*[standing ovation lasts 2 minutes]*

*Wow. Wow. I can't tell you, I can't begin to tell you how awesome that is. Thank you.*

*I know. I know what it is. You can't fool me. I know. You're into chicks with one arm, aren't you? Nothing's sexier than a girl with a stump, am I right? You sick fucks.*

*I don't blame you. There's a lot to love. Obviously. But let's run it down in case some of you haven't thought it through. One-armed girls can't flip you off and multitask. They can be like [holds up stump], but you don't get the full finger thing. You have to infer from the look on their faces. That was hard for me to cope with. I'm a busy person and I need to be sure people know when I'm telling them to fuck off. So, I've had to adapt.*

*You wanna know the worst one? The one I did not see coming? Wiping your ass. I was a righty, and I challenge each and every one of you next time you take a shit, try your non-dominant hand. Now imagine that your first shit where you've got to wipe with your* idiot hand comes after loads of opioid-based painkillers and three straight days of hospital Jell-o. It was a harrowing activity but I've learned how to deal with it in the bathroom and…well, there's no easy transition for this, but the bedroom, too. One-armed girls work a lot harder in the bedroom, fellas. Trust me on that.

Need proof? You know how, like, a hand job is considered a lesser sexual activity? For me, that's the highest form of foreplay. I mean, I've got one arm, so if I'm jerking you off, you've got my attention. I'm not scrolling through my phone, I'm not playing with my hair, I'm all about you at that point. Eye contact. Lots of eye contact because I can't do anything else because I've got one arm and you've got one dick. One-to-one attention. And, trust me, I'm gonna fucking own it. I will make this so much weirder and so much hotter for you that your dick will never get hard for a two army again. I will break you…single handedly.

I'm going to talk about my arm some more, so if that makes you uncomfortable [holds up stump]. But, to be honest, I think I've earned it.

[applause]

I've got a little bit of a unique perspective on the whole thing because I wasn't born without an arm, so I know how guys used to look at me. When I was on the subway, I would get the quick up and down, you know. I'd get the, "I'd do her if the cancer was spreading," or, "She might fun if I were on work release from the penitentiary." You know, that kind of thing.

But now I get one of two looks. The first is the, "Okay, okay, that's an okay-looking girl, right, her face is fine, I guess, nice rack, I'll just continue looking at her body and…AHHHHH!" Seriously, I was on the subway a few weeks ago and this guy asked me if anyone was sitting next to me, and when he saw I had one arm, he literally jumped back. Then he said, "Sorry, I didn't realize." Realize what? I've *got one arm. My stump doesn't leak anything, it's a fucking stump, it's a piece of skin. I'm a person, I have one arm. It's fine.*

*He didn't sit next to me. And you know what? I put my two feet up on his seat. [holds up stump].*

*The other type of look I get from men now is the same sort of thing, you know, the face, the tits, but then they get to the arm and they're like, "OH, HELL YES!" What I'm saying is I get hit on more now than at any other time in my life.*

*[applause]*

*Hey, everyone wants a story, right? And since you're here or you're watching this on premium cable, I presume you all know mine. I tell ya, I've got a killer party story. It'll light up the fucking room. It's so good HBO bought this show and we're filming tonight, and that's so awesome because I love HBO. This is my first comedy special, so when they came to me with a contract, I made all kinds of demands. One of them was, "Can someone sit me down and tell me what Westworld is about?" I've watched that show for twelve hours and can't tell you a plot.*

*I asked to know why The Sopranos ended the way it did. This is a true story, it apparently really pissed off one of the executives when I asked them that, because he gets asked that ALL THE TIME. Like, he can't go out to dinner without some asshole screaming, "Did they kill Tony Soprano?" and he has to say, "You can believe what you want to believe," which people do not like hearing.*

*Yeah, so, let's get this out of the way early. I was in The Square, not far from here, a few months ago when the owner lost his mind, freaked out, and killed comics Terry Richardson, Sammy Platter, and Jerrod Seybourne. He almost killed Jackie Carmichael, he almost killed a great new comic you haven't heard of yet named Braden Bond, and he almost killed me [holds up stump]. He killed an aspiring comic by the name of Raoul Sanchez, who I never met but*

*I've talked to his family and he seemed like a very decent, ambitious, hard-working guy.*

*Jaff Maul also killed his longtime girlfriend, a woman named Calista Jones, who I had also never met, but who died fighting like hell. She fought with everything she had. Absolutely everything. She didn't make it, but she died with a strength most of us can only hope to ever have. I think about her a lot.*

*I have dick jokes coming up, seriously. I know that brought the room, like, way down, but I've got jokes about boners, I've got a whole five minutes on period sex, I might do some fart material later on if I feel like it. It's coming up, just hang on. Trust me, we can get serious for a second. It'll be okay. Just go with me for a second. [WAVES STUMP]*

*So, I read an article in the New York Post leading up to the show tonight talking about whether or not I'd give details on that night, and if there's one thing I don't want to do, it's disappoint the New York fucking Post. The newspaper that adds "nude" and "headless" into most of their headlines can be a tad, what's the word, sensational from time to time. So, yeah, let's not disappoint them. And I'm not stupid. I know you came here to see the stump. Gentleman, my eyes are up here.*

*The question I get most often, the biggest question I get asked, is, "Do you feel like a real life final girl?" You all know what a "final girl" is, right? She's the girl in the horror movie that survives and beats off the monster at the end while all of her friends are butchered around her? I, seriously, get that question more often than any other, and everyone who asks it thinks they're so funny, like no one else has ever seen a horror movie, or, more importantly, like it's okay to ask me that question. These guys, and it's always guys, I don't know what they think I'm going to say. I really don't. But they sure as shit don't expect this.*

*[pulls a photo out of her back pocket] [camera zooms in]*

*It's my arm after the doctors cut it off. I took this picture in the hospital to remember what it looked like before I had it cremated. Or this one.*

*[takes out another photo]*

*It's a photo of Jackie Carmichael in recovery. Notice the lack of an eye. Or this one.*

*[takes out one more photo]*

*It's a police scene photo of the bodies of Jerrod and Terry, stacked at the bottom of the stairs. This is the one that always gets them because most of these guys, and it's always guys, used to worship Terry Stafford. He was a very funny guy who was also a predator who raped women who came into his orbit. He took a bullet in the head to give me more time to escape. I'm grateful every day for that. He was good for something. But I didn't escape at that moment and Jaff Maul, the owner of The Square, shot me in the arm. [holds up stump]. Oh, and I managed to call the cops and the one who showed up and did his job fearlessly and professionally got stabbed through the throat and died choking on his own blood. He had a nine-year-old daughter who misses him every day. His name was Officer Mick Brunzell.*

*[one minute of sustained applause]*

*That's what being a "final girl" feels like. Living with those images in your head, on a loop, every waking second of every fucking day.*

*And to be fair, these guys, and they're always guys, get it so wrong. If anyone is the final girl, if there's a hero in this story, it's Jackie fucking Carmichael.*

*[applause]*

*That's right, she deserves your applause and your worship because she's the queen bitch mayor of bad ass town. I pray you're never in a situation like I was in, but if you are, I pray double hard to*

Jesus and Krishna and Buddha and Mohammed and every God out there that you have a friend like Jackie Carmichael fighting by your side. She was the one who got me out of there. She was the one who was strong enough to care for everyone who had gotten hurt.

Imagine being trapped in a room with a madman outside trying to get in and still having the strength, the fucking strength, to take care of someone else. To care about someone else's humanity so deeply and truly that you tend to their wounds and whisper encouragement and just hold them, even when it puts your life at risk. That's Jackie fucking Carmichael, and if you ever meet her, give her a really big hug, but watch the eyepatch. She's still kind of raw about it.

One more thing, then we'll get to the jokes, I promise.

The next question I get asked most often is, "How has your life changed since the incident?"

[holds up stump]

And that's not fair. What they mean is, "How is your outlook different?" and that one I don't mind answering because, you know, it doesn't treat me as some sort of pop culture plaything but an actual person with feelings and motivations.

The answer is really simple. I was never a shy person. It sounds weird, but you meet a lot of shy people in stand-up comedy. Some people only come alive on stage, and I was never one of those people. What you see is mostly what you get on or off stage, but that's not so true anymore. Aside from two truckloads of trauma and PTSD, the biggest thing that has changed is I'm taking my lead from Jackie. I'm trying to be more caring about people. Kinder, I guess. I touch people more. It's weird, it took me losing my arm to touch people more, but it's worth it. This city is hard and cold and it can really suck, and I can tell you, you have every right to be afraid of people, but it's worth breaking through that fear and showing people you care. It really is. And that's more than enough talk about that.

*Oh, and since I'm making news here, Terry Stafford once sexually assaulted Jackie in a hotel in Texas.*

*Okay, now that that's out of the way, I flew here on Delta. A first-class flight on Delta is usually an oxymoron, but I got recognized for the first time, which was completely weird. So, I'm sitting there, drunk on power and alcohol...*

# Lights Out

It was about three weeks after her stand-up special was broadcast that Taylor got a knock on the door of her apartment.

The attack was six months in the rearview but it was still part of her daily life, both from an interior and exterior standpoint, and a lot closer than it appeared. Directly after everyone had gotten out of The Square, she was the only one conscious, and as such, she had been the one the cops had gone to for facts. She talked and talked until she passed out, only to wake up and talk some more. After the cops, the media phone calls started coming, and they were so numerous and plentiful Jackie's agent had called her and suggested a press conference.

The agent was a delightful man named Steve who was patient and calm, with a soothing baritone that was exactly what she needed at that moment. He walked her through what would happen, what she would be required to do, and asked her if she could do it. Earlier that same day, the doctors had informed Taylor that, despite their best efforts, they were recommending amputation of her arm just above the elbow. etween that, the attention and the trauma, it was too much to process.

So she went to talk to Jackie.

Jackie's list of injuries read like a medical horror novel. She had broken bones in her face and a cracked vertebrae in her neck, her eye was long gone, a severe concussion, and damage to her lungs from the smoke would reduce her lung capacity permanently. Still, she had woken up recently and Taylor went to see her. The same couldn't be said for Braden, who remained in a coma, but his prognosis was not terrible. On Taylor's end, she still had her arm, but it was bandaged completely, no skin visible between the tip of her finger and mid shoulder. She had lost feeling just beloiw the elbow a few days ago, which was a bad sign.

The second the two women saw each other, they started crying. Neither of them could articulate why.

"I'm so happy to see you," Taylor said.

"Hey, I'm happy to be seeing anything."

They spent the next twenty minutes going over their various war wounds and could have easily spent twenty more if it wasn't for Taylor's cell phone going off. She had asked for a new one, and Steve had provided, complete with all her old contacts, believe it or not. It was Steve calling and Taylor needed to get to the point.

"Steve wants me to go out there and talk to the press," Taylor said, suddenly feeling self-conscious about using such an old-fashioned term as "press." "I don't know. There are so many reasons not to."

"You want a good reason to do it?"

Taylor nodded, and Jackie had a big grin on her face.

"I've never heard you do stand-up," Jackie began. "But I've been in the game a long time, so can I take a guess at some of your act? You're clever, I bet. With that sexy deep voice of yours, I bet you're not just out there doing jokes about airline food. You talk about relationships and men and occasionally throw in stuff about how you don't relate to other women. Am I close?"

"Pretty close," Taylor said. "That's kind of embarrassing."

"Don't be embarrassed," she said. "When you started doing stand-up, who did you see? Who were the big ones? Amy Schumer? Sarah Silverman? Those are your girls, am I right?"

"Yeah. Some of them."

"Of course! Those are some seriously funny comics. That's great, but I'm going to tell you a secret about every great stand-up I've ever met. They figured out who they are and what they see. They're not trying to be anyone else. They know."

The coughing started quietly and quickly ramped up. Jackie was already on oxygen, the tube in her nose hissing every few seconds. A few of the very expensive-looking machines at her bedside began to beep, but Jackie pulled it together after a minute or so.

"As I was saying," she said, smiling, "I've been thinking about you. I'm laying here and I'm thinking, I don't know if you know who you are. So I'm going to tell you."

"You are?"

"Yes, I am. You're the girl who stares down the barrel of a gun and says, 'Fuck you.'"

Taylor felt like she had just had her first kiss. She blushed, and couldn't stare Jackie in the face no matter how hard she tired.

"Sammy, God rest his soul, was a basically decent dude. But he stared down the barrel of a gun and shit his pants. Like I said, I've been thinking, and I think Jaff got real unlucky because there were seven of us in there, right?"

After doing a quick bit of math, Taylor came to eight. She had, out of necessity, read the police report of the incident and realized the full extent of Jaff's madness. He had killed one of his employees, a man named Raoul she had never met but wanted to make sure she never forgot.

"There was an employee named Raoul," she said. "I think you're missing him."

"You're right, I was. That was that first shot we heard."

"Yeah. Plus, his body was behind the stage. Or on the stage. I don't remember. Either way, we didn't see it."

Both got very quiet for a second, remembering their time in The F Pit. For a second, Taylor's chest got tight and she shook it off as best she could. Each night since her escape, she had awoken to the same feeling of tightness and rising fear and she hoped it wasn't something she couldn't get under control.

"Raoul aside," Jackie continued, "of the seven of us, there were five fighters. Five people who stared back into a gun and told Jaff to go fuck himself. He got unlucky and we beat him. It took a lot of our flesh and blood but we beat him and we wouldn't have done it without you."

Taylor was crying and a smile crept across Jackie's face.

"Or me. I did a lot."

"You did so much," Taylor said, unable to crack a joke. She hated when that superpower was taken from her, but there was nothing wrong with sincerity at this point.

"I know we don't know each other, but I love you, kiddo," she said.

The women embraced and made it a point after that to see each other every day they were in the hospital. Soon, Braden came out of his coma and joined them. He recovered quickly, but his road was a long one. The two women would visit him and they would take turns roasting the nurses who thought they were the greatest patients on the face of the Earth.

Jackie, who was having a hard time with recovery and trauma but had her wits about her, coached Taylor through the press conference and she gave a detailed statement on behalf of the survivors. It was at that press conference she had first encountered the "final girl" question and shrugged it off. She didn't give a lot of detail, answered all the questions she could, and made front page news across the country. That afternoon, HBO called.

From there it was a whirlwind of activity. She was writing material and fielding calls the day after the surgery to remove her arm. Steve, Jackie's agent, signed Taylor and talked to her every day about the offers that had come in. She did a few more interviews, signed a book deal (to be co-authored by Braden and Jackie, of course), and even fielded a marriage proposal from a local morning DJ who had faked his way into the hospital with a bouquet of flowers and a ring. On some level, it was everything she dreamed of. On another, she fought every day with trauma, guilt, depression, and pain.

And then she got out of the hospital, she did the special, which was critically acclaimed, she kept in touch with Jackie and Braden, and things remained busy but not nearly as crazy. That is, until the knock on her apartment door three weeks after the stand-up special aired.

The man at the door was older, wrinkled, and mostly bald but very respectable looking. He was on the shorter side, but still had a broad-shouldered look and wore his plaid shirt as if it were a uniform. He also had a brown satchel across his chest. Aside from her grandparents, she didn't know anyone in this age range and was a little alarmed to see the man at her door.

He brandished a card with Steve's name on it.

"Hello, ma'am," he said. "Your agent said I should come by and talk to you."

Without a compelling reason not to, she let him in. Something about his eyes and very measured way of speaking led her to believe she was not only safe, but that something important was about to happen.

"Thank you," the man said. "My name is…well, it used to be Detective Brad Hoffman. I spent fifty years with the NYPD but I've been off the force for a while now."

"Can I get you anything to drink?" Taylor felt the desire to be kind to the man, even to the point of putting a cover on the end of her amputated arm.

"No, thank you," he said. "I won't waste your time. ma'am, I

279

investigated a case in April of 1986 that I think is going to be of interest to you, given recent events."

"Okay, but I wasn't born in 1986," Taylor said, not quite sure how to sit in the presence of a police detective. She crossed and uncrossed her legs nervously. "I don't get it."

"I've got two reasons you should care," Detective Hoffman said. "First, it was a shooting that seemed to come out of nowhere, much like your situation a few months ago."

If it was possible to convey a complex idea like "respect" through a tone of voice, the retired detective was pulling it off, Taylor thought.

"Second, it happened at the same address."

"Pardon me?"

"The exact same address," he said. "In 1986, a man named Daniel Salceda went on a rampage. He had a much higher body count than your incident, I'm afraid."

Taylor's head started to swim and she went to steady herself, only to realize one of her hands wasn't there. This had been happening a lot since the surgery, where muscle memory put her at risk instead of helping her.

All of a sudden, Taylor understood. Looking at Detective Hoffman, she was certain he did as well.

"What's your first name?" she asked. "Sorry, I missed it."

"Brad."

"Brad, you're talking about the voice, aren't you?"

Since she had gotten out of The Square, she hadn't mentioned the voice to anyone except Jackie or Braden, who both weren't quite sure what to make of it. Jackie had heard it but she was on the road to passing out at that point and Braden nodded but never said whether or not he believed her. They had talked about it as a group and came to the conclusion they had heard the same thing, but had agreed to not talk about it in public or, really, in private. It was one of those things that had no upside to talking about.

Detective Hoffman gave her an inquisitive look, and for a second, she wasn't sure she hadn't lost her mind.

"I've never heard it called that, but I think we're on the same page," he said. "A woman, talking to you, encouraging violence. Does that sound familiar?"

"It does," Taylor said. "But she wasn't encouraging me to hurt anyone. She was almost...taunting me. She told me—"

"Told you that you couldn't leave," the detective finished.

"Brad," Taylor said after a long beat. "Not to be vulgar, but you're freaking me the fuck out."

A smile briefly skirted across the old man's face and vanished just as quickly.

"I was one of the first officers on the scene for the Big Dan Salceda shooting," he said. "It's haunted me for a long time, so I started doing research. May I?"

He motioned to the satchel, now situated across his stomach. She nodded and he opened it and pulled out a thick file folder. It hit with a thud onto Taylor's coffee table and he delicately unwound the string keeping it all tied together.

"The thing that haunted me, truly, was Big Dan didn't give any indication that he was having trouble," Hoffman said. "I knew him. That was my bodega, the one I went to in my neighborhood, and he was the same as he ever was. No months of bad behavior leading up to this, no major changes in life that I knew about, nothing. Just one day he woke up and gunned down enough people to fill a subway car."

Taylor's stomach started to drop. She didn't know Jaff Maul very well, but given what others said about him, Hoffman's description fit like a tight-fitting skirt. Jaff wasn't loved, but was generally liked and had given no hint or preview of what he was planning to do. That is, if he was planning it at all. During her recovery, she had read a lot about the idea of someone snapping and going on a murderous rampage, and turns out it's not as common as you might think. A lot of cases attributed to someone snapping were actually mentally ill men who just hid their intentions well and had been planning violence for a long time.

This situation felt different, and it wasn't just because Taylor was close to it. Jaff had seemed not just resolute, but obsessed with killing everyone in that club. The man in front of her had a theory, which was wild, but still a theory, as to why.

"At the same address," Taylor said, making sure she understood.

"At the same address," Detective Hoffman said. "I know this is a lot to take in and it's…a pretty crazy thing to hear, so if you don't want to discuss it right now—"

"No, no," Taylor said. "Please. This feels, I don't know, important."

He smiled, his eyes kind and tired. Rifling through the pages on the coffee table, he hunted for a page in particular and placed it, gently, in front of her. The sheer amount of material likely represented years of research, Taylor figured. This old man had clearly spent a good bit of his retirement on this case that had plagued him and he had fallen down a gaping rabbit hole full of ghosts.

On the page the detective flipped to was a series of dates and names Taylor didn't recognize.

"What am I looking at?"

"The Square is located in a business district that goes way back to the founding of the city," Hoffman said. "It was never a strictly residential area. Always businesses. And what you're looking at is all the businesses and owners that have ever existed on that spot. And this…"

He produced another piece of paper, this time with dates and descriptions of violent crime on them.

"This is what happened at that very spot. It started back here with the Stick and Thistle," he said. "It was a bar and it was owned by a woman named Maggie Moguely. We don't have any photos of her."

The name floated through Taylor like a ghost. It sounded familiar and like a threat at the same time and she had no doubt the voice she had heard belonged to Maggie Moguely.

"Was she who…was she talking to Jaff? And to me?"

"Well, that question presupposes the existence of an afterlife, a link between that afterlife and our world, the ability of spirits to influence the living, and that Maggie Moguely was one very motivated and angry ghost. I know none of this to be true."

"But if you had to guess?"

The ex-detective swiped his fingers over his wrinkled brow and let out a deep sigh, clearly not wanting to weigh in on the existential. Taylor understood. When she was in high school, a friend of hers had insisted she had seen an alien, swore up and down that it was true, and told the story dozens of times to her friends and others who had come seeking details. It hurt her reputation, of course, but while Taylor had always admired the fact that she had stuck to her guns, it didn't stop anyone in the school from thinking less of her.

"Let's try this," Hoffman said. "You heard someone speaking to you. Do you mind me asking what they said?"

Of course, Taylor had not shared this with anyone except Jackie and Braden, both of whom agreed that information might not be great to go spreading around. There was an online theory, one shared by at least one detective in the NYPD, that one or all of them were involved in the killings in one way or the other. Talking about voices wouldn't help that case any, even if it was what she had experienced.

Still, Hoffman seemed old school in his approach and demeanor, not the type to gossip, spread rumors or overshare. didn't seem like he was genuinely what he looked like—an old detective who had seen something he couldn't explain and who had a theory. Plus, she was dying to talk to someone outside the group about it and get their take. If this had actually happened to her and there was a history of this, that mean she wasn't crazy and she had experienced something supernatural.

"It…" Taylor started. "It was a woman's voice. Definitely. And it said, 'Nobody leaves,' over and over. It was threatening. At one point it asked me to kill myself."

Her voice was getting softer and Hoffman was responding in kind, leaning toward her and making sure his voice was even and safe. He nodded, as if he knew exactly what was happening.

"I'd like to show you something else. You might find it upsetting."

"Well, I'll never play the piano again, so I think we're past upsetting."

"You used to play the piano?"

"No," Taylor said, forgetting she was dealing with a civilian. "Comedy is how I respond to uncomfortable situations."

"Ah."

The thick file now well spread out, Hoffman produced a photo that Taylor recognized all too well. It was The F Pit taken after the incident was over. Apparently, the fire had spread down the stairs and into the room, as part of the carpet was burned away and puddles of water had collected from the firefighter's spraying down the room.

Part of the back wall had been burned away and the photo showed a firefighter pulling it apart with his gloved hands. Taylor peered inside the hole and a shock ran from her brain to the base of her spine, causing her to visibly shiver.

Inside the hole was a sign, likely made of wood, though it was hard to tell. The edges were faded into oblivion and only traces remained of the elegant, old-timey script poplar on signs during the day. While she couldn't make out the whole thing, the part she could make out was more than enough.

"No one leaves," she said.

Hoffman flipped to another photo, this one just of the sign.

"I have a friend at the Smithsonian," he said. "She verified it for me. Did a little work on Photoshop to fill in the blanks."

The sign, now free from the confines of the wall, was worse now that Taylor saw the whole picture. She couldn't say why, but the reality of the sign was nothing short of terrifying.

"Stick and Thistle," Hoffman read. "So grand, no one leaves."

"That's…" Taylor started, but didn't know how to finish. It was as if her brain had clamped onto the words and couldn't unclamp.

"Like I said," Hoffman piped up after ten seconds or so, "any theory predisposes much."

Suddenly the questions came flooding into Taylor's brain, fast and furious, and she opened her mouth to speak, but Hoffman cut her off.

"The reason I'm here today isn't to scare you," he said. "I'm not even here to ask for your help to stop it from happening again. All I wanted is for you to know that you were caught up in something bigger, just like I was when I shot Big Dan Salceda so long ago. I found solace in that over the years. I hope you do as well."

He produced a card from his breast pocket and put it in her hand, holding a long time. His touch was rough and he smiled at her.

"That's my phone number," he said. "You may want to call the second I leave, you may never want to call at all. I would recommend you do your own research if you're interested. I can help if that's something you want to do."

He let go of her hand and she let it drop to her side.

"Remember," Hoffman said, gathering up his material from the table and returning it to his satchel. "You were part of something bigger."

For someone who spoke for a living, Taylor wasn't sure what to say as the man got up and made his way toward the door. That didn't last long. The comic took over.

"Maybe we could put up a sign in the window, you know?" she said. "Malicious spirit crossing. Don't start a business. You may murder your friends."

"It's a thought," Hoffman said. "But people don't listen."

With that he was out the door, leaving Taylor with a big question about whether or not she wanted to learn more.

***

When the story broke about what had happened at The Square, there was a two- to three-week period where Taylor, Braden, and Jackie couldn't go out in public. Their faces were on the cover of newspapers and alt weeklies alike, news stations camped outside the window of each of their hospital rooms, and old videos of their stand-up trended on social media. But, as with everything, by the time Hoffman visited Taylor the media attention had died down and the three survivors could meet for a quiet drink. Or what passed for a quiet drink in New York.

It was a Tuesday prior to happy hour the first time they got together. Jackie was not eager to get back on the road to do comedy, at least not right away, and the next season of *The Dapper* didn't start shooting for another month. She was glad for the down time, and the producers had promised her all the time she needed to recover, but she was getting a little antsy and ready to get back to work. Plus, it gave her time to get used to her new eyepatch, which was white with rainbows on it.

Both Braden and Taylor could book most clubs in the country and were working on several projects at once for the first time in their careers.

"I love being here, but I wish I had taken, literally, any other path," Braden said after a big swig of his IPA. "It's not guilt, exactly. It's more, I don't know, sadness."

Normally, they would all crack jokes at his expense, but Jackie didn't have that comic sharpness in her much anymore. Taylor thought of two or three lines, but also didn't say them, wanting to respect Braden as opposed to some weird sense of decorum. When they were in the hospital, they had made dozens of inappropriate jokes, mostly at the expense of Taylor's lost arm, which she wrote down and had used in her act.

Since they were cleared to leave, they just weren't in the mood to bust each other's balls. Which was weird.

Plus, Taylor had some pretty heavy information to drop on them.

"I know what you mean," she said, responding to Braden. "Thanks for hanging out. I had a visitor the other night that I'm still trying to figure out how to process, to be honest."

She told Jackie and Braden about Detective Hoffman, everything he had said and the research he'd done, watching her friends' faces closely. No one gave a hint about what they were thinking until she had finished. In fact, after she was done, nobody said anything. Braden stared into his beer and Jackie was somewhere else, her eyes starting off into the middle distance.

"I don't know what to think, either," she finally said. "It's out there. I'm not the type of person who usually believes in that sort of shit, but—"

"I believe it."

Jackie's voice was steady, making more of a proclamation than a statement.

"I know it sounds nuts, but I knew Jaff more than the rest of you. He could be a grump, sure, but at the end of the day he ran The Square because he loved being surrounded by artists. He never really wanted to be one of us, but he really liked being the guy who gave us a place to do our thing. That's something close to a sense of purpose, you know?"

She broke her gaze with nothing and grabbed Taylor's hand. Taylor wasn't sure why but it felt nice.

"Even if he was harboring all sorts of rage, going as far as he did doesn't really wash," Braden added.

"Toward the end there was this moment where he came at me, when I was behind the bar," Jackie continued. "There was nothing left of the dude I knew. It was something else, something really fucking rank and evil. So you tell me there's the ghost of some Irish lady from three hundred years that took him over and turned him into that thing that attacked me, that makes as much sense as what I saw in the club that night."

Since she had escaped The Square, she had worked hard to try to get certain images out of her head—Jaff shooting Terry in the head, the look on what was left of Jerrod's face, the screaming bright light and blaring music. These thoughts would suddenly appear, like a jump scare, in her mind and she was working with a therapist to react to these thoughts in a healthy way. The thoughts came charging at her again as Jackie spoke and she had to try hard not to lose focus on what they were talking about.

Braden noticed as Taylor shut her eyes for a little too long.

"Is it any easier to think some guy went completely crazy and tried to kill everyone?" he asked.

"I don't fucking know," Taylor said, breathing deeply. "This detective, he kept telling me if a ghost or something is to blame, that presupposes an afterlife, ghosts, that ghosts can affect people, all sorts of shit. I don't think there's such a thing as ghosts, but if there was a ghost or a spirit or whatever, it can go die in a fucking fire. I'm not talking about this anymore. Not saying anything about this ever again, that seems like it's going to be really easy for me. It might be the easiest thing I do for a long time."

"And you don't think we owe it to the next person who moves in there? We shouldn't give some sort of warning?"

Taylor smiled.

"And tell them what, exactly? There's no version of this where we don't come off like a couple of crazy people."

Jackie let go of her hand and smiled.

"This is where you and I differ, my dear," she said. "I'm far too old to give half a fuck about what strangers think of me. The next person who buys that place, they are getting a visit from me, one way or the other."

"Of course that's what you'd say," Braden said.

Taylor smiled at that. He was right, and Taylor had said so during her show and Jackie hadn't done anything to acknowledge the praise. She was who she was, compassionate even when confronted by horror and blood. Strong even when she could have easily justified being weak. She was who Taylor wanted to be when she grew up, and she felt a little swell of pride thinking that she was on her way.

"HEY!"

The sound was loud, even in a somewhat noisy bar, and all three of them knew exactly what it meant. The guy and his two friends, each sporting a dumber hairstyle than the last, came over to the table. One of them was hunting for a pen.

"You're, uh, you're those three comedians who…um…"

"Were almost murdered by a ghost?" Braden said. Taylor kicked him from under the table.

"No, that's not it," the man said. "You were in that club, The Square, right? I mean, I noticed a one-armed chick when we came in, but it just now dawned on me."

"What a gentleman," Jackie said. "It's not everyone who notices a one-armed chick."

The man stared back at them, a little unsure what to say next or what vibe was being directed toward him. Taylor took away all confusion.

"If you fuck off for a bit, I'll wave to you on the way out. With my one arm."

Braden snorted and the guys got the message, one of them

muttering as they, indeed, fucked off back to their table.

"You really going to wave at them?" Jackie asked.

"I don't know," Taylor said. "But it was a good joke."

# Epilogue

It was a great space.

Jay Laub watched as construction workers reinforced the ceiling, put up drywall, worked on the electrical systems, and more. It didn't look like much now, all hallowed out and empty, but it was going to be amazing when it was done.

He'd had the idea for a long time. The space would be brightly lit, very minimal, no big, gaudy art on the walls, and a kitchen that would take its time and prepare with quality. The aesthetic would not be written on the walls. It would be a place you could meet for a casual encounter or a place you could bring your laptop and get some work done. For years, Jay's vision of a clean space in the middle of a dirty city had been near the front of his mind, and when Bitcoin came along and he bought low and sold high, it was finally time.

The Little Rim, he would call it. If he breathed in deep, he could almost smell the coffee brewing.

And he had bought it for a song! He had been looking around Manhattan, and knew going in the prices were going to be astronomical. Real estate in cities was where the mega rich parked their money, both legal and illegal, and prices were always through the roof. But his first foray into locations had left him straight up gobsmacked. Then, just when he thought The Little Rim was a lot dead, he found the great space.

Several thousand square feet. A basement for storage, maybe a kitchen. Beautiful location. Dark past, sure, but who the hell cared?

The real estate agent had been sure to tell him about it, and he had vaguely remembered the story. Terry Stafford had died in there. Some guy had gone crazy and killed a few people. There was a mural on the side of the building that he would paint over. Truth be told, you could find a place like that in every city in America, more or less. Gun violence or whatever it was definitely was not going to stop him from buying a great location that was a full decimal place cheaper than his nearest option. Besides, it might draw some traffic out of curiosity. It was a win-win.

It was such a win-win that Jay was down there, every day, watching The Little Rim work its way into existence. Things were coming along nicely. He had even found some neat stuff downstairs—an old broken sign that had been torn apart but must have been nice in its day, a safe that was still closed for some reason in what used to be an office, a filing cabinet that was still full of files. He had a guy coming later that afternoon to open the safe. Whatever was inside was his now.

As he was watching the work come together, he felt someone tap him on the shoulder. In the city, that's never a good thing.

"Hello."

The woman was stout, her hair big, and she was vaguely familiar. She had scars up and down her face and was sporting an eyepatch with rainbows on it.

"Do you have just a moment?"

Jay was going to give a standard "I'm happy with my religion and I don't want to buy anything" speech he used to ward off solicitors on the street, but she looked really familiar and he hesitated. It was all she needed.

"You're the new owner of this joint?"

"Yes," Jay said. "I...I think I know you?"

"I've been on TV. I'm Jackie."

He still wasn't placing the woman, but he took her word for it and shook her hand. Her grip was strong and she held it longer than she should have.

"So you're renovating this place?"

"Yeah," Jay said, giving in to the fact that he was going to have an interaction with this person. "We open in a little over two months."

"So I've read," she said. "The Little Rim, is that right?"

Jay was confused. He hadn't done any promotion as of yet, hadn't even started a Facebook page. The only way she could have known that was if she had read some of the documentation he submitted when purchasing the place.

She read it all on his face.

"You'd be surprised what you can learn from public records," she said, slapping him on the back and laughing. "Don't worry. I'm not here to fuck with your business, dude. Far from it. I'm here to help."

The woman hunted around in her bag and gave him a file folder.

"What I'm giving you is a history of your new joint," she said. "I have no idea what kind of guy you are. Maybe you're open to this sort of stuff. Maybe you're not. All I can tell you is you were warned."

"What the hell does that mean, I was warned?"

The lady gave a small smile, her one eye sparkling.

"Read this," she said. "And do what you're gonna do."

Jay watched her walk away. There was a bounce in her step, a little bit of joy as she crossed the street to a waiting Uber. She was the most upbeat one-eyed person he'd ever seen.

Lacking any direct project in front of him, Jay's attention drifted to the file she'd handed him. Inside was a police report, some pages photocopied out of a book, a timeline, and a sealed letter. He went straight for it, tearing at the envelope with one hand and flipping the paper open.

The letter was hand written on very nice stationary. There were three signatures at the bottom. He read the contents, chuckled a little bit to himself, and put the letter back in the file, closing it and tossing it in a pile with other documents that needed his attention.

"Weirdos," he said to himself.

It was one thing to talk to other people about your beliefs, but to warn someone about ghosts in the building you were moving into was a different matter entirely. The more he thought about it, the madder it made him. Who the hell did these people think they were? Here he was, trying to start a small business, doing the very thing most valued in this country, and they were going to come in and tell him there was a ghost that was going to mess with his head? That was garbage.

A harsh wind blew, and on the wind, Jay swore he could have heard a voice say something.

A few minutes later, the safecracker arrived. Within minutes, he had the small safe open, where Jay found a ledger, an envelope with a few hundred dollars cash, a small revolver, and a box of ammunition.

"I'll just leave that in there," Jay thought to himself. "If all this is someone's idea of a joke, it's not funny."

# ABOUT THE AUTHOR

Mike Bockoven writes thriller/horror novels while his kids are in gymnastics class or at piano lessons. He lives with his wife, Sarah, two daughters, Emaline and Tessa and an exceptionally dumb wiener dog names Sherlock. He is the author of FANTASTICLAND. You can find him at his website, mikebockoven.com, on Facebook (facebook.com/ Bockovenbooks) and on Twitter @mikebockoven. He lives in Grand Island, Nebraska.